J. S. Fletcher

Mistress Spitfire

a plain account of certain episodes in the history of Richard Coope, Gent., and of

his cousin Mistress Alison French, at the time of the Revolution, 1642-1644

J. S. Fletcher

Mistress Spitfire
a plain account of certain episodes in the history of Richard Coope, Gent., and of his cousin Mistress Alison French, at the time of the Revolution, 1642-1644

ISBN/EAN: 9783337227906

Printed in Europe, USA, Canada, Australia, Japan

Cover: Foto ©Andreas Hilbeck / pixelio.de

More available books at **www.hansebooks.com**

STRESS SPITFIRE

A Plain Account of Certain
Episodes in the History of
Richard Coope, Gent., and
of his Cousin, Mistress
Alison French, at the Time
of the Revolution, 1642-1644

REVISED AND EDITED
FROM THE ORIGINAL MS.

BY

J. S. FLETCHER

AUTHOR OF

" WHEN CHARLES THE FIRST WAS KING," ▮▮▮▮▮▮

London

J. M. DENT & CO.

CHICAGO: A. C. McCLURG & CO.

1897

To

MY FRIEND LIZZIE

The Frontispiece to this book is by Mr J. Walter West, and the Map has been specially drawn by Mr Lewis Kaberry.

CONTENTS

CONTENTS

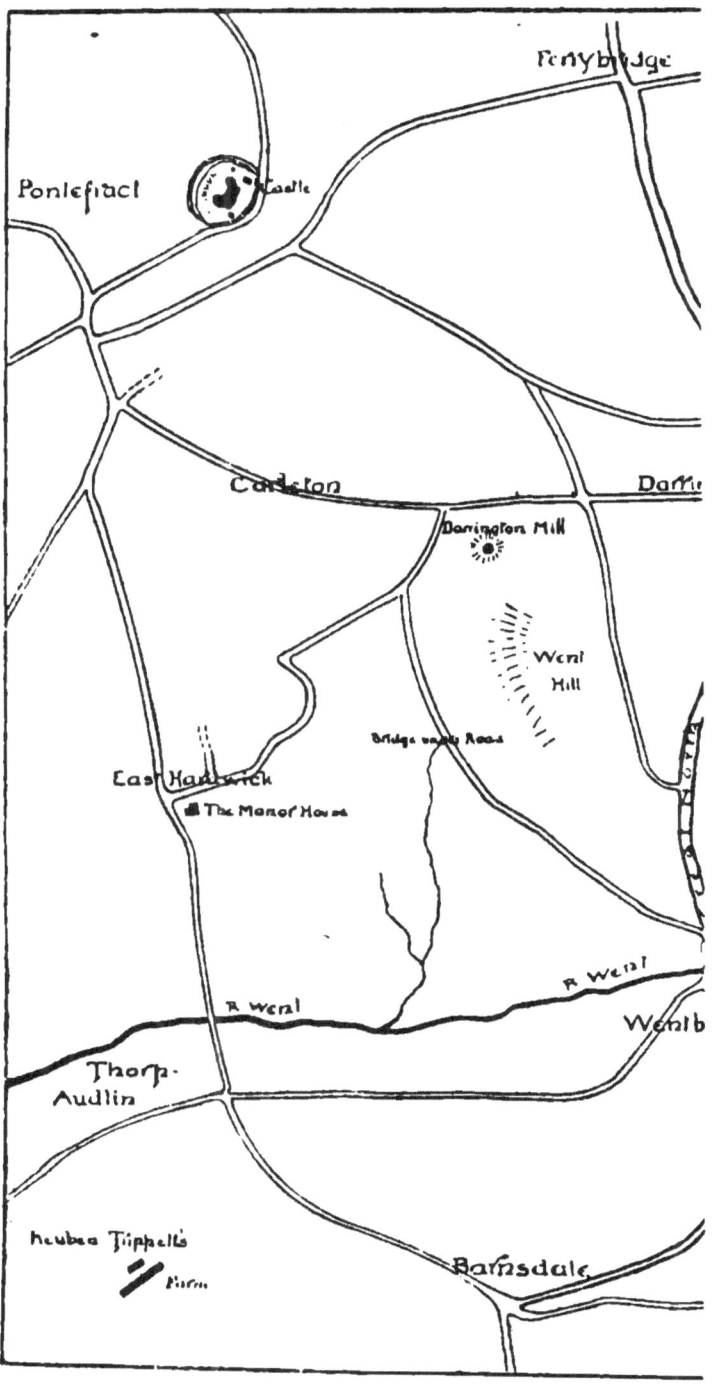

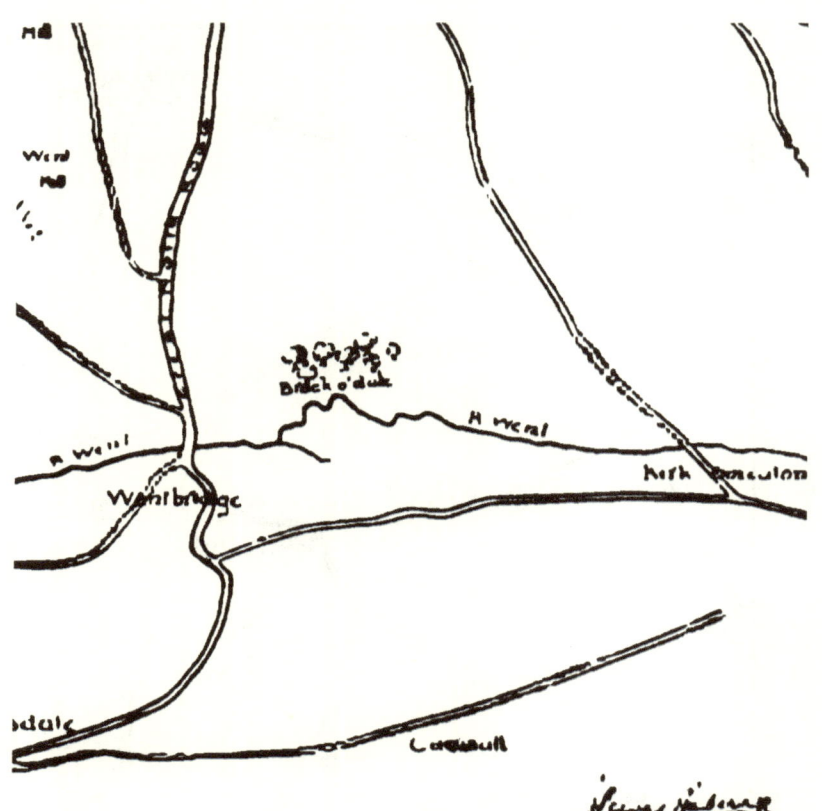

Chapter I

Of certain Events which happened at East Hardwick Manor House, August 27-28, 1642.

I

AT seven of the clock I turned away from the window, where, for a full hour, I had stood flattening my nose against the pane in a vain attempt to see something of interest in the dripping garden or the dank meadows outside. Sir Nicholas moved in his deep chair by the fire and then groaned, his old enemy catching him afresh and tweaking his great toe. Seeing that his pain had awakened him I went over and stood at his side. I saw the firelight glint on his frosted hair, and it woke in me some sleeping memory of a by gone winter. Yet then it was August, and had been a bright one, but that day we had suffered from a heavy rain which came with the dawn and kept pouring itself upon us without ceasing, so that no man putting his nose out o' doors could have

A   1

said with certainty whether he sniffed April or November in the air. As for me, I was heartily sick of it and everything, and when my uncle's silvery hair reminded me of winter I thought regretfully of the previous Christmas and of Mistress Catherine and the mistletoe that then hung over the very spot where I now stood watching Sir Nicholas making wry faces at his foot.

"Plague!" says he, "Plague on this toe of mine! Let me counsel thee, nephew—but what o'clock is it? God's body! I must ha' slept, gout or no gout, why, I must ha' slept an hour."

"An hour and a half, sir, by the clock," says I. "But, by the time that I have watched at the window, a year, at the least."

"Ha! Dull, eh? Why, nephew, I make little doubt that thou hast employed thyself in some fashion that was not altogether—the devil fly away with my toe!—not altogether without amusement. Thy thoughts, now—what, when I was thy age I could ha' mused by the day together on something pleasant. Ha! I mind me of a day that I passed under a beech tree —I was then in love—I cut her name and mine—they were enclosed in a heart, and through the thicker part of it I carved an arrow. Cupid, eh, nephew?—and—and——"

"But I, sir," says I, "have no maiden to think of, seeing that none thinks of me."

"Why," says he, with an arch look in his eyes, "that's but a poor reason, Dick, for God's faith, there are many men think of maidens that never think of them! Is there—plague take it, nephew! sit thee down like a Christian rather than stand lolling there on one leg like a dancing Frenchman. Is there, I say, no little pastry-cook's wench in all Oxford that thou hast not set eyes on since Easter, and thought softly of? Ha, Dick, I mind me——"

But in the midst of his memories the pain in his toe seized him so violently that he screamed to me to fetch Barbara, who came leisurely from the housekeeper's room, and bade me go forth and leave her with him, which I was not loth to do. And being heartily wearied and sick of the rain, and my poor uncle's gout, and the house, which I had kept all day, I threw my cloak about me and lounged into the porch, and stood there, one shoulder against the wall, staring at the raindrops which pattered in the courtyard, and made a musical tinkle in every pool.

But there was naught in the courtyard or in the land beyond it likely to rouse me out of that dullness of spirit into which I was fast falling. The walls were dripping wet, there were rivulets of shiny water in the road outside, and across that lay the fields, as befogged and gray with the long day's weeping as ever I saw them in autumn. 'Twas still early in the evening— the previous night I had seen the top of Pomfret church as I leaned against that door at the same hour—but already there was in the air a misty darkness accompanied by a chilling cold that searched its way through my thick cloak. I half regretted that I had not set out that morning for Doncaster, where I had promised to spend a day or two with my college friend, Matthew Richardson. 'Twould have been a wet ride thither, certainly, but what matter when I should have had good company and profitable conversation at the end of it? When Sir Nicholas had a touch of the gout he was neither company nor conversation for any man save in the way of quarrelling, and therefore I had kept away from him most of that day, striving to amuse myself with such books as he possessed in his justice room, or with the old guns and muskets that stood in racks on his walls. I never could abide a wet day in a country house—in a town house it makes little difference, I think, for there are diversions and amusements of one sort and another, let alone a man's occupation, but in the country I am minded to be abroad, on foot or on horseback, and to be kept inside by a day's rain is exceeding irksome to me. So I stood in the porch feeling in no very good humour that August evening, and still the rain continued to fall.

There were, perhaps, more matters than one to trouble me that night. Here was I, Richard Coope, a young man of one-and-twenty years, at that time a scholar of Pembroke College in the University of Oxford, destined by my uncle, Sir Nicholas, to be one thing, while I myself mightily desired to be another. Because my father, John Coope, died young, leaving me no fortune, Sir Nicholas had taken me in hand, kindly enough, and had charged himself with my up-bringing and education. He was minded to send me to the bar, for something had persuaded him that I should at least become Lord High Chancellor, and add new glory to the family name. And that had been well enow, had I myself possessed the least liking for the quips and quiddities of the law, which, as a matter of fact, I hated like

poison. My taste was for other matters—wholly
and first of all for the finer things in literature,
such as a rare book, or tract, a copy of
elegant rhymes, or a page or so of prose that
was worth the third reading. I had made verses
myself in hours which should have been devoted
to what the folk called serious business; and
though there were often great law-books propped
before me, my eyes took in little of their contents, so long as a broadsheet of ballads or such-
like intercepted their gaze. After that — and
'twas a taste that no man need be ashamed of,
I take it—I cared for naught so much as the
sights and sounds of country life, and the peaceful
occupations that are their accompaniment. What
I desired for myself was that Sir Nicholas should
let me live my own life in his old house, and leave
me his estate when he died, so that I, like him,
might be a country gentleman, and want for
naught. I never could see any objection to
that notion—it was not as if I cared for great
riches, or had any desire to rise to perilous
heights in the world. My uncle, 'tis true, was
not a rich man, as some would count riches; but
there was his Manor House, with its comfortable
surroundings and a thousand pounds a year where-
with to maintain it in quiet dignity; and there

was none to whom he could leave it but me and my cousin, Mistress Alison French, who was already provided for, seeing that her own father was alive and a well-to-do man. To my thinking, the life of a country gentleman would suit me well — I should breed cattle and sheep, and occasionally compose a set of well-turned verses after the fashion of Sidney, whom I admired greatly, and more than all, I should have the scent of hawthorn blossoms and of the brown soil, instead of the stink of those musty parchments which I never could abide.

Now, Sir Nicholas and I had talked these matters over that morning, and we had differed, as we always did—at least, upon this particular question. He was all for what he called my advancement—I was for a quiet life after my own fashion.

"'Slife!" said he, after hearing my notions for the twentieth time; "to hear thee talk, boy, one would think that all the life and energy had gone out of us Coopes. And, beshrew me, so it has, for thou and I are the last of the lot, and I am too old to lift finger again."

"I am willing enough to lift finger, sir," I answered. "You would not find me wanting if

occasion arose to fasten up the doors and stand a
siege——"

"Why, faith," said he, "and that may come ere
long, in these times."

"But in the law, to which you destined me,
there is precious little lifting of fingers save with
a goose's quill in them," said I. "Every man to
his taste, sir; 'tis a saying that I learnt from
yourself."

He looked at me meditatively.

"First and last," said he, "I have laid out as
much as a thousand pound upon thee, Dick."

"Sir," I said, "you have never doubted my
gratitude."

"Thou art a good lad," he answered. "I have
not. But a thousand pound—'tis a great sum to
be thrown away. I think, Dick, the law must
occupy thee. What man, a Coope can achieve
aught that he sets his mind to! Thy father,
now, was Registrar to the Archbishop—I make
no doubt he would have been Vicar-General and
Chancellor of the Diocese if death had not removed him. As for thee, with all the advantages
I have given thee, thou should'st at least become
Lord Chief-Justice. 'Lord Chief-Justice Coope'
—'tis a high-sounding title, though I see no
reason why not Lord Chancellor Coope. How-

ever, when that comes I shall be dead and gone. In the days of thy greatness, Dick, forget not to come here at times. The old place will make a country house for thee—thou canst turn aside to it in journeying 'twixt London and York— 'twill be but poor lodging for a Lord Chancellor, but——"

As I stood watching the rain patter on the flags I remembered this, and laughed for the first time that day. Sir Nicholas was so certain of the things of which I was filled with doubt that his assurance gave me vast entertainment. He had regarded me as a future Lord Chancellor from my boyhood, and now it was too late to persuade him that such dignity was beyond my reach and capabilities. I began to wonder whether it was worth while to attempt persuasion upon him. In the very nature of things he could not live many years, being then much beyond three-score : it would therefore become me to follow his behests while he lived, and study my own inclinations when he was dead. I think it was the laughter which woke in me on remembering his prophecies as to my great state that moved me to this sensible re-flection—howbeit, some of my gloom shifted itself, and I turned inside to make enquiry after my good relative and see if I could do aught to entertain him until his bed-time.

II.

Because of the rainy night Barbara had caused a rousing fire to be lighted in the great kitchen, and near this as I passed through were grouped the half-dozen serving men and lads whom Sir Nicholas kept in his employ. Two of them were ancient retainers; the remainder, lads that helped in the stables and with the cattle, and led an easy life under the old knight's rule. Of the two elder men, one, Gregory, stood behind his master's chair at meals, and kept the key of the cellar; the other, Jasper, was half-hind and half-steward. These two, as I turned into the kitchen, stood a little apart from the rest, conversing with Barbara. Gregory, holding in one hand his great bunch of keys and in the other a flask which he had just brought from the cellar, stood open-mouthed listening to Jasper; Barbara, her hands on her plump sides, stood by him, wide-eyed and eager. The lads at the fire watched these three, and from the scullery door two kitchen wenches peeped wonderingly at Jasper's nodding head.

Gregory brought me to a stand with an appealing look.

"Master Richard," says he, in a whisper, "if so be you'll pause a moment, sir—Sir Nicholas is comfortable, thank God—there's a little matter ____"

"What is it?" says I.

"Jasper has come in from Pomfret, Master Richard," he says, still whispering; "with the seven load of wheat a' went, and has returned with great news."

"Exceeding great news," says Jasper, shaking his head. "And the wheat, Master Richard, sir——"

"Come," says I, impatient, "what's your news, Jasper—out with it, and let the wheat rest."

"We were afraid to let the master hear it, Master Richard," says Gregory. "'Tis of an upsetting nature——"

"'Tis news of war, Master Richard," says Jasper, interrupting him. "The King and the Parliament is going to fight. I heard it talked of in Pomfret market. They do say that the fighting has begun—somewhere in the south country, I think—but I was that put about over the wheat that I didn't rightly catch all particulars. But they were certain that it's war at last, and the castle is to be garrisoned for the king."

Now there was naught much to be surprised at in this, for it was what we had expected for many a long day. We had heard rumours of it all that month, and it was well known that the country gentlemen all over the riding were making themselves ready against such time as the fight 'twixt King and Commons should come to a head. But now that the final news came to me I felt some little shock, one reason of which you shall presently understand. Also I felt some debate within my own mind as to my uncle's position and safety. His Manor House of East Hardwick stood within three miles of the Castle of Pomfret, and I had little doubt that the latter would eventually become a centre of active operations, in which case the neighbouring houses of any importance were not unlikely to suffer at the hands of beleaguering troops. These things I thought of as I listened to Jasper's news.

"Say naught to the lads and maidens," says I. "They'll only blab it over the village within the hour. I will mention it to Sir Nicholas myself——"

"Pray God it bring not another fit of his complaint!" says Barbara. "'A suffered a terrible twinge after you was gone out, Master Dick."

" 'Twill be more likely to make him forget it," I answers, going towards the door which led into the great hall. But before I could lay hands on the latch, there came a great stamping of feet in the porch outside and a loud voice calling for a groom. The lads tumbled out, with Jasper in their rear, and presently there came blustering in a great man of loud voice, demanding Sir Nicholas, and protesting that the night was not fit for a dog to be out in. He caught sight of me and stared, and came stamping across the kitchen with a wet hand outstretched.

" That should be young Dick," says he. " 'Tis a long time since I saw thee, youngster—wast then a lad the height o' my knee. Art grown a man now, and hast sinews of thy own, I warrant me."

" 'Tis Sir Jarvis Cutler," whispered Gregory, as I took the man's hand.

" Thou art right, old cock!" says Sir Jarvis. " Gad! I like the look of thy nose and of the bottle thou carriest. And how does my old friend Sir Nicholas, young Dick—well and hearty, I hope—for there's need of him now, i'faith."

" I fear that need must still be needy, then, sir,"

says I. "My uncle suffers much at present, and stirs only from his couch to his chair."

"'Sdeath!" says he. "'Tis bad news, that—but, what, he will find a substitute in thee, I doubt not. Hark thee, Dick, I have ridden hither from Stainborough, and my horse, poor beast, 'tis hard put to it—we will not to Pomfret to-night—there's no hurry—see to it that my horse is cared for—Sir Nicholas, I am sure, will grudge neither it nor me a night's lodging. And help me to some dry gear, lad, that I may go in and see thy uncle—'od's body, as bad a night as ever I was out in!"

So I sent Gregory to tell Sir Nicholas of Sir Jarvis Cutler's arrival and to prepare food and drink, and I had Sir Jarvis to my own chamber in order to provide him with dry clothes.

"We are much of a build, thou and I," says he. "Faith, thou hast grown mightily o' late, lad. But thou art more for books than swords, eh, Dick? Why, so Sir Nicholas gave me to understand, but in these times there'll be more sword-work than book-work, boy—aye, marry!"

"Then the war has broke out, sir?" says I. "We heard something of it, but our news was scanty."

"'Tis true enough," he says, struggling some-

what with his garments. "Faith, I can give thee
an inch or maybe two in the shoulders, Master
Dick. Yes, lad, true enough—His sacred Majesty
hath set up his flag against the rebels and
traitors."

"His Majesty hath set up his flag?" I says.
"When and where, sir, might that be?"

"At Nottingham, lad, five days ago. I myself
was there at the time, and came north with
charges and messages enow to fill better heads
than mine. But let us to Sir Nicholas, Dick.
I have much to say to him."

We found my uncle greatly excited over the
arrival of Sir Jarvis, and giving orders as to
food and drink to Gregory, who was laying a
table close to the hearth. He made an effort
to rise from his chair as we entered, but the
gout tweaked his toe, and he sat there, groaning
and making wry faces as he stretched out his
hand to the knight.

"Plague on this gout!" says he. "It prevents
me from playing my part, Sir Jarvis, as I should;
but you are welcome, indeed. Gregory, a flask
of my Tokay—fine stuff, Sir Jarvis, on such a
night as this. Draw near to the fire, Sir Jarvis.
Dick, thy manners, boy—give Sir Jarvis a seat
near me—'tis parlous weather, Sir Jarvis, and

must needs have its effect on them that have crops out."

"There are other matters than crops to think of, neighbour," says Sir Jarvis. "If crops were all——"

"Ah, you bring us news? We hear rumours o' things in this quarter, but unless a neighbour visits us——"

"The King hath declared war against the rebels," says Sir Jarvis. "His Majesty set up the Royal Standard at Nottingham five days ago. I marvel you have not heard it sooner."

"Jasper heard it in Pomfret this afternoon," I says. "I was coming to tell you of it, sir, just as Sir Jarvis arrived."

"God save His Majesty!" says my uncle. He sat staring at the blazing logs in the hearth. "It vexes me sore that I cannot lift sword in his honour. Once upon a time——"

"Aye," says Sir Jarvis, "the dog cannot always run, neighbour! Howbeit——"

He addressed himself to the good things which Gregory set before him. While he ate and drank I slipped away and went to my own chamber to think over the news which he had brought. For me it bore a significance which I was not able to explain to either Sir Jarvis Cutler or my uncle,

nor indeed to any one in the Manor House. I
have said that when I heard definite rumour of it
from Jasper it gave me some sort of shock. And
the reason was that I now knew the time for
action was at hand. I and others of my way
of thinking had banded ourselves together at
Oxford, and had taken oath that when the
moment came for striking a blow for the rights
and liberties of Englishmen we would give in
our open adherence to the Parliamentarians, and
do our best to bring to an end the tyrannical
rule under which good men and true citizens
had long suffered. There was scarce one of
our society that did not spring from a
Royalist family, even as I myself did, and for
that reason we had been obliged to keep our
tongues strictly guarded ; saying naught, though
we heard much. We were all young men of a
certain turn of thought, that is to say, our
philosophical studies, prosecuted for the most
part according to our own tastes, had led us
to favour republicanism rather than monarchy,
and this in spite of the fact that we were
surrounded by every influence likely to make
our opinion tend in the opposite direction
Now, we had resolved that whenever war should
break out, as we felt it must, our theories should

B

find their practical outcome in taking arms in defence of the popular cause, and so as soon as I heard the definite news brought by Sir Jarvis Cutler I knew that ere long there must be open breach between my uncle and myself. I had hoped that this might never be, for I knew Sir Nicholas would bitterly resent what he would term my treachery to the King. However, I could not take my hand from the plough even had I wished, for I was bound by a solemn oath. And, indeed, save for Sir Nicholas's sake I had no wish to do so, I, like many a young man of those times, being heartily sick of the cruelties and oppressions under which so many of my countrymen suffered.

I was now sorry that I had not ridden over to Doncaster that day to my friend Matthew Richardson, who was one of our society, and acted as a kind of centre round which the rest of us revolved. I should have been glad of his counsel—besides which I knew that he would be in possession of full information as to all that was going on. It was apparent to me that I should shortly have to declare myself, for Sir Nicholas would certainly design my assistance for the King, and that, let come what might, I knew could never be given. So I sat there some time, wondering what would next happen, and wishing that things might be so ordered that no breach should occur between me and my worthy relative. But presently there came a tapping at my chamber door, and Gregory pushed in his head to inform me that a man waited my coming in the porch below.

"'A seems to have ridden hard and far," said Gregory, as we went down the stair together. "Pray God he ask not a night's lodging, Master Dick, for Sir Jarvis's beast has got our only empty stall, and the night is too wild to turn one of our own horses into the fold."

"'Twill but be some post that brings me a letter," I answered. "I shall not invite him to tarry."   .

"A mug of ale, sir," said Gregory. "Maybe he would stay long enough for that. If you——"

I nodded, and crossing the kitchen shut the door behind me. There was a lamp hanging in the porch, and by its light I saw the messenger —a thick-set fellow—standing in the doorway, muffled to the eyes in his cloak, and holding his horse's bridle over his arm, across which the brute thrust a wet nose that sniffed at the light.

"Good-even, friend," says I, standing before him.

"Good-even, master," he answers, scanning me very close. "A wet night and foul ways."

"Aye," says I.

"Master Richard Coope, I think?" says he.

"The same, friend," says I.

He fumbled at his reins and drew the horse nearer to him with a movement of his hand.

"The sword of the Lord," he says in a low voice, looking full at me.

"And of Gideon!" says I.

He plunged his free hand into his breast and brought out a packet, which he presented to me without loss of time.

"That is my duty, master," says he; "the rest you know as well as I. I will now go on my ways—there is more to be done to-night, bad as the weather is."

He backed his horse from the door. I followed him into the still falling rain. He had one foot in the stirrup as I spoke to him.

"This is not my house," I says, speaking low, "but I could get you food and drink if you have need."

"None, master," says he. "At such times as these we must take no risk for the sake of carnal delights."

"But is there no answer to this packet?" I says. "Did not they that sent you——"

"You will answer the message in person, master, I doubt not," he says. "Fare you well—the Lord protect you."

The darkness swallowed him up ere he reached the open door of the courtyard, but I lingered a moment in the porch and listened to the sound of his horse's feet on the road outside. I heard him ride to the corner. The horse broke into a quick trot: I knew by the sound that the man was making along the road to Pomfret.

I went back into the house. A stable-lad nodded his head by the kitchen fire, and Gregory was coming from the cellar with a mug of ale.

"'Tis for the man without, Master Richard," says he. "On such a night——"

"The man is gone," says I. "He would stay for naught—'tis but a book he has brought me—drink the ale yourself, Gregory."

I hastened to my own chamber and broke the seal of the packet, which bore my name and address in Matthew Richardson's hand. There was little writing within for anybody to read, but the lines signified much to my eyes.

'That which you wot of," it ran, "has come

to pass, and it now behoves us to do what we are resolved upon. Within twenty-four hours of your receipt of this, then, you will join me at the third milestone on the road between Doncaster and Sheffield.—M. R."

As I finished reading this brief epistle for the second time, Gregory came tapping at my door again.

"Your uncle is asking for you, Master Richard," says he. "Sir Jarvis has finished his supper, and they are talking of the war—Lord help us all !— though, indeed, it seems as if Sir Nicholas forgot his pains in discussing of fights and such-like. But I misdoubt that to-morrow——"

He lighted me down the stair, shaking his grey hair and muttering to himself. In the great kitchen he left me, and I went over to the hearth and placed Matthew Richardson's letter amidst the glowing cinders. I stood there until I saw it crumble into white ashes.

III.

When I went into the hall, my uncle and Sir Jarvis sat in their chairs by the hearth, the great screen protecting them from the draught, and the

fire piled up with logs, and glowing so bright
that you had fancied it was a winter's night rather
than an August evening. On the table between
them stood a second flask of Sir Nicholas's
Tokay, and I observed that in his excitement my
good uncle had filled his own glass and sipped
largely from it, which was a bad thing for his
gout, and to be paid for afterwards. Sir Jarvis
Cutler was smoking tobacco from a pipe—a new-
fangled habit which I knew my uncle could not
abide, but which he evidently forgave in a guest
so much after his own heart.

"Sit thee down, Dick," says Sir Nicholas.
"Od's body, I wondered what had got thee.
These boys, Sir Jarvis, will for ever be at their
books—pour thyself out a glass of wine, Richard :
'tis vastly different stuff, I warrant me, to what
you find in your common rooms at Oxford. Sir
Jarvis, spare not—there is more where that came
from—if it were not for the gout I would help
you to crack more bottles than one. Nay, Dick,
forget thy books and rhymes, man !—this is no
time for a long face."

"With due respect, neighbour," says Sir Jarvis,
"'tis a time that will bring long faces enow.
But as for books, I agree—'tis rather a time for
swords than words. Thou wilt have to lay aside

the pen, lad," he says, turning himself to me, "and take up the sword."

"I trust not, sir," says I. "I have no mind to see fighting 'twixt folk of one speech and blood."

"Why," says he, "that's well said from one point o' view, but neither here nor there at this present. For fighting there will be, aye, 'twixt father and son, and brother and cousin."

"Say, rather," chimes in Sir Nicholas, "'twixt loyal and disloyal, faithful and unfaithful. A plague on all rebels, say I!"

"I have been telling thy good uncle, Dick," says Sir Jarvis, pressing fresh tobacco into the bowl of his pipe, "of what there is afoot in these parts amongst those of us that are true to the King's Majesty. Now that his Highness hath necessities we must needs help him with ourselves and our substance. There's been a meeting in York, Dick, amongst certain of us—but for his plaguey gout your good uncle had been there—and we came to a decision—no hangers back, Sir Nicholas—to do what we could, and that's our best. Some have given a hundred pound, some three hundred, some five—'od's body! why trouble about the amounts?—each gentleman has done what he could—it mounts

up in some cases to as much as ten thousand
pound. Then men are being enlisted, and are
to be maintained at our charges—a costly business, Sir Nicholas, but one that must be endured.
And now that His Majesty's flag is raised in
defiance of these traitors, we are forming a
garrison for Pomfret Castle, and it shall go hard
with us, but we'll hold it against every rebel of
them."

"Tell the lad what names you have amongst
you, Sir Jarvis," says my uncle. "'Tis a
fine list of worthy and gallant gentlemen,
and any man should be proud to join their
company."

"Why, first," says Sir Jarvis, "there's Colonel
Lowther, that will govern and command us, and
with him Colonel Wheatley and Colonel Middle-
ton. As for the gentlemen Volunteers, we have
formed them into four divisions. Colonel Grey
will lead the first, Sir Richard Hutton the second,
Sir John Ramsden the third, and Sir George
Wentworth the fourth. I myself am second in
command to Sir John, and I warrant thee, Master
Dick, we have some pretty fellows with us, as
have all the other captains. Some hundred and
thirty gallant gentlemen we are in all; but we
can find room for more, and as thy worthy uncle

is beyond fighting at this moment, why, we will make a place for thee, his representative."

" Sir," says I, " you're very kind ; but I have no mind for wars and battles. My occupations are of a peaceful nature ; if I fight it must be with pens and parchment for weapons rather than pikes and swords."

" 'Slife, Dick ! " exclaims my uncle, peevishly. " This is no time for peaceful acts, man."

" 'Twas but this morning you counselled me not to be led astray from my profession that is to be, sir," says I ; " and I've thought things over, and decided to follow your wise advice. If I am to be Lord Chancellor, 'tis time I gave more heed to my books."

" Tut, tut ! " says he, still more peevish, for his toe began to tweak him again. " Since morning, lad, a good many things have happened. We must needs deny ourselves for the king's sake, and 'tis my wish that you should assist our neigh-bours in keeping Pomfret Castle for His Majesty. Say no more on't : Sir Jarvis, fill your glass."

" I doubt the prospect of war has little charm for thee, Master Dick," says Sir Jarvis, eying me in a fashion I had no liking for.

" I am not a soldier," says I, putting as much ill-humour into my voice as I could, for I was

playing a part, and wished to do it well. "And
I am not minded to engage in brawls——"

"Brawls!" he cries. "'Sdeath, lad, thou hadst
best not use that word before one of His Majesty's
officers! Brawls, quotha! Why, boy——"

"Fie on thee, Dick!" says my uncle. "Fie!
Brawls, indeed! Why, 'tis the most righteous of
quarrels into which His Majesty hath entered.
Say no more, Sir Jarvis; the lad hath been bred
to papers and books, but he will fight well enough,
I warrant you, when he is once shown the trick of
the thing. I wish I had had thee trained in fence,
Dick; but I never thought there would be occasion
for thy use of it. Sir Jarvis, help yourself to the
bottle. Nay, man, be not sparing—who knows
what there may not be in store of hard work to-
morrow? If it were not for this plaguey gout of
mine, I would help you more freely; but, i'faith,
friend, I am in sore pain, and will ask your leave
to go to my bed. Dick, play the host to Sir
Jarvis, boy. Spare not the Tokay, Sir Jarvis
—Gregory will serve you."

Now, when Gregory and Barbara between them
had helped my uncle to his own chamber, Sir
Jarvis and I sat before the fire, not over lively
companions. He smoked his tobacco, and from
time to time refilled his glass, and now and then

he cast sidelong glances at me, who watched him out of my eye-corners.

"Thou art not too fond of the king, then, Master Dick?" says he at last, glancing at me.

"Sir," says I; "I know no reason why I should discuss His Majesty with you or any man."

"Aye," says he; "I have heard that answer before, and know what it means, lad. Faith, you may deceive the old knight upstairs, but not the one that sits with you down below. I have heard there is disaffection amongst some of you young Oxford sparks — aye, I heard it a six - month since."

"'Tis a matter of complete indifference to me, sir," I says, as cool as I could.

"'Od's body, lad!" he exclaims with a sudden fervour. "Thou art prettily unconcerned about these things, but if I met an enemy to the king I would run him through as soon as look at him!"

"Would you, sir?" says I.

"Aye, would I!" says he. "Were he my brother, aye, or father, I would, Master Dick."

I laid hands on the flask and poured myself out a glassful.

"Here's your health, sir," I says, bowing to him.

"I never thought to find thee disaffected," says he, taking no heed of my compliment.

" Have you done so, sir ? " I asks him.

He favoured me with a hard look.

" Faith ! " he says, half muttering to himself.
" I don't find much enthusiasm in you."

" You forget, sir," I answers, " that I am to be
a lawyer. 'Tis not my trade to show my feelings,
but rather to conceal them."

" Be damned to your feelings ! " he raps out.
" 'Slife, man, there are half the lads in England
shouting for one side or t'other to-night, instead
o' sitting as you do with a face as long as those
parchments you pour over."

" I am quite agreeable, sir," says I. " Let them
shout—I suppose I have a right to preserve my
voice for the courts of law."

" Oh, preserve it ! " he answers.

" Will you take some more wine, sir ? " I says
very polite, and pushing the flask towards him.

He stared at me from under his bushy eyebrows
and laid his pipe on the table.

" No ! " he says. He rose and stretched himself
on the hearth, his big body seeming to eclipse the
leaping flames. " I'll to bed," he says. " Good-
night—and more spunk to you. Master Richard,"
and he strode across the hall to the door.

I jumped up at that.

" By God ! " says I, a sudden passion raging

within me.   "If occasion should ever serve, Sir
Jarvis, you shall see what spunk I have!"

With his hand on the door he turned and looked
long at me, as I leaned forward over the table
staring straight into his eyes.

"Aha!" says he at last.   "I see how it is—
egad, Dick, I thought it strange if I could not
draw thee!   Well—well—as I said before, 'twill
be house against house, and brother against
brother, aye, and son against father.   Good-night
to thee, Dick."   He swung through the door and
left it open.   I heard his heavy tread on the
kitchen flags, and then the clank of his sword's
heel as it caught each stair.   I stood there in the
same attitude until all was still again.   The fire
crackled behind me.   I suddenly bethought me
of the letter which Matthew Richardson had sent
me, and ran out to the kitchen hearth, half afraid
that some scrap of it might have escaped the
flames.   The fire had smouldered away; it was
all dead ashes; and before it sat Jasper, his
hands folded across his stomach, fast asleep.

IV.

When I came into the hall next morning it was
later than my usual hour for appearing before my

uncle. I had slept ill during the first part of the night, and kept my bed late in consequence. During the night the weather had changed, and the sun was now shining brightly across the meadows and the garden outside our windows. My uncle, evidently relieved of his pain to some extent, sat at the table, breaking his fast, but there was no sign of Sir Jarvis Cutler.

"Thou art late, Dick," says my uncle as I made my obeisance to him, "and Sir Jarvis is well on his way to Pomfret if a' be not there already. In these times, lad, one must stir one's self and be up and about."

"I trust that your pain is relieved, sir," says I, feeling glad that our guest had departed.

"Why," he answers, stifling a groan, "'tis certainly somewhat abated, nephew, and I have made shift to walk with a stick from my own chamber. In these days"—this time the groan came in spite of his rare fortitude—"a man must not think as much of his own ills and aches as of his Majesty's necessities. It behoves me, Sir Nicholas Coope, knighted by His Majesty's father, to do my duty, nephew Dick—even as it behoves thee to do thine."

"I trust, sir," says I, "that you will not find me wanting in my duty to you."

"I've no doubt of that, boy," says he, with a keen look at me, "but I wish thou wouldst show a little more enthusiasm for the good cause. 'Od's body, mightst ha' been a crop-eared Anabaptist last night, by thy long face, instead of a Royalist gentleman!"

"Why, sir," I rejoins, "to my mind there is no occasion for rejoicing at the prospect before us. It seems to me time for weeping and mourning rather than laughing and carousing. I see no pleasure in watching Englishmen slay Englishmen."

"Thou art a curious dull dog, Dick," says my uncle, giving me a queer look. "'Sdeath, man— why, when I was thy age it would have rejoiced me to see prospect of a broken head or two. But this is neither here nor there when there's business to talk of. Touching this matter of the garrisoning of Pomfret for the king, Dick, I have promised Sir Jarvis that thou shalt fill the place which I should have taken myself. Thou shalt not go empty-handed, either, lad—thou shalt have a good horse and good money, and a man—Robin shall attend thee—he has a pretty knowledge of many things that will be useful to thee. As for the law, it must wait. 'Tis a pity, but we must do the king's behests first of all."

Now I was by that time in a tight corner, and felt myself fairly put to it. But into Pomfret Castle I would not go, and so there was naught for it but to say my say.

"With all respect, sir," says I, "I humbly venture to disagree with you. I have no wish to volunteer under Sir Jarvis Cutler, or any other gentleman. I desire to prosecute my studies, and to further my own advantage, as you have always desired me to do. I have no taste for wars, and least of all for a war of this sort. So I beg you, sir, to permit me to return to my peaceful avocations, and do what I can with them until such time as peace may be mercifully vouchsafed to us again."

Which was all most damnable hypocrisy, seeing that I was as much filled with desire for war as he himself, and as ardently wishful that my cause might triumph as he was that his might succeed. But 'twas pardonable, I think, for I did it to avoid giving the old man more pain than was necessary. If I had told him in so many words that I was leaving him to join the Parliamentarian army it had killed him, of a surety; to leave him under the impression that I was returning to my studies would only disappoint and grieve him.

C

He stared at me across the table, and I saw the veins swell in his forehead.

" 'Od's life!" he says. " I believe thou art naught but a tame cock after all. Do I understand thee, nephew, to refuse service to His Majesty, and to prefer thy stinking parchments and musty folios to the sword and pistol?"

"Infinitely, sir," says I, lying harder than ever.

He got up from the table, gave a deep sigh, and hobbled over to his chair. I ran forward to help him : he pushed me away testily.

"Leave women's work to women," he says, giving me a spiteful look. "Lord! that thou hadst been a lass, and Alison French a man!"

" I am not the less a man because I am a man of peace, sir," I answers, more damnably hypocritical than ever.

"Confound your cool manners!" says he, losing his temper. " 'Od's body, a pretty fellow you have turned out, setting yourself against the king's interests! Now hark thee, nephew—either go to Sir Jarvis and take service under him as I desire, or else leave here at once and return to thy books and parchments : I'll have no laggards dangling about my hall in time o' war."

"Dear sir," says I. " I was about to ask your

permission to return to Oxford this day. 'Tis still far from term time, but there is a professor there with whom I am anxious to continue my reading."

"Aye," he says, as if to himself. "Aye—oh, return at once! I could not abide to see thee playing with books when thou shouldst be practising fence."

"Then I have your leave, sir?" I asks him, abusing myself inwardly for my deceit, now as it was for his own sake.

"Oh, take it, nephew," he answers. "Take it, by all means." He turned himself to the fire and tapped his stick impatiently on the hearth. "I am disappointed in thee, Dick," he says, presently. "'Slife, what are all the young men coming to? Had it been Alison, now—what art loitering there for?" he screams. "Get thee ready, boy—get thee ready and go—go! We are going to have war and bloodshed—thou wilt faint if the scullery - wench gets her finger pricked!"

So it came about that within the hour my horse stood saddled and bridled in the courtyard and I was ready to depart. I went in to say farewell to my uncle and found him cold and ceremonious.

"I wish thee a safe journey, nephew," says he. "When it will be possible to ask thee to visit me again is more than I can say, seeing that the times are so troublous. Hold—here is money in this purse—"

"Dear sir," says I. "I am already furnished through your generosity, and shall want for nought yet awhile."

He stared at me, and then returned the purse to his drawer, from which he took out a sealed packet.

"You ride south, nephew?" says he, "Be good enough to call at my brother French's house as you go towards Doncaster, and deliver this letter to your cousin." He put the packet into my hand. He looked at me narrowly. "By God, Dick!" he says, suddenly, losing his politeness, "I never thought to see the day when a Coope would run away from a bit o' fighting. Get thee gone—get thee gone, boy!"

So I was perforce obliged to ride away from the Manor House leaving a wrong impression behind me. And yet, of two evils I think I chose the lesser one, for it was better that my uncle should believe me a coward, loving the peaceful occupations of art and letters more than the alarms of war, than that he should know me

to be what he would have termed a renegade, a
traitor, an enemy to God, king, and country.
Nay, if he had known the true facts of the case I
doubt if he would have allowed me to leave him
at all — he would rather have sent me under
strong guard to Pomfret Castle and bade Colonel
Lowther deal with me for a rebel.

At the top of the hill over against Thorpe
village I turned in my stirrups and looked back
at East Hardwick. I saw the roof of the Manor
House beyond the trees, and as I watched I
caught the flutter of gay colours from the pole
at its north gable. Sir Nicholas had caused
to be hoisted the royal standard, in defiance,
doubtless, of all the disaffected in those parts.
It waved against the light breeze, and I looked
at it again and at the roof beneath it ere I
clapped spurs to my horse and went on towards
the Barnsdale woods.

It was then drawing near to eleven o'clock in
the forenoon, and though the roads were heavy
because of the previous day's rain, I had time
enough and to spare, both in doing my uncle's
errand and in keeping my rendezvous with
Matthew Richardson. As for the errand I had
little pleasure in undertaking it, for my cousin
Alison French and myself had never met in

all our lives without falling out. She had the hot quick temper of all the French's, and was as ready to give as she was to resent a sharp word. That, indeed, was the memory which I had retained of her since our last meeting, which was many years previously, she being then but a chit of a girl and I a boy of some twelve years. As I rode along I recalled one little incident in which both had played a part.

"As if," quoth she, "I cared for a great lubberly boy like you! Why, there are lads in the village——"

"There are lasses in the village too!" said I, not to be outdone. "And half-a-dozen of them that are prettier than you."

We were standing in Sir Nicholas's kitchen-garden at the time, at a spot where Jasper had recently set down a row of raspberry canes. She snatched one of them up and began to belabour me soundly across head and shoulders, caring nothing where the blows fell. I remembered with a whimsical sense of humour that at first I had not known what to do, but that at last I had twisted the cane out of her little hands and broken it across my knee, whereupon she had burst into tears. In truth, she was a curious creature as a child, and I had little relish

in the prospect of meeting her again, so I determined that if I came across some trusty servant
in Francis French's park, I would give him the
packet and go on my way.

But as chance would have it, I had hardly just
turned out of the highroad when whom should
I light upon but Mistress Alison herself, going
abroad with two great hounds, whom she kept
to heel with a stout whip.   Although I had
seen naught of her for nine years I knew her
again at once, for there was no mistaking the
flash of her hawk's eye nor the quick fashion
in which she turned it on myself.   But she
had forgotten me, and at that I felt some
natural pique, and resented her forgetfulness.

"Mistress Alison French?" says I, drawing
rein at her side, and staring hard at her beauty
as I swung my cap to the saddle bow.

"The same, sir," says she, that quick glance
of hers mixed with a little wonder. "But——"
and then she recognised me. "Ah," says she,
"'tis Dick Coope! So you know me, Dick,
although——"

"Although you have grown so monstrous handsome, cousin," says I, a little rudely.

"'Tis just because you yourself are a proper-
looking man that I did not recognise you," she

said with a frown. "You were as ungainly a
boy as ever I saw, Master Richard, and I don't
think your manners are improved even now."

I said naught, but sat staring at her. She had
grown to a divine tallness, her figure was as
plump and ripe as a woman's should be, there was
a rich colour in her cheeks, and a fine glossiness
in her dark hair that was mighty taking. As for
her mouth it was as sweet a morsel as a man
could wish to taste, and I could see that if her
eyes would melt they would put one in such a
way as few women can—they were so full of
that swimming roguishness that can become
tender and alluring. Howbeit, she kept them
hard enough at that time.

"And what brings Master Dick here?" asks
she, fingering her whip.

"This packet, fair cousin," says I, and handed
her Sir Nicholas's letter.

"From my uncle," she says. "You give me
leave to read it, cousin? I can ill bide delay of
any sort."

"'Tis reward enough," says I teasingly, "to sit
by and gaze on so much beauty."

But at that she frowned heavily, and when she
cut the silk and was fairly amongst the crabbed
lines within, she frowned still more, and once I

saw her white teeth close on the pretty nether
lip and crush the blood out of it, whereby I
guessed that Sir Nicholas had given her news that
was none too sweet. And at last she folds up
the sheet with a rustle and whips it into her
breast, and looks at me with a glance that had
made the great Turk himself shake in his shoes.

"So you prefer books to swords, Master
Richard?" says she.

"Did I say so?" says I.

And for very love of sport I laughed mock-
ingly. She drew herself up to her full height—
egad! I had never seen aught so taking!—and
her pretty mouth curled itself, while the rich
colour flushed over her dark cheek.

"Good-day to you, Master Poltroon!" says she.

"Good-day to you, Mistress Spitfire!" says I.

And with mutual consent we turned our backs
on one another. But I laughed long and loud as
I trotted away to keep my tryst.

Chapter II

Of my Meeting with my Kinsman, Anthony Dacre, at the Wayside Inn — of my Further Adventures, my Disinheritance by Sir Nicholas, and my Doings with the Parliamentarians—and of my Employment on an Important Mission by General Oliver Cromwell.

I.

IT was but little beyond noon when I turned out of Francis French's park into the highroad, and I suddenly bethought myself that if I went immediately to the trysting place I should be as like as not to cool my heels there for some time ere Matthew Richardson joined me. His message had required me to meet him within twenty-four hours, and of the twenty-four there were still some seven or eight to run. "Faith!" says I to myself, "he might have been more explicit—does he expect me to sit by the wayside like a tinker who puts his mare in the hedge-bottom to graze for her supper?" And I went on somewhat out of humour, and that not altogether because of Matthew's thoughtlessness. To

42

tell truth, Mistress Alison's last words, though
I had laughed at them, had stung me rather
sharply and roused a certain anger in me. Now
that I was out of her presence I felt her scorn
more than while I sat watching her. "So I am
to be flouted by every chit of a lass, am I?" says
I, with some bitterness. But on the instant my
humour changed, and I fell to laughter again at
the thought of her looks when I paid her back
in her own coin. "What care I?" says I, shaking
my bridle reins. "Here's for whatever comes
next," and so I cantered forward.

At the joining of the roads against Hickleton,
I came to a wayside inn of so inviting a sort
that I involuntarily pulled up my beast and
asked myself whether it were not some time since
breakfast. I then discovered that I was pro-
digiously hungry, and so made no more ado, but
rode into the yard and handed over my horse to
the hostler, bidding him take good care of it, as
it was my sole dependence for a long journey.
The fellow looked at it somewhat curiously.

"I could swear, master," says he, "that this is
of old Sir Nicholas Coope's breeding—we have its
marrow in yonder stable at this moment—'tis a
mare that Master Dacre of Foxclough rides—I
never saw two beasts more alike."

"Aye?" says I. "Why, truly, thou hast a rare eye, lad—but what is Master Dacre's mare doing in your stable?"

"Master Dacre's within," says he, nodding his head towards the inn.

"Oh!" says I, and stands staring at the door, somewhat nonplussed. I had not expected to meet any of my kinsfolk just then and scarce relished the notion. "Come," says I to myself, "what signifies Anthony Dacre?—we're as near strangers as may be," and I once more bade the man see to my horse, and walked into the house.

They seemed somewhat quiet inside — there were but two or three men drinking in the kitchen, and the landlord leaned idly against the corner of the settle, his hands tucked under the wide apron that covered his capacious paunch. At sight of me he started into activity. My eyes cast about them in search of Anthony —the landlord noted it, and thought I looked for a place worthy of my condition. "If your honour will but step into the parlour," says he, and flings the door open before me. So I slips in, and there sat Anthony Dacre with a jug of ripe ale before him and some trifle of food such as a wayside inn affords to chance comers. He gave me a glance as I stepped within the room, and I saw that he did not recognise me, which was naught to be surprised at for we had not met those seven years. For a moment, then, I stood staring at him, half doubtful whether to make myself known, or to go on my way without recognising him. Faith! I have since wondered many's the time indeed, whether much of what followed might not have been prevented if I had turned on my heel and left Anthony to refresh himself in peace.

Now this man Anthony — at that time my senior by some three years, and as proper a looking man as you might desire to set eyes on — was the son of old Stephen Dacre of Foxclough House, that was related to Sir Nicholas Coope by his marriage with Mistress Dorothy, the old knight's youngest sister. As for old Stephen and his wife they were both dead, and all that they had, which was but little, now lay in Master Anthony's hands. A poor parcel of land it was, that manor of Foxclough, the soil being stony in one place and marshy in another, and old Stephen had done naught to improve it, but had rather drained its feeble resources in order to keep up his roystering habits, much to the grief and perturbation of Sir Nicholas, who was given to frugality, though hospitable as a gentleman

should be. Thus Master Anthony had but little
to live and keep up his small state upon, and
since he was well minded to do as his father
and grandfather had done before him and live
as royally as might be, there was naught for him
but to curse his fate and sharpen up his wits
to his own betterment. And so far as his own
wits were concerned he saw no better chance, I
suppose, of improving his condition than by
courting the society of Sir Nicholas, and seeking
to ingratiate himself in the old knight's favour.
Thus it was that when we were lads together
Anthony was constantly at the Manor House,
and made himself rival to me (though indeed I
knew naught of it at the time, being young and
unlearned in such matters), in my uncle's affec-
tions. But there was something occurred between
them—I never knew what it was—which alien-
ated them, or, rather, which caused Sir Nicholas
to look with disfavour upon Anthony, and after
that the latter never came to the Manor House
that I knew of, nor did my uncle ever speak of
him except to say now and then that Anthony
was a real Dacre, and would be a scapegrace and
roysterer all the days of his life.

Until I met Anthony at the inn I had not
heard of him for some two years. It was said

that he had gone to the wars, and that Foxclough
—which was a half-ruined barn of a house when
old Stephen died — was closed. Then it was
thought that he was dead, or had gone across
seas in search of treasure. Certainly, it had
never mattered a straw to me whether he was
dead or alive, here or there. I knew naught of
his secret desires for Sir Nicholas's land and
money, and it would have made no difference
to me if I had known of them. But since he
was a kinsman, and we had been lads together—
at which time, I, as the younger, had somewhat
admired him—I made up my mind to speak to
him now that we had met accidentally.

"You have forgotten me, Master Anthony,"
says I, standing before him at the table while
the landlord lingered at the door waiting for my
commands.

He paused in the act of lifting his cup to his
lips, and stared at me.

"Why —" says he, "I am somewhat—is it
Dick Coope?" he says, half-recognising me.
"Lord! I did not know thee, Dick."

He stretched out his hand across the table.
"Sit down, lad," says he. "We will drink a cup
together—let me recommend this ale to thee.
But perchance thou wouldst like a flask of ——"

"Ale for me," says I, "It's all I am like to get for awhile, and maybe more than I shall get."

"Oh!" says he, and looks at me curiously. "Aye? Well, every man knows his situation best, Dick. Let me see, 'tis some time since we set eyes on each other, I think."

"Some seven or eight years, I should think," says I, sitting down before him at the table.

"Aye, it must be all that," says he. "And how goes the old knight, my worshipful uncle—od's zounds, he and I had a sore difference the last time we met, Dick. But you'll know all there is to know of that, no doubt."

"Nay," says I, "I don't—Sir Nicholas can be as close as any man when he likes."

"I should ha' thought he'd have had no secrets from thee," says he. "Art a lucky man, Dick, to be heir to so snug a little property, and I lay the old knight has a nice warm sum put away in some old stocking. As for me," he says, spreading out his hands, "here I sit, as needy a poor devil as any scare-crow in a road-side field."

Now I know not what it was that moved me to it, but there was something in me that morning which prompted me to say all that I

thought, whether it were wise to say it or not.
It may be that my parting with Sir Nicholas,
and that last stinging epithet bestowed upon
me by Mistress Alison, had disposed me to seek
consolation from the first person I met; certain
it is, that sitting there with Anthony Dacre,
who was well-nigh a stranger to me, I had
no more sense than to tell him all that was
in my mind.

"Aye," says he again, "as needy as any scare-
crow, Dick, and maybe needier, seeing that he
wants naught, and I want all."

"Why?" says I, "I don't know that you're
alone there, Anthony. Your estate——"

"A patch of stones and bog," grumbles he.

"It will feed something," says I.

"A score miserable cattle," says he.

"Why," says I, "but that's something. Now
here I am with naught."

He looked across the table at me in a sudden
surprise, and if I had kept my wits about me, I
should have noticed his quick curious glance.

"Hast never quarrelled with Sir Nicholas!"
says he. "Gadzooks, I thought thou wert—well,
well," he says, laughing, "then I am not the only
one of his relations to disagree with the old
knight, it seems. But what has parted you,

Dick?—I understood you were a sort of young Sir Nicholas already."

" 'Tis a political difference," says I, like the fool that I was.

"Hah!" says he. "I can well believe it in these times. And for which side art thou, Dick?—hark thee," he says, bending across the table to me, "I'm not afraid to tell thee, lad, that my sympathies are all with the Parliament. 'Sdeath, I have been considering this last week or so whether I won't join with them—'tis a gentle-manly occupation, that of arms."

" 'Tis what I am about to adopt," says I.

"I trust on the right side," says he.

"I am for the Parliament," says I, stoutly.

"Aye, and Sir Nicholas is a staunch King and Church man," he says. "Well, well—so you differed on that point, eh?"

"Something like it," says I. "He would have had me go into garrison at Pomfret Castle under Sir Jarvis Cutler."

"A man must never give up his principles," says he. "You stood by yours, of course, Dick?"

"As you see," says I, feeling somewhat impor-tant, and being foolishly willing to parade it.

"I fear the old knight will disinherit thee, Dick," says he, regarding me closely. "Even

as he did me some seven years ago because
I dared to contradict him on some trifling
matter. 'Tis a touchy old cock, and can ill
bide opposition from any man."

"Faith," says I, "Can he bide it from a
woman? He is like to have it in plenty if
I know aught," I says, the memory of my
little scene with Mistress Alison still fresh in
my mind.

"Oh!" says he. "Is he so? And how may
that be, Dick?"

"He has sent for Alison French," says I,
draining my cup.

"Our cousin Alison, eh?" says he, still curious.
"Aye, he had always a tender spot in his heart
for the lass."

"Will he preserve it?" says I. "She has
the sharpest tongue that e'er I heard."

He looked at me with interest. "I ha'nt seen
her this two year," says he. "She bade fair
to be a fine woman."

"Fine enough," says I. "But preserve me
from her tongue—'tis keen as a newly-whetted
sword."

"You seem to bear some lively recollection
on't," says he, looking at me with amusement.
"Well, well—I seem to have come home to

some strange news. But thou art not off, man—
sit out another jug of ale with me."

"I must be gone," says I. "I am riding south."

"And I am for my old ruin of a house," he
answers. "I have not set eyes on't this two
year, Dick. I must see to it, I doubt—and
then for the wars."

"Belike we shall meet there," says I, and
shakes him by the hand and goes out to my
horse. As I rode away from the inn I saw
him come to the door and gaze after me. He
threw me a wave of his hand as I turned the
corner.

II.

STILL in a sore discontent with myself and
my recent doings, I jogged forward through
Hickleton and Sprotborough to Warmsworth, and
coming to the trysting-place about four o'clock
of the afternoon, sat me down by the road-
side and waited until such time as my friend
Matthew Richardson should make his appearance. As for my horse, I tied him up to the
mile post and bade him crop the grass within
reach to his heart's content. "Yes," says I,
"eat while thou canst, poor beast—God only

knows what cheer we shall have in the days
that are coming!" By which you may perceive
that I had no great joy at the prospect before
me. Now this may seem strange, and yet 'twas
not strange, for, as I have told you before, I
had never much inclination for such an active
life as a soldier must needs live, and still less
for the privations that fighting men are neces-
sarily put to. But having put my hand to
the plough—by which I mean, having sworn
to embrace, and if need be, to fight for the
popular cause—I was bound in honour not to
look back. And surely my sympathies were
all in favour of the cause I had espoused — it
was but a natural sluggishness that made me
hanker after peaceful pursuits at a time when
most men were furbishing up their old weapons
with uncommon zeal.

About five o'clock came Matthew Richardson,
mounted on a good horse, and full of enthusiasm and fervour. He greeted me with warmth,
but was somewhat taken aback on perceiving that
I was not armed.

"Why, what?" says he, staring at me. "Is
it thus you ride to war, friend Richard? Where
be thy accoutrements, thy armour, thy greaves,
thy sword and spear——"

"You forget," says I, "that I am escaped from a house where every weapon is sacred to the cause of the King's Majesty. "'Tis a marvel that I have come hither at all."

"Ah!" says he, "I forgot, 'tis true, that your uncle is a staunch Royalist. Well, but we must arm thee, Richard, at the first opportunity. I have friends in Derbyshire," he says, musingly, "that will fit thee out, I think. So now to horse and let us onward."

"Whither away first?" says I.

"To Northampton, lad. 'Tis there that Essex is gathering the army in which lies all the hope of England. A brave array it is," he says, "judging by all that I hear."

"I have heard naught of it," says I, as we jogged along. "Until last night I did not even know that war had broken out."

"You are welcome to such news as I have," says he, and for the next hour he entertained me with information about the doings of the Parliamentarians. The Earl of Essex, it seemed, had been named general-in-chief and had appointed various officers to serve under him, amongst whom were Kimbolton, Stamford, Holles, Hampden, Cholmley, and Wharton. Lord Bedford was general of the cavalry, and had

under his command some five thousand men,
captained by lords and commoners, of whom
Cromwell was one and Ireton another. "Three
and twenty thousand men, horse and foot, there
are," says Matthew. "Truly, the oppressor hath
need to quail and quake before them!"

"'Tis certainly a goodly array to hear of," says I.

"Yes," says he, with enthusiasm, "and 'tis
representative of the will of the people, Dick.
Shouldst hear all that I have heard of the sacri-
fices that have been made! High and low, rich
and poor—faith, lad! I had not thought that the
popular cause had so many friends. But yesterday comes Geoffery Scales—thou knowest Geoff?
—he will meet us at Mansfield on our way—and
tells me that when he was in London t'other
week, there was the wildest enthusiasm for the
Parliament. Why, there has been plate of gold
and silver sent in for melting, and women of
fashion have given their gew-gaws, and the poorer
sort their rings and little ornaments—praise be
to God!" he says, with a sudden fervour. "It
rejoiceth my soul exceedingly to perceive so
vigorous a feeling in favour of liberty."

"Why," says I, "but is there not an equal
feeling on t'other side, Matthew? It seems to
me," says I, "that for every ounce of enthusiasm

on our side the Royalists can show another, and maybe more, on theirs."

"Thou art come out of a Royalist hot-bed," he says, not over well pleased. "I trust they have not shaken thy faith at all, Richard?"

"Marry, no," I says. "I daresay 'tis strong as thine, lad, though I do not show it in just thy fashion. Thou art a dreamer, a visionary, a man of fine and airy spirit, friend Matthew, and thou dost see far into the future, whereas I am slow as an ox at thought, and mighty sluggish into the bargain. Howbeit, I will strike as many blows as you like for the good cause."

"Yes," says he, his eyes kindling, "and what a cause it is! Thou callest me a visionary, Dick—why man, 'tis true I have seen the rarest things in my dreams of what this nation may be, once freed from the ancient oppression."

"Aye, and what shall she be, Matthew?" says I. "That is, if our side wins?"

"If our side wins?" he says angrily, turning hastily upon me. "If our side wins! Why, man, we are bound to win—wherever yet in the world's history was there a popular cause that was not successful in the end? But to thy question—why, Dick, we shall set aside the tyrant and all his unholy crew, and after that

we shall govern the nation in justice and righteousness and there will be abiding peace in the
land."

"The Lord grant it!" says I, with a sigh.
"Faith!—'tis precisely what I desire. Let us
press on, Matthew, and hasten its coming."

So we went forward, joined by one or other of
our fellows at various places along the road.
Some of them were enthusiasts like Matthew
Richardson, who believed that they had a heaven-
sent mission to bring about the millennium by
resort to arms, others were like myself, in full
sympathy with the wrongs of the nation, who
had come to the sorrowful conclusion that naught
but war would settle matters, and had therefore
resolved to join the Parliamentary forces. Five-
and-twenty of us there were altogether, all
students of the ancient University of Oxford,
who rode into Northampton under Matthew
Richardson's command to take service under
Essex, every man bringing his own horse and
his own gear, and each resolved to do his best
for the cause.

Now if this were a chronicle of my doings with
the Parliamentarian army I could here set down
the history of many things which happened to
me during my service under its flag, for in good

sooth those were stirring times and I saw much
of what went on.   But this is a plain account of
the most notable passage in my own life and in
that of Alison French, my cousin, and all that I
have so far writ is as it were a prolegomena to
the important business of my story.   But since
you may know where I was, and what I was
occupied with during the period which elapsed
'twixt my leaving the Manor House in 1642
and returning to it in 1644, let me tell you
that I was engaged in fighting the battles of
the people in no paltry fashion.   Faith! when
any man talks to me of the glories of war I
laugh in my sleeve at him for a fool that knows
naught of his subject.   I was in Ireton's troop
during those two years, and know as much of
bloody heads, empty bellies, and sleeping out
o' doors, as the best of them.   The marvel is,
looking back upon it from the standpoint of
a greybeard, that I endured so much privation
and discomfort, who had all my life been accustomed to gentle living and soft quarters.   But
we were young, and young folks, especially if
they have any enthusiasm for a cause, or dogged
belief in its righteousness, will endure a deal.
Now I had little enthusiasm, but much dogged
belief, and when I had finally assumed the steel

helmet and mastered the long sword of a trooper,
there was in me a grim determination to fight
for the true cause that made me regardless of
either a raw wound or a couch of damp straw.

III.

From the time that I said farewell to Anthony
Dacre at the door of the wayside inn until June
of the following year I never heard aught of my
relatives, though they, as it appeared—thanks
to Master Anthony—heard no little of me. I
was here and there with the army under Essex
all that autumn and winter of 1642-43, and truth
to tell, we had no very brave times of it.   There
was discontent and despondency, and also there
was disease and desertion, and there was the
affair at Kingston Bridge where we let the king
escape us in the most childish fashion, and these
matters did us little good, as you may believe.
The king was negotiating, and quibbling, and
lying, at Oxford, and nobody was sorry when
spring came and put an end to all the talk and
writing.   Essex reunited his army, and there
was not a man of us that did not look forward to
the resumption of hostilities.   It was Hampden's
notion that we should immediately invest Oxford,

which was at that time ill calculated to withstand
a siege, but Essex thought differently, and made
for Reading, which he reduced after a ten days'
siege. About the middle of June we approached
Oxford and fixed our headquarters at Thame,
within ten miles of the city, and it was while
we lay there that I received news of my relations
at the Manor House.

There came into my tent one afternoon a tall
fellow that first stared about him with an air
of great curiosity, and then enquired if he spoke
to Master Richard Coope.

" You do, master," says I.

" My name is Stephen Morrel," says he.

" I never heard on't before," I says. " Have
you business with me, Master Morrel ? "

He lugged a packet out of his breast and held
it towards me so that I could see the hand-
writing.

" Do you recognise that fist, Master Coope ? "
says he.

" Why ! " says I. " 'Tis my uncle's." There
was no mistaking the crabbed up and down
strokes. " Sit you down, Master Morrel," I
says. " Faith ! I had no idea that you carried
news to me."

" Why," says he, " I know naught about the

news, Master Coope. But suffer me," he says, seating himself, " to give you some account of the manner in which this packet came into my hands."

" With the greatest joy in the world," says I. " But don't be long in your story, for I am mighty impatient to read my uncle's letter."

" I will waste no words," says he, settling himself in a fashion that made me think he intended at least an hour's discourse. " It was after this fashion," he says. " You must know, Master Coope, that I set out from the North some three weeks ago, bearing despatches from Sir Thomas Fairfax to the Earl of Essex. 'Tis a mighty desperate thing, let me tell you, this carrying of despatches through a lonely country where you may as like as not be stopped by stray parties of the enemy, or fall across some town or village that is mad for the King's Majesty. What do you think, Master Coope, on that point ? "

" Sir," says I, " I am so exceeding loth to interrupt you that I shall not trouble you with my thoughts. This packet, now—? "

" Aye, to be sure," says he, " Well, Master Coope, I progressed safely through divers difficulties—though, indeed, I had one adventure twixt Northallerton and York that has elements of danger in't—until I had passed the town of Pomfret by some two miles, when my horse had the ill-fortune to fall and cut its right knee very severely. As you may believe, this put me in a sad position, for my orders were imperative. Now as I stood there, wondering what to do, there came along the road an old gentleman of exceeding fine presence, and with him the handsomest young gentlewoman that I have seen this many a day. 'Sir,' says I, 'I am in sore trouble, and crave your assistance. My horse has cut its knee somewhat severely—if your stable is at hand suffer me to lead him there that I may wash and bandage his wound.' 'Of a surety!' says he, very prompt and polite. But he suddenly looked at me from head to foot. 'What art thou?' he says, with rank suspicion in his eyes. 'Sir,' says I, 'I am an officer in the Parliamentarian forces.' 'A rebel!' says he. 'A renegade! Get thee gone, traitor—expect no help from me—shouldst hang from yonder oak!' 'Sir,' says I, 'I entreat you to forget that I am your foe, and beg you only to remember that I am a gentleman, a Christian, and in need.'"

"Faith!" says I, "you touched him in a sore place there."

" So I perceived," says he, " for he immediately
straightened himself up and looked at me very
fierce. ' Hah ! ' says he. ' Bring thy horse after
us — I have forgotten thy first description of
thyself, young man.' So I walked after him,
the young gentlewoman having gone on before,
and presently he turns aside into an ancient
courtyard that lay within the gates of an old
manor-house. 'There,' says he, 'take thy beast
into the stable and doctor him — God forbid
that I should not do thee mercy, even if thou
art an enemy.' ' Sir,' says I, ' I am no enemy
to you, but your very much obliged servant.'
' Tut, tut,' says he, and goes into his house.
So I made for the stable with my horse and
there put his wound to rights, and felt thankful
that I had fared so well. But my story is
wearisome to you, Master Coope ? "

" Sir," says I, " since you introduced my
worshipful uncle into it, it has possessed the
keenest interest for me."

" Well," he says, " while I was repairing the
damage to my beast's knee, the old gentleman,
your uncle, came to me again and looked at me
with some curiosity. ' So thou art in good sooth,
a rebel?' says he, at last. ' Sir,' says I, ' I am what
you call a rebel, and you are what I call a rebel.'

'Tis a mere difference of opinion between us.'
'Hah!' says he. 'Well I grieve for thee, young
man.' Be advised; go home, and serve the
king loyally.' 'Sir,' I says, 'I serve a greater
Power than the king, and am on its business
now.' At that he walks up and down the
stable awhile with his head bent and his hands
behind his back."

"A favourite position of his," says I, my
thoughts going back to other times.

"Then he comes back to me and looks me
squarely in the face. 'Art thou by any chance
going nigh to the army commanded by the
traitor Essex?' says he. 'Sir,' I says, 'as
between Royalist and Parliamentarian, no; as
between gentleman and gentleman, yes.' He
takes another turn or two. 'I have a lad, my
nephew, with that army,' says he. 'Wilt thou
take a message to him! 'Of a surety,' says I,
'if I should chance to come across him.' 'I
have no certain news of his whereabouts,' says
he, 'but if thou canst find him—his name it is
Richard Coope—tell him that—nay,' he says,
'why should not I write him letters with my
own hand?' 'Why not, indeed?' says I. 'But
canst thou tarry?' says he. 'Sir,' says I, 'I will
tarry an hour to please you.' Now at that he

bustled me into the house and had me into his
hall, where I found the young gentlewoman I
spoke of plying her distaff, and conversing with
a man of sinister countenance, yet handsome
withal——"

"Anthony Dacre!" says I.

"That indeed was his name. Well, the old
gentleman bids the girl see to my wants, and
faith! she caused to be set up before me a
noble collation, with good wine, but not one
word would she exchange with me of conversation, but was as coldly polite as you can imagine.
However, the man talked with me somewhat
freely, and seemed desirous of hearing something
of my business, as to which, you may be sure,
I said naught to him. After a time back comes
the old knight and gives me this packet, whereupon I took my leave. The sinister-faced man
came forth with me. 'As you are riding
towards Doncaster,' says he, 'I will set you on
your road for a mile or two.' ''Tis agreeable,'
says I, and away we rode at an easy pace.
Now within the half-hour we came to a steep
bit of road where there were many trees on
either side."

"'Tis Barnsdale," says I, mighty interested.

"I don't know the name," says he, "but I

E

have lively recollections of what took place there. This fellow that was riding at my side suddenly whips out a pistol and presents it at my face. 'Give me that packet!' says he. 'If you value your life, give it to me on the instant!' Now I then knew what I was dealing with, so I made a rapid movement with my horse and suddenly knocked the pistol out of the fellow's hand, and had drawn my own ere he could get at his sword. 'Softly, good sir,' says I, and lets him see that I meant to shoot him at the least sign of resistance. 'What is your meaning?' I says. But he began to scowl and swear, whereupon I relieved him of his weapons and secured them to my own saddle-bow. 'I perceive,' says I, 'that this packet bears some news for Master Richard Coope which you have no mind for him to receive. 'Now,' I says, 'I don't know where Master Coope is, or if he be dead or alive, but if the latter I'll see that this letter reaches him.' And with that I left him—'and here,' he says, handing me the packet, 'is your worshipful uncle's epistle, Master Richard—and faith! I think you'll acknowledge that I had some slight adventures in carrying it safe to you.' "

And with that he went out of the tent ere I could thank him for his kindness.

IV.

"HERE'S a pretty puzzle!" says I to myself, staring at my uncle's letter, and full of wonder as to its contents. "What on earth is that fellow Anthony up to now that he should try to shoot a man who happens to be carrying me a packet from Sir Nicholas? Faith!" says I, cutting the strings, "there seems to be something queer in all this—let's see what the good old knight has been minded to write to me."

Now Sir Nicholas's letter ran thus—I transcribe it from the original, which is strictly preserved with my other family papers :—

"NEPHEW RICHARD,

"As Providence will have it there is put into my power to-day the chance of holding some communication with you, and I hasten to avail myself of the same, and to take my pen in hand to write to you, though indeed I have no certain knowledge as to whether you be alive or dead. However, if you be alive I trust these may reach you, so that haply you may repent of your exceeding naughtiness upon hearing my admonition thereon, and be turned once more to better ways. Thou art my only brother's only child, and 'tis a sore vexing of the spirit to me that thou shouldst so strangely depart from those paths of virtue in which I strove to make thee walk. But let me address myself to the immediate purpose with which I write to you. It must be done in few words, for the messenger is in sore haste to be gone on his evil errand. God forgive me for lending assistance to an enemy of the king!—'Swounds, I would not have done it, but that he appealed to me as a Christian, and that I thought there might be some chance of communicating through him with thee, Dick.

" I understood, nephew, when you left me, that you were there and then returning to your studies at Oxford. This was displeasing to me, for I had wished you to fight for the King's Majesty, but after all there was naught of absolute evil in your desire or your faintheartedness. And yet two days are not gone by after your departure when in comes my other nephew, Anthony Dacre, whom I had dismissed years ago in your favour, Dick, and tells me that he met thee carousing in some wayside inn, and declaring thy intention of joining thyself to the rebels. 'Sdeath, it was a

marvel that I did not there and then run him
through with my sword! I never heard tell of
such a thing as a Coope fighting against his
sovereign—'tis most marvellous. But he assured
me in the most solemn fashion that he spake the
truth. I trust in God, nephew, that he lied, and
yet I fear me he did not, for I have since heard
that thou and Lawyer Richardson's son, and some
other of your college friends and acquaintance,
have attached yourselves to the enemy, being
hot-headed young fools. Still I am loth to believe
aught that I hear against thee, Dick, for a Coope
should always serve the king whose good pleasure
it was to make me a knight.

"I know not whether these will ever reach thee,
for I have really no knowledge of where thou art,
but I now write to inform thee that if thou hast
indeed joined the rebels all is over between thee
and me. I trust to hear better news, or at any
rate that thou wilt repent even at the eleventh
hour—I could find it in my heart to forgive thee,
nephew, even then—and return to thy proper
place, instead of consorting with a pack of
scoundrelly crop-eared knaves that would dis-
grace Tyburn.

"I would have thee know that Anthony Dacre
—whom I like not—is for ever pressing his

attentions upon Mistress Alison, thy cousin, whom I had always meant thee to marry. I cannot tell whether the wench favours him or not.

"I beseech thee, nephew, if these should come to thy hand and find thee a rebel, to repent thee of thy naughtiness, and to immediately abjure thy errors and return home. I am sore vexed at thy froward conduct, and shall visit thee sharply for it, but as I am a merciful man and stand in *loco parentis*, as the saying is, to thee, I shall also reserve for thee my forgiveness on condition that you do henceforward fight on the right side.

"Anthony Dacre told me that you spoke disrespectfully of me and of Alison when he met you at the wayside inn as you was on your way to the wars. I should joy to know that in this, as in that other matter, A. D. was a liar—as I firmly believe him to be, being much inclined that way.

"How hast thou managed for money? Alas —I wish I knew whether these words will ever come under thy notice.

> "I rest thy affectionate kinsman,
>
> "NICHOLAS COOPE, Knt."

Post-Scriptum.—"The messenger, being still at his meat, I open this to tell thee, Dick, that we had yesterday a litter of fourteen young pigs from the old sow, and that thy bay mare gave us a fine foal about a sen'night ago. The land is looking very well hereabouts, and so far we have had none of our stock or produce carried off by your rascally Parliamentarians, though we have twice contributed liberally to the needs of passing regiments of the king's forces, which, to be sure, was our bounden duty. My gout is a deal better—I am in hopes to harness myself and go to the wars yet.

"If all that A. D. says of thee is true, I am minded to cut thee off altogether. So no more at this present from thy uncle."

I laid this letter aside with many diverse feelings. It showed to me plainly that that precious rascal Anthony had drawn me out as we sat at the wayside inn, and had forthwith blabbed all I had said to Sir Nicholas, embellishing his news, doubtless, with a deal of his own invention and ornament. "If ever there comes a chance, Master Anthony," says I, "I'll pay you for your kindness." And yet, going by the letter, was there aught untrue in what Anthony had evidently told them at the Manor House? It was true that I had left Sir Nicholas under a false impression; it was true that I had joined

the Parliamentarians; it was true that I had
spoken of Mistress Alison French in a way that
was aught but .respectful. "Lord!" says I to
myself, "What a position am I placed in by
my own folly." And yet I was conscious of
naught wrong in my conduct. I had left Sir
Nicholas as I did in order to spare his feelings
(and to save him from locking me up, as he surely
would have done had he known my true
thoughts), I had joined the Parliamentarians
because I honestly agreed with them; and if
I had said aught sharp about my cousin, why,
it was because she had spoke sharply to me.
"The mischief was," thinks I, "to say aught at
all to Anthony—I should have kept my thoughts
to myself."

Now, I cared naught about Anthony and his
lies, or about Alison's disdain of me, but I had
an honest affection for the old knight, and felt
that I must endeavour to set myself right with
him, and therefore I went about the camp,
seeking Stephen Morrel, under the hope that
he was presently to travel North again with
despatches. And finding that he was, I sat
down and wrote a long letter to my uncle,
wherein I set out all my conduct, excusing
myself in naught, but putting my own case

boldly and in a manful way, and claiming the
right to think for myself in these vexed matters.
Also I assured him of my unfailing love and
respect for himself, and begged him to allow
me—these troublous times over—to pay him
my duty in person. All this I wrote and more,
and two days later committed the packet to
the care of Morrel, who was riding North with
despatches from Essex to Fairfax. But as ill-
luck would have it my letter was never delivered,
for Morrel was taken prisoner by the Royalists
ere he had well got out of Oxfordshire and was
shot, and so Sir Nicholas was left in ignorance
of me and my motives for a long time. Howbeit
there came at last a chance for me to put myself
right with him, and it was the seizing of it that
led me to the most important adventure of my
life.

Upon the twenty-seventh day of October,
1644, was fought the second battle of Newbury.
Essex was ill, and the army was commanded by
Manchester, who had with him Cromwell as
general of the cavalry. Which of us it was
that had the advantage I cannot say—the king
retired upon Oxford, but there was no pursuit
of him. Some said there was a difference of
opinion between Manchester and Cromwell, and

as to that I know naught either. What I do know is that on the following morning I was fetched to Cromwell's tent, where I found him sealing a despatch, and conversing with Ireton. He looked me up and down, with that keen glance of his, which seemed to read a man's thoughts on the instant.

" You are a Yorkshireman ? " says he.

" I am, sir," says I.

" I have here a despatch of the strictest importance for Sir Thomas Fairfax, who is now investing the castle at Pomfret," says he. " I think you are the man to carry it."

" Sir," says I, " I am at your orders."

He sat looking at me, his fingers playing drum-taps on the sealed packet.

" This," says he, " must not be permitted to fall into the hands of the enemy. 'Twixt Sheffield and Pomfret they are now in full force. I think you, as a native of that part, should circumvent them."

" I'll undertake that, too," says I.

" What do you propose ? " says he.

" Not to travel like this," says I, with a glance at my uniform. " I'll go as a travelling scholar— I have my old suit at hand."

" Begone," says he, and hands over the packet.

He kept his thumb and finger on one corner of it, and looked me squarely in the face. "If this should fall into the enemy's hand," he says, and pauses. He let the packet go. "You will be on your way in an hour, Master Coope," says he, and waves me out.

I was out of the camp in half-an-hour after that, and on my way northward. I wore my old suit, and out of one pocket stuck a Livy, and out of the other a Horace. As for the packet for Sir Thomas Fairfax, it was sewed within the lining of my doublet. I had ridden a good ten mile before I remembered that my mission would give me the opportunity of waiting upon Sir Nicholas. That, I think, added some zest to my adventure, for I was honestly anxious to see the good old knight once more.

Now, I made good speed in my journey, and met with little hindrance until the afternoon of the fourth day, when I was brought up by as unfortunate an accident as a man in my position could encounter. My horse, which had left Sheffield that morning, seemingly fresh and fit for the last stage of his journey, suddenly fell dead under me on the roadside 'twixt Hickleton and Barnsdale, leaving me staring at him with as rueful thoughts as ever I had in my life. It was then four o'clock in the afternoon, and by six I had trudged forward to Barnsdale. There, pausing under the trees, I stood to catch a glimpse of the Manor House in the distance. I laid my hand on the packet hidden in my doublet. " That must be delivered ere nightfall," says I. But I was dead tired, and by no means certain as to how my resolution was to be carried out.

Chapter III

I.

I WAS by this time on the threshold, as it were, of my destination, for only a short seven miles lay 'twixt me and Fairfax's headquarters, but seven miles to a weary man is no light thing to venture on, and the packet which lay in my doublet was of a strict importance. However, fate being plainly against me, I ceased to fight with it, and resolved to rest for awhile, leaning against a beech tree that was damp and black with the November mists, debating in my mind as to the advisability of doing this or that.

" Faith ! " says I to myself at last. " With my knowledge of the country it shall go hard if I don't reach Pomfret to-night, and on a good horse, too. And so let's see for such means as the neighbourhood affords."

As luck would have it the barking of a dog
across the fields reminded me of a farmhouse
that stood there. 'Twas a lonely place, lying a
long way back from the road, and so well hidden
by great trees that you might have passed it,
going north or south, and never caught a glimpse
of its gables. I had forgotten it quite till the dog
barked. " Egad ! " says I, hearing him. " Here's
the very thing for me. Reuben Trippett's bay
mare will carry me across this seven miles in a
trice, and I'll take her without as much as a ' by
your leave,' if only the stable-door be open." And
without pausing to reflect upon such questions as
to whether Reuben still lived there, and if the
bay mare (which he had lent me more than once
in by-gone days) was still his property, I climbed
the hedge at the next convenient opening, and
made my way across the dank meadows towards
the farmhouse.

By this time the night was closing in, very dull
and misty, and as there was no light in Reuben
Trippett's window by which to guide my steps,
I had some little difficulty in finding my way.
There were three fields to cross, and in the middle
one I called to mind a wide stretch of marshy
land in which as a lad I had gathered many a
handful of rare butter-bums. " Keep me out o'

that!" says I to myself, but the words were scarce out of my mouth when into it I flops, to my sore discomfort, and the sad besmirching of my breeches. But having met with it—and floundered out on t'other side after some difficulty —I knew where I was, and so went forward until at last I saw the farmhouse chimneys make a faint outline against the grey sky. There was a glint of light through a crack in the kitchen shutters. "Softly does it," says I, and I crept along the wall till the sneck of the fold gate lay in my hand. "Why, this," I says, chuckling to myself, "is the rarest adventure"—and so I was across the rotting straw in the fold and at the stable-door quicker than a star can shoot. "These cobble-stones," thinks I, "must be covered up, or they'll hear the mare's feet on 'em"—and I ran across to the tumbril in the middle of the fold and brought back an armful of straw and spread it carefully over the stones. "And pray God," I says, "that old Reuben hears naught, for his blunderbuss will spread pepper-corns over a good twenty yards!"

The stable door was unlocked—there was naught for me to do but lift the sneck and enter. Once inside I stood listening. On the instant I knew that there were no horses there. The place was cold, damp, evil-smelling, and silent as a dead-house. Now a stable in which horses have their habitation is warm as one's own bed at getting-up time, and so I knew from its very coldness that neither the bay mare nor any other mare or horse stood ready to hand. And I was outside again in a moment and standing on the straw that I had laid down so carefully just before, with my brains busily wondering what had come to Reuben Trippett, whose stables and byres had always been full of cattle.

As I stood stroking my chin, I minded me of the chink in the kitchen window. "I'll peep within," says I, "whatever comes of it," for I was in the mood for adventures that night. And so, crossing the fold with cautious steps I approached the window very gingerly, and put my eye to the crack through which the light streamed. And seeing that within which interested me more than a little, I kept it there and took a longer and steadier look.

There was naught in that kitchen (which I remembered as being well stocked with house stuff of all sorts) in the way of plenishing but a rickety table, a mouldering settle, and a crazy chair. The lath and plaster hung from the ceiling and walls in strips—'twas plain to me that old

Reuben was either gathered to his fathers and sleeping quiet in Badsworth churchyard, or gone elsewhere. Nevertheless, there was human life in the place, and it was the form under which it came that surprised me. Three men sat on the settle, and a fourth leaned against the jamb of the black, empty fire-place, the fifth sat on the broken chair with his back to the window through which I peered. One of the three on the settle I recognised for Jack Bargery, as villainous a rogue as all Osgoldcross, either Upper or Lower, could show, the men on each side of him and the fellow leaning against the jamb I had no knowledge of. But the figure in the chair, and mark you, I saw nought of it but the back, which made a black mass against the light of the candle burning on the table, seemed somewhat familiar to me and set some memories itching in my brain. And then a sudden turn of the man's head brought it all back to me, and I knew him at once for my precious kinsman, Anthony Dacre.

" Ho-ho!" thinks I to myself. " Here's a pretty meeting by candle-light. What may these five sweet gentlemen be about?" I says. And because my curiosity was aroused I straight forgot everything, Cromwell's despatch and all, in a rare desire to hear what the fellows were talking of.

F

But 'twas no good straining my ear, for there was a thick pane of dullish glass 'twixt me and them, and I could make naught out, though I heard a mumbling sound, and saw their jaws move now and then. And just because 'twas Anthony Dacre that seemed to be doing all the talking, the others only putting in an occasional yea or nay, my curiosity warmed to boiling point and must needs be satisfied. So for the second time that night I began to cast about for means.

Now, in the old times, I knew every inch of the land round about my uncle's estate, and the farm-steads were as familiar to me as the pump in our own stable-yard. I remembered, as I stood with my eye to the crack in the shutter, that in the rear of Reuben Trippett's kitchen there was a lattice at which the maids used to hand in the milk-pails from the byre. 'Twas a matter of thin strips of lath, and in the daytime was left swinging as the wind liked, but in the night a shutter came down over it, and was secured by a bolt. If the shutter, by any good or ill luck,—I cared not which it might properly be called,—had been left up when the house was deserted, I should be able from the byre to hear every word spoken in the kitchen as well as if I had been inside. So, remembering this, I stole round the corner of the house to the byre, all agog to hear what mischief Master Dacre, that scamp Bargery, and t'other three were compassing. That it was mischief I never doubted for a moment; there was not an honest pair of eyes amongst the four that I had seen, and I remembered Anthony's for more years than I could then call to mind.

The byre, like the stable, was cold and empty. I warrant me there had been no cows in it for a twelve-month. I had grown somewhat heated by my adventures in the bog, and the chill stuck to my bones and made me shiver. One glance at the far end of the mistal, however, helped me to forget cold and everything. They had forgotten to put down the shutter when they left the old house, and the lattice window made dim bars of shadow against the swimming light of the candle. There was naught left to me but to steal gently along the slimy walls of the byre (ugh! I can feel the damp of them now, and snuff their fetid odour, which then came thick and heavy to my nostrils) until I came to the lattice. And since I dared not venture to stick my head before it, lest the fellows within should catch sight of me, I got as near to the window frame as I dared, and listened with more attention than I had ever given, I think, to aught before.

Anthony Dacre was speaking when I put my ear as close to the latch as I dared, but he had evidently come to the tail of his sentence, and I could make little sense of it.

"Fair or foul," says he, to wind up; "fair or foul."

"And more foul than fair, I warrant me," thinks I. "A deal more o' the foul than the fair, Master Anthony, if I know aught o' thee." And I composed myself to hear somewhat more.

I heard a shuffling of feet on the kitchen floor, as if each man nudged his neighbour's knee.

"Come," says Anthony; "is there ne'er a tongue amongst the lot o' you?"

The man Bargery spoke—I knew his voice, too.

"Why," says he, "'tis like this: what use is speaking till we know Master Dacre's plans? Or are we as soldiers that march under sealed orders?"

"Ah!" says another; "well put."

"Why," says Anthony, "I see no objection to telling you all that's in my mind—why not? The main object's in your knowledge already; 'tis the details that you're curious about, eh?"

"There might be cutting of throats, and such like," said another. "'Tis best we should know. Forewarned is forearmed, so they say."

"Listen, then," says Anthony. "Faith, I think you'll say 'tis as pretty a bit o' contrivance as was ever devised. Sir Nicholas, as you know, has made himself something beyond obnoxious to the Parliamentarians, and I saw a rare chance in that. So this morning I goes to Fairfax in his camp, and professes my devotion to the Parliament, and then spins him a long yarn about Sir Nicholas Coope and his efforts to keep the king's flag flying over his old barn of a house. And, 'sdeath, lads! I played my cards so well that I got a warrant from him to apprehend my worthy relative, and take him before Fairfax. Here 'tis—there's Fairfax's own seal and fist."

I heard a murmuring growl from the four men, and the shuffle of their feet as they drew near to the table to inspect the paper.

"But——" says Bargery.

"When I've finished," says Anthony Dacre. "Now, here's my plan: we shall go, the five of us, and apprehend Sir Nicholas, and thus get admission to the house, the door o' which my pretty mistress keeps so persistently shut in my face. If the old knight calls up his fellows, we must give them as many tastes of cold steel as will suffice for their supper. I have little fear of trouble in that quarter, however."

"There are four stout men i' the house," says Bargery, "and as many arms as would set up a troop."

"What are four men to five, with Fairfax's warrant behind them? And thy four men—zounds, there is but old Gregory, and ancient Jasper, and two lads that cannot tell the difference 'twixt a musket and Sir Nicholas's cane! Besides, we go in peace—leave it to me to make fair professions. I look not for any fighting—nevertheless, 'tis as well to be prepared. But hark ye, lads, I have a second paper from Fairfax that I set more store by than the first. Look at that for a piece o' rare generalship."

I heard the shuffle of their feet again as the men approached the table, and a murmuring as if none of the four could read over well. "'Tis such a crabbed fist," says Bargery at last, and they shuffled back to the hearth and the settle.

"But plain enough for all I want," says Anthony. "'Tis a safe conduct, lads, granted at the request of Master Anthony Dacre to Mistress Alison French, so that she may pass through any opposition of the Parliamentary troops to her father's house. Now ye see my plan, eh? We shall go to the old knight and arrest him, but I shall be so full of concern and care for my cousin that I shall tell 'em great tales of my procuring this favour for her lest she should experience discomfort."

"But," says Bargery, "they tell me that she sets great store by the old man, and she'll therefore let it count heavy against you that you come to hale him out o' the house."

"And I thought o' that, too," says Anthony. "And so I arranged that two of Fairfax's troopers should accompany us to the house. We shall, therefore, be seven to four if it comes to fighting. Now, hark ye, lads, this is the whole manner of it. At nine o'clock to-night we meet the troopers at the corner of Hardwick village. They, Bargery there, and myself, go to the Manor House, and seek admission—t'other three o' you wait me in the lane that leads past Hundhill. We gain admission, and I, very sorrowful, crave private audience of Sir Nicholas. I tell him how it grieves me that he and I should think differently on these matters of state, but that I am at least an honest man. Then I go on to say that I have learnt in the camp that Fairfax has issued a warrant against him, and that being personally much concerned because of it, I am come with the troopers myself to see that no indignity is offered him. Eh, you follow my notions?"

"Excellent!" says Bargery. "I see the reason on't."

"Then I brings out my safe conduct for Mistress Alison," continues Anthony, "and offers her myself and three o' my own men as escort along the road. Once the old knight is off to Fairfax's camp, she will set out with me and you three that have waited for us, towards Doncaster. And as for the rest," he says, with a laugh, "why, I need say naught of it. And now, lads, we'll make arrangements for our meeting."

Then there was a silence, and I wondered what they were doing, and whether I had best not slip away ere they came out of the house. But I think the four men must have been staring at each other, each wanting to say something that was on his mind. For presently one of them, a fellow with as hoarse a voice as ever I heard, growls out, "And our pay, Master Dacre; ye han't said e'er a word o' that." At that I pricked up my ears. "Ha, ha!" says I. "Now there's a chance for honest men." But as luck would have it there was no falling out amongst these rogues, for Anthony promised to satisfy their demands, and presently they talked of parting. Thereat I stole away from the hatch and into the fields. The night had come on as black as a dog's throat, and I found it hard work to make my way back to the road, but, faith! I had so much to think of that I never once stayed to consider the whereabouts of the marshy ground. And it was most likely, because I never remembered it, that I missed it and went sailing along in the darkness, comfortable enough—for I never thought of the discomfort—until I found myself in the hedge which separated me from the road. That I had not perceived, but I forgave it, for all that it had run various thorns into tender parts o' my body. And so I climbed over it—having hurried alongside it till I found a post and rails— and stood on the road, once more wondering what to do next.

"Here's a pretty coil!" says I. "Egad, Master Anthony, I used to trounce thee in the old days —why did I not give thee such a trouncing that thou hadst never needed more?"

But what was the good of that? The thing was to do—not to stand there thinking. But as thought goes before action—at least with wise men—I gave two minutes to it. And this is what I thought: First, it was plain that my rascally kinsman, Anthony Dacre, whom I there and then prayed God to utterly confound, meditated some serious injury to Mistress Alison French, and was minded to stop at naught, not even the seizure of Sir Nicholas himself by force, in order to compass his evil intentions. Second : There was nobody but myself who, knowing his plans, could warn my uncle and cousin of their danger. Third : I had a packet from Cromwell to Fairfax in my breast, which I was in honour bound to deliver as quickly as I might. Fourth : It seemed but a Christian-like thing to stay at my uncle's house and tell him and Alison of that villain Anthony's notions concerning them. Fifth : What was I going to do ?—go straight on to Fairfax's camp, or proceed to the Manor House ? Sixth : Why the dickens should I interfere on behalf of Sir Nicholas (who had misunderstood me) or of my cousin Alison (who had—to my face, too !—called me a poltroon). Seventh : I hated Anthony Dacre, and would give much to circumvent him. Eighth : Blood is a deal thicker than water. Ninth : If I made haste I could inform Sir Nicholas, speak a word of warning in my cousin's ear, and go forward to Pomfret before nine o'clock. And tenth : Soldier of the Parliamentary army as I was, and faithful to the cause of the people, and to the special trust that their leaders had reposed in me, I

would see Parliament, people, Cromwell, Fairfax,
and everything, damned before Anthony Dacre
should have his will of an old man and an innocent girl !

" But God send," says I to myself, " that there
be no need of it !" And I set off along the
road at a round pace. The night seemed to
grow darker, and there is something in me—
and there was a deal more of it in those days—
that cannot abear darkness, but I trotted along,
being pretty sound in wind and limb, keeping
my ears open for any noise, until I came to the
cross roads, having Thorpe on one side o' me
and Wentbridge on t'other. And here a notion
struck me, for which I thanked God many a
time in the days to come. There were two
brothers, John and Humphrey Stirk, yeomen,
exceeding true and honest fellows, that lived in
their farmhouse at Thorpe, and farmed their
own bit of land—egad ! they were the very men
to do a good deed ! I had played with 'em
many a time when we were lads together, and
so had little Alison, and I knew that they would
put themselves out of the way to serve either
her or me. The thought of them came into my
mind as I trotted up to the cross roads, and
so I never stopped in my run but turned the

corner to the left and went forward to their house.
There was a light in the kitchen window—and so
I was within, half-breathless, holding a hand of
each, and looking from one honest pair of eyes
to another.

"God save us!" says Humphrey. "'Tis Master
Dick!" "We thought you was at the wars,"
says Jack. "And, faith, you look as if you had
been!" "Natheless," says Humphrey, "we're
glad to see you home again—and sit you down,
Master Dick," says he.

But there was no thought of sitting down in
my mind. And in a few words I had told them
sufficient of what I knew, and had begged their
assistance. "Willing enough," says Humphrey.
As for Jack, he says naught, but goes to the wall
and takes down his musket. "There's powder and
shot," says Humphrey, "in the cupboard," and
he lays hands on his own musket, that stood in
the corner. "Let's have enow of both, brother,"
he says, and Jack nods his head. "Trust me,"
says Jack. "'Tis but poor work to go fowling
with a single charge."

And so within five minutes of seeing their
lighted window I was back in the road again,
with one on each side of me, and all three of
us making our way towards my uncle's house.

" Anthony," I says to myself, " will have a greet-
ing that he recks not of." And I laughed at the
thought of it. But my laughter died away quick
when I reflected upon everything. In good
sooth, chance, fate, or Providence, had put me
in as tight a corner as a man could wish to be
out of.

III.

As we hurried along the road I made up my
mind as to my course of action. I would go to
the Manor House and warn my uncle and Alison
of their danger, and leave with them John and
Humphrey as a bodyguard. That done I would
make my way across the fields and through
Carleton to Fairfax's camp before Pomfret. I
would tell him of my wayside adventure, and
beg his protection for Sir Nicholas and my cousin,
and straightway return to East Hardwick. My
credentials were from Cromwell himself—I felt
assured that Fairfax would grant any request I
made to him. One thing, however, was certain—
I could not, although it was my strict duty to do
so, go forward to Pomfret without giving my
relations warning of their danger.

Neither John nor Humphrey were lads of

many words, and so there was little talk between us till we came to the Manor House. It stood gaunt and gloomy against the sky, and dark as the night was, I saw the king's flag still flapping against the staff above the gable. There was a faint light in one or two of the windows that overlooked the garden, but in the courtyard everything was dark. The great door was fast, and the stone lions above it seemed to threaten us as we tried the latch. But there were holes in the wall that had served me for stepping-stones to the top many a time, and within a minute we were on t'other side and making softly for the house door. It was some minutes before any response came to our knock, but at last we heard the shuffle of feet within, and then Jasper's voice asking who we were. Now we were not minded to shout and bawl so that folk in the street could hear us, if any were about, so I put my lips to the great keyhole and calling Jasper by name, whispered to him my own. I heard him utter some sound of great surprise, but he began to undo the bolts and bars, and presently held the door open a few inches and looked out at us from over his lanthorn. "The Lord ha' mercy!" says he, "I thought it must be your spirit, Master Richard. And is that

John and Humphrey Stirk that's with you? But we thought you was at the wars and——"

"Let's in, Jasper," says I, pushing my way past him with John and Humphrey close at my heels. "And hark ye, Jasper, bolt and bar the door again—is every door and shutter secure for the night?"

"Lor-a-massy, Master Dick, is there aught wrong? Yes, indeed, Master Dick, everything is fast for we're abiding in parlous times and never know who's about. But——"

"Go round the house, Jasper," says I. "Say naught to anybody, but go round and see that all's fast. Bolt, bar, and chain—we may have to stand a siege this night. And now let's within — where is Mistress Alison?" But ere he could answer me the door into the great kitchen opened, and Mistress Alison herself stood before us. She carried a lamp in one hand and held it up as she stopped on the threshold to look at us. Faith, I shall never forget her as she was at that moment, looking as proud and impatient as only a woman of her sort can!

"Who——?" she says, staring from Jasper to us, with a haughty interrogation in her eyes and the curve of her mouth. "Ah!" she says, sud-

denly recognising me. "Mr Richard Coope," she
says, and stares straight into my eyes with a
contempt that brought the blood to my face.

"Mistress," says I, hurriedly, "this is no time
for talk nor for quarrels. By chance or providence
I have learned that Sir Nicholas and yourself
are in great peril, and I have come here to warn
you of it, and have brought John and Humphrey
to protect you."

"Indeed," says she. But she stood there in
the doorway making no offer to permit us into
the kitchen.

"Let me see my uncle," says I. "He must
be warned of his peril at once."

"Your uncle is in his bed, sir," she answers,
still keeping her place. "He is ill, and is not
to be disturbed by anyone."

"Then let me see you within, mistress, that I
may tell you my news," says I.

"You can tell it to me here, sir," she says.

"Then, by God, I won't!" I raps out, losing
my temper under her provocation. "Look you,
cousin, I am perilling myself to serve you, and
you treat me like a dog! Is it mannerly to keep
me and my friends standing here as if we were
beggars?"

I saw the colour flash into her cheeks at that,

and she stepped back into the kitchen with a
motion to us to follow. As we came into the
glare of the lights I noticed, though it was no
time for thinking of such matters, that her beauty
was of the rarest sort and had deepened since I
had last set eyes on it. She stood by the fire,
one hand resting on the back of a chair, the other
still holding the lamp—faith! 'twas the prettiest
sight to see her thus with her fine gown and the
dainty slippers peeping from beneath it, and her
face turned to me with the scorn still lingering in
the delicate lines of her mouth.

"Now, sir?" says she.

But I glanced at the lads who waited in one
corner. "What we have to say is private," says
I. "Is there no more private room in the house
than this?" I says. But she would take no hint,
only she nodded her head to the serving-lads
and they slunk into the scullery.

"Madam," says I, "you seem to forget that
I am Sir Nicholas's nephew and a gentleman."

She turned and looked me from head to foot
and from foot to head. "A renegade!" she
says, and looks straight into my eyes. "Your
news, sir! I have no time to waste in bandying
compliments or exchanging opinions."

G

"Faith, madam," says I, "but you've no objection to applying epithets. But renegade or no, I am here to serve you and my uncle, and so I'll tell you all about it," and I straightway proceeded to give her a faithful account of all that I had overheard in the kitchen at Reuben Trippett's old farmstead. She heard me without a sign or a word, save that when I mentioned Anthony Dacre's name her lip curled with a rare scorn ('sdeath, I wish he had been there to see it!) and her white fingers closed tighter over the rail of the chair. But when she had heard me to the end, and I had told her my plans for their protection, she did not soften a whit, but looked at me with the same cold, hard dislike.

"I thank you, sir," says she, very icily. "It was the act of a gentleman to warn us." She seemed to melt there somewhat. "And now I will not trouble you to delay your departure longer"—she hardened again—"we are in no need of assistance."

"Nay," says I, "but that's just what you are in need of, mistress! 'Tis foolish to belittle your danger—Anthony Dacre——"

"I have no fear of him," says she, very contemptuous, in her own high manner. "And as for Fairfax's troopers, they will not gain admittance to the house. I myself will see to the bolts and bars."

"But," says I, "'tis not a matter of bolts and bars that will prevent them. Bethink you, they will force an entrance and seize Sir Nicholas."

"He is ill in his bed," says she. "They cannot move him."

"They will stop at naught," says I. "Come, cousin, be advised. Let John and Humphrey stay with you, and allow me to return as quickly as I can. 'Tis what my uncle would do."

"I am able to think for myself, sir," says she. "And I have come to my own opinion in the matter. And so I thank you for your good offices and decline your further help."

And there she stood, still looking disdainfully at me, as if I had been some upstart that had dared to address her. "Here's a pretty coil!" says I, and looks at John and Humphrey. "By your leave, madam," I says, and pulls my two companions aside. "What shall we do?" I says. "If we leave this spirited lass to have her own way there will be mischief. What do you advise?" And we all three looked at each other.

"Why," says John at last, "I should pay no manner of heed to her."

"Nor me," says Humphrey.

"'Tis a man's job," says John.

"Aye," says Humphrey.

"If I were you, Master Dick," says John, "I should call in Jasper and Gregory and the lads, tell 'em the trouble, and take counsel for defending the house. As for me and Humphrey," he says, "here we stay while need be."

"Well said," says Humphrey.

But I was half afraid as I turned to Mistress Alison.

"Madam," says I, very respectful, "I am sorry to do aught against your will, but I have taken counsel with my friends here, and for your own sake and for my uncle's, I cannot agree to your wishes. And so, mistress, you must be pleased to leave this matter in my hands to settle as I please."

"What," she says, "you dare——"

"Madam," says I. "No daring about it. You will please to regard me as master in this house, my uncle being a-bed, and leave me to do what I think good. John and Humphrey," I says, "get the men together, and let us set the matter before them," and as they made for the scullery I turned and gave her a long stare. She flushed crimson from neck to forehead, and looked at me with a sudden rage.

"How dare you!" she says. "How dare you!"

"Cousin," says I. "I dare aught. I know what you think of me, and for that I neither care nor fret. But when it comes to a contest 'twixt us I am not going to be beaten by a woman. And so I'll let you see which of us two is the stronger. Faith!" I says, "'tis for your own good. Renegade as I am, I'm perilling my neck to save you."

She stood looking at me with more wonder than I had ever seen in a woman's eyes. "I am mistress here," says she at last.

"Not while I am master," says I, coolly. "And as I have but a short ten minutes wherein to be master I shall exact the strictest obedience. Dare but to question one of my orders, madam, and I shall have you locked in your chamber." And with that I gave her a look that was meant to be as hard as one of her own, and marched forward to meet old Gregory, who was coming in with the others. But ere I could speak to him in runs one of the lads to say that four men on horseback were asking admission at the courtyard door. "They're here!" says John Stirk. And so there I was caged, with Cromwell's despatch in my doublet that should by that time have been delivered to Fairfax. " Present needs first !" says I, and I settled down to the business of the moment.

Chapter IV

Of Various Events of Importance which took place during one night, and caused us considerable Uneasiness and other Emotions.

I.

As they began to knock at the door, at first with a certain gentleness, but afterwards in as peremptory a manner as if the king himself had waited without, I turned to my cousin again, and again favoured her with a hard look. She stared at me with a rising indignation in her eyes, but I saw a questioning look in them that nerved me to preserve my stern attitude.

"Mistress," says I, "the enemy is at our gate, and we must perforce parley with him. There is no one amongst us better fitted to that task than yourself. And so, mistress," I says, still keeping my eyes on hers, "I must ask you to take your orders from me after this fashion. First——"

But here she broke in upon me, standing very straight, and holding her head very high, and looking me up and down as if I had been some country lout that had dared to address her.

"Master Richard Coope," says she, "I take no man's orders, and yours least of all. Your orders!" she says, with fine scorn. "*Your* orders!"

"Nay, mistress," says I, "we do but waste time. Do not let us waste more in explanations. You will not only take my orders, but what is more, you will do them. What! will you oppose your girlish whims and fancies to Sir Nicholas's good estate?"

"Insolent!" says she, her pretty face all aflame. "*You* to speak—I must be dreaming or going mad," she says, suddenly.

"Why," says I, "'tis a pity indeed if you are, cousin, for we have no time to listen to dreams or to deal with mad folk, nor with mutineers either," says I, putting on my sternest air again, "so come, mistress, let us to business——"

"Prithee, madam," says old Barbara, "do what Master Richard asks of you, else we shall all be murdered in cold blood. Thank the Lord, say I, that Master Richard should happen in on the nick o' time," she says, "a man is a rare comfortable thing to have in a house at times like these."

But Mistress Alison gives her a cold stare and looks at me. "What is it that you wish, sir?" she says. "Since I am in your power——"

"Nay, cousin," says I, forgetting all my stern manner in a trice, "it is to serve you that—but come, accompany me and John here to the chamber over the door; I wish you to speak with these men through the window. And believe me," I says, lowering my voice as she walked at my side, "I am deeply grieved to give you so much trouble, but 'tis necessary for both my uncle's sake and your own. And so——"

"Nay, sir," says she. "Spare me fine speeches, I pray you. You have taken the affairs of this house into your own hands, and since I am only a woman you compel me to do what I should not do if I were a man. Pray you insult me not as well as injure me."

"Oh," says I, "if you will so mischievously pervert things, mistress, why——"

But we had come to the little casement overlooking the courtyard. In the darkness we could but barely see the men on horseback below us. Three of them remained a little distance away and held the horse of the fourth, the crown of whose hat we perceived outside the porch beneath us. He was knocking at the door, this time very loudly. " Stand back," says I to John, and drew back myself into the middle of the room. " Now, cousin," I says, "open the casement, and ask who is there, and demand his business."

" You must put words into my mouth, then, sir," says she, fumbling at the latch.

" You have wit enough of your own, cousin," I answers her. " Use it with your accustomed sharpness, I pray."

And to that she made no answer, but I could fancy that her eyes flashed in the darkness, and that she bit her lips for pure vexation. However she opened the window and leant out. " Who are you that knock honest folk up at this hour ? " she cries. " And what is your business that you bring a troop of men into the courtyard ? "

" Ah ! " says Anthony Dacre from below. " Cousin, 'tis I—I am glad to find you here— I had feared you might have returned home. Prithee, come down and unbar the door, cousin —I have important news for you."

" I can hear it quite well here," says she.

" Why," says he, " I can't stand here and bawl it at the top o' my voice, cousin."

" My ears are very quick," she answers. " I daresay I shall hear it if you whisper it."

" But 'tis of the last importance," he says, "and besides, I have friends with me."

" So I perceive," she says, coolly. "And neither you nor they are coming within the house. So you better tell me your business at once, Master Dacre."

I heard him smother an oath. "Ah!" says he. "So you are still as vixenish as ever, fair cousin? But we are coming into the house, and so you had best be civil to us while we are without, lest——"

" Spare your threats," she says scornfully. " I care no more for them than for your civility. And so, if you will not tell me your business I shall shut the window."

" Oh," says he. " Pretty treatment indeed! Then let me tell you, mistress, that here are with me certain troopers from Fairfax's regiment who carry a warrant for Sir Nicholas's arrest. What do you think to that, eh? Gadzooks, I came here to see that the old knight suffered no hurt or inconvenience, and that yourself was protected, and you treat me like a thief! Come, cousin, 'tis a sad business, but war is a strange matter. You had best open the door at once— these troopers are not used to be kept waiting."

" Then let them go whence they came," she

says. "They will wait here long enough if they don't."

"Then you will not open?" he says, uneasily, and as if he could not believe his ears.

"I said so once," she answers.

"Why, then," says he. "I am sorry for you, cousin. I can do naught to help you if you continue in your obstinacy. These troopers will break in upon you, and——"

"Oh," she says, "a truce to your talk, Master Dacre. Let me say a word to you," she says. "Now listen; if you and your precious companions dare to lay a finger on door or window of this house we will shoot you for the vermin that you are—and so now we understand each other, Master Anthony Dacre," says she, and slams the casement in his face.

"Bravo, cousin!" says I. "Bravo! There was no need to give orders—your own——"

"Oh," says she, "spare your breath, sir. I spoke for myself, not for you."

"Ah!" says I. "Was it indeed so? Then perhaps, mistress, you will be good enough to show me where those arms are with which you are going to exterminate the vermin in the court-yard? For I doubt not, in spite of all your brave words, that they will attack the house, and in that case we had best be prepared to make good your promise."

And by that time, being returned to the great kitchen, I called everybody together, men and women, and held a council of war. And first of all we looked to the arms. In the hall there was a sufficiency of muskets and fowling-pieces, ranged in racks, together with numerous pistols, most of which were in bad need of cleaning. It turned out that Jasper and one of the lads had lately cast a quantity of bullets, and that three small kegs of gunpowder had been brought in but the week previous. We were therefore fairly ammunitioned, and I immediately armed every man amongst us with a gun, a powder horn, and twenty bullets, bidding each to shoot so straight, if need arose, that not a shot should be wasted. And this done, I proceeded to take a rapid survey of our position, and to consider how we might best turn it to account.

Now, my uncle's house was one of those ancient buildings which stand on three sides of a square, and the courtyard was enclosed on all but one side—the north—where it was separated by a high wall and wide gateway from the road. There was a great advantage to us in this, for the only door which opened from the courtyard

to the house was that at which Alison had parleyed with Anthony Dacre, and as it stood
exactly in the centre of the inner side, it could
be commanded from the windows of the other
sides of the square. It was a strong door of
stout oak, liberally studded with great nails, and
secured by as many bolts and chains as there
are Sundays in a year, and we now further
strengthened it by dragging a great table into
the porch and driving it between the door and
the wall. This done, there was naught but to
post two of my small army in such positions as
would command a view of the door from without. Fortunately for us, there were on the
ground floor, looking into the courtyard, but two
windows, and both of these I instantly secured
in such a fashion that nothing but a battering-
ram could have broken through them. On the
next floor there were more windows, and at
two of these, one on each side the courtyard, I
stationed Gregory and Jasper, with orders to fire
on anyone approaching the door that stood full
in their view. These two were favourably placed,
for they could keep the wall of the house between
themselves and the enemy, and at the same time
point their pieces through a broken pane of the
windows.

Of the safety of the door which gave access from the courtyard to the house I had little fear ; but there were three other doors which caused me some uneasiness. To the front of the house, looking towards Barnsdale and the south, there was a great door which opened into my uncle's flower-garden ; on the right hand, opening out of the room in which he kept his dried herbs, was a smaller one through which he often passed to walk along a sheltered path ; on the left-hand, opening out of the scullery, there was a door into the stable-yard. Now Anthony Dacre knew all these doors as well as I did, and would obviously select the weakest for his point of attack. The first thing to do, then, was to strengthen each of them. To this we at once set to work, bringing down great bedsteads, heavy chests, and whatever loose wood we could find in the house, and piling it up in such a fashion that if pressure were brought to bear on it from without, it would but drive our barricades tighter against the stout walls within. But this done, a great difficulty presented itself to my mind—all these doors being flush with the several walls in which they were built how could I place my men where they might command them ? I had found that easy in the case of the courtyard door, because two sides of the house overlooked it, but it was impossible as regarded the other three doors, and all I could do was to post men at the corner windows of the second floor with orders to fire on the enemy if they appeared to be approaching the doors with mischievous intent.

Now, as to the windows—I suppose that when they built these old houses (my uncle had often boasted to me that his was erected in the days of I forget which Henry) they had always in their minds the fear of a siege, and so the windows on the ground floor were as few as could well be, and each was supplied with exceeding strong bolts and bars that closed over stout shutters of oak. I saw to it that each was further barricaded and strengthened by the piling up against it of the heaviest furniture in each room—and when that was done there appeared to be no more that we could do towards making the old house stronger than it was. So now I took a survey of my arrangements, and found that they worked after this fashion: Gregory and Jasper were posted at upper windows on each side of the courtyard, commanding the porch-door; John and Humphrey Stirk were at windows looking out into the front garden; the two oldest lads, Peter and Benjamin, were stationed at a window which overlooked the stable-yard ; and the third lad, Walter, being very young, I ordered to run from one post to the other, supplying them with ammunition, or bringing them food or drink, as need required. The window overlooking the door which opened into the west garden I reserved to myself, feeling that an occasional surveillance of it would suffice. To Barbara and one of her maids I gave charge of the commissariat arrangements, and bade her stint none of my little army, having previously satisfied myself that there was provender in the house sufficient to last us six weeks. As for my fair cousin I requested her to attend upon Sir Nicholas, and to employ the other maid's time in the like direction.

And now, all these matters being attended to —and it had taken some little time, I promise you !—and the enemy being still debating matters amongst themselves in the courtyard—I had taken occasional observations of them through the window above the porch—I suddenly turned dead tired and sat me down on the settle in the kitchen, feeling curiously faint and hungry. I had sent an ample ration and a mug of ale to each of my men, but I myself had tasted neither bite nor sup for I know not how many hours. "Alack, Barbara, old lass !" says I, thinking there was nobody but herself and myself in the kitchen, "times are altered since I was last here! If my poor uncle had been on his legs instead of in his bed, I should ha' been invited to eat and drink—faith, I ha' touched naught since——"

But at the word Mistress Alison steps out o' the gloom, and in the glare of the firelight I saw her cheek aflame with the rarest crimson. "I crave your pardon, cousin!" says she—'egad, 'twas the first time she had so styled me since I entered the house—"I have forgotten my duty because of all this trouble. Barbara, see that Master Coope is served—nay," she says, "I will see to it myself," and she bustles about, and brings me meat and drink, and sets it with her own fair hands on the table before me. "Cousin," says I, looking hard at her, "I thank you. I am sorry," I says, and then stops, not knowing what more, nor what I had meant, to say. "But I thank you," I says. "Indeed, I am both hungry and thirsty."

"I am sorry, too," she says—but she did not look at me, her eyes being fixed on the fire—"I should have invited you to eat." She stood there, lingering, and still she would not look at me. "I fear," she says at last, and faith, there was a still brighter crimson in her cheeks, "I fear

I have been somewhat hasty—and—and—I thank
you for—for what you are doing for Sir Nicholas,
cousin Richard," — and suddenly she turned,
and gave me one shamefaced sort o' look, and
fled up the stairs.

Heigh-ho! I believe it was then that I fell in
love with thee, my sweet! Lord! what a colour,
and what eyes she had!

II.

Being now considerably refreshed, and having
reviewed my situation as I sat at meat, with
the result that I made up my mind to attend to
the business of the moment, and leave all thoughts
of the future until such time as they must perforce
be settled with, I arose from the table and went
the round of my men, whom I found very vigilant
and ready to discharge their several duties when
need arose. It was then close on midnight and
we had been invaded for nearly two hours, but so
far, the enemy had remained quiescent, and had
not so much as re-demanded our submission. He
continued very peaceful, and appeared to have tem-
porarily withdrawn his forces. When I reached
the window at which I had posted Gregory, I
found that the courtyard was empty, and that

all was so still and peaceful, save for the sighing
of a somewhat angry wind, that no one would
have guessed we were withstanding a siege.   But
there was naught to reassure us in that.

"What are they after, think you?" says I, as
I peered over Gregory's shoulder into the darkness without.   "They seem to have drawn off
altogether at this present moment."

"I warrant me they are not far away," says he.
"They put their heads together and talked awhile
after Mistress French had spoken with them out
of the window, and then they wheeled about and
passed the gate.   And it's my firm opinion,
Master Richard," he says, "that at this moment
they're foddering their horses in our stables,
though being appointed to stand here," he says,
"I can't decide that matter for myself."

"I'll go round to the east side o' the house,"
says I, and set off along the corridors to the
window at which I had stationed Peter and Benjamin.   "Now, lads," says I, coming up to them,
"any signs of the enemy?"

"They're in the stables, Master Richard," says
Peter.   "We watched them come in at the gate
from the lane an hour ago.   First, there was four
came together, and then three more followed after
them.   And they've turned out our horses," says

he, pointing to some dark shapes that stood disconsolate enough in the middle of the stable-yard, "and put their own beasts in the stalls."

The door of the stable stood opposite the window at which we were watching. It was one of those doors that have two halves, and the upper one they had left open, so that we had an excellent view into the stable. They had lighted the lanthorn that hung from the roof, and I could just see the candle that swealed and sputtered in it. Now and then, one or other of Anthony's gang passed and repassed the square of light. They were evidently making their cattle comfortable on my uncle's provender, and the thought of it raised within me a roguish desire, such as a lad might have felt, to spoil their sport. The swinging lanthorn and its glare of yellow light gave me a thought. "Isn't Master John Stirk a famous hand with his gun?" says I to the lads. "I have surely heard something o' the sort in bygone times," I says. "A rare hand, surely," says Peter. "A' can hit—— "

But I was hurrying along the corridor towards the post at which I had stationed John and Humphrey. I passed near my uncle's chamber on the way, and from a little distance saw Mistress Alison with her hand on the latch of the door.

She bore a bowl of some sick man's slop or other, and had no eyes for me, so I went on to find the two brothers leaning against the wall by the garden window, and gazing in silence into the gloom outside. " All's well here," says John, as I came up. " We heard footsteps on the path once, but 'tis a good hour ago, and they must ha' withdrawn for awhile."

" They are in the stables," says I, " foddering their beasts on Sir Nicholas's corn, no doubt. And since all's quiet at present," I says, " come you with me, John—I lay Humphrey will guard your post for a moment," and I led him back to where Peter and Benjamin stood staring at the light in the stable. " You are a good marksman, they tell me," I says. " Can you hit that lanthorn, do you think ? "

" Aye," he says, fingering his musket, " but not so well from here as from below. " There's a little window in the scullery, Master Richard, that I ha' sometimes made use of to talk with the maids. I could hit it from that."

" Come on," I says, and we went downstairs. " We will give these rascals a lesson," says I, as we turned into the scullery. " Now, John, mark the candle, and out she goes."

He opened the little window—'twas no more

than a pane of dull glass a foot square—and
pushed out the barrel of his musket. On the
instant the explosion followed, and the light in
the stable disappeared. We heard the crash of
the lanthorn as it was driven against the wall,
and the sudden stamping and kicking of
frightened horses.

"'Tis as dark as the grave," says John, closing
the window carefully. "Let 'em feel their way
to the corn-bins," he says, and we turned to go to
our several posts again.

However, before we were at the head of the
great staircase there came new developments,
which rather startled me and gave a different
turn to affairs. The silence of the night—which
had seemed twice as deep since John Stirk discharged his piece—was suddenly broken by
what appeared to be a regular fusilade, and at
the same moment a loud crashing of glass and
splintering of woodwork gave us notice that at
last we were under fire. Close upon their noise
followed a shrill scream from the corridor where
we had left Peter and Benjamin.

"Somebody's hit!" says I, and we ran along
the passages. Ere we had taken many steps our
feet grated on broken glass or kicked against
fragments of woodwork. At the corner of the

corridor leading to Sir Nicholas's room stood Mistress Alison, holding a lamp above her head and gazing towards us with anxious looks. "No lights!" roars I. "Go back, cousin—you give them a chance to see us," and I hurried Peter and Benjamin along the passage into an inner chamber, where we might strike a light without danger. "I'm hit somewhere," says Peter. "I can feel the blood running." But it was only a deep scratch that he had got in his cheek, from which the blood ran pretty freely into his neckcloth. "Off you go to Barbara for a clout," says I, and went back with John and Benjamin to the corridor. The night air was blowing in raw and cold, for all the window was shot away. "It's a lucky thing we wasn't in front on't, Master Richard," says Benjamin. "They must ha' fired all their pieces at it."

There was no great harm done by this first brush, though I was somewhat regretful when I saw the wreck that I had not allowed our enemies to burn their candle unmolested. However, they made no attempt to relight the lanthorn, and as we could see naught of them in the stable-yard, I made Benjamin fetch a great mattress from the nearest sleeping chamber, and with this we blocked up the open casement as well as we could. But we had no sooner got it into place than new matters called for my attention. A door opened suddenly and we heard a scuffle of voices, first Mistress Alison's, then Sir Nicholas's, thin, piping, but exceeding angry. "Here's more to do!" says I, and set off for my uncle's room, followed by John Stirk. "This," says I to my-self, "will be harder work than fighting," but I went boldly within the chamber. The old knight, startled, doubtless, by the firing, had got himself out of bed and now sat on the side, furious be-cause my cousin endeavoured to persuade him to return to his pillows.

"What the murrain!" says he. "'Od's wounds, wench, am I a child to be—'od's death," he says, suddenly catching sight o' me, "nephew Dick, as I live! So we are in the hands of the rebels, Alison? Faith, I never thought to see a nephew o' mine assault me in my own house!"

"Sir," says I, "I am here to defend you, and I present you with my very humble duty."

But something seemed to twitch his poor old face as I spoke, and he fell back on his bed. "Oh," says my cousin, "leave us, sir, leave us, and send Barbara to me quick!" And so John and I bundled out of the chamber, sore bewildered.

III.

During the remaining hours of that night our enemies gave us no more trouble than the mere observing of their movements. It appeared to me from what I could make out, as I went from one man to another, that they remained in the stable, and were of an uncommon quietness. "Hatching their plans, no doubt," says I, and was not unthankful that things wore their present complexion. I had no great love of fighting in the dark, and I considered, moreover, that our chances were better in the daytime, when we could use our eyes to some advantage, than in such a night as that when we could scarce see aught at twenty yards' distance. However, though they made no further motion towards attacking us, I saw to it that a strict watch was kept, and moved from post to post constantly, lest any of my sentinels should forget themselves and fall asleep. So the night passed, and in a somewhat sombre and melancholy fashion, for there was a mournful wind without, and in my uncle's chamber the old man himself lay grievously sick and in constant need of Mistress Alison's ministrations.

About six o'clock in the morning, a grey light being then apparent in the eastward heaven above Went Hill, I found John and Humphrey Stirk with their chins resting on their muskets, and their mouths as wide agape as young blackbirds are when the old bird comes home with a worm in her beak. "Ha!" says I. "By your faces, lads, 'tis high time you were relieved. Away with you to the kitchen, and bid Barbara see to food and drink for you while I keep guard. We are ill-mannered, but you shall have an hour's relief while there's a chance," I says, bundling them off, and feeling that it were scurvy behaviour to treat volunteers less considerately. So they thanked me and withdrew, and having been on my legs all night I sat me down near the window and stared at the grey sky outside. "Faith!" says I, yawning, "here's a pretty state of things that I have come into. Look upon thyself, Dick," I says, "as a dead man, over whom they have already said 'Ashes to ashes.' For thou wilt certainly be shot if thou stayest here, and hanged if thou dost escape. However, there's no use in repining nor in reflecting. Shot or hanged, what matter a century hence?"

And yet, as I sat there, I could not help but reflect, though I can with great honesty say that I did not repine. I think it must have been my

liking for philosophic questionings that made me
reflect in the fashion I did, for, in sooth, all my
thoughts turned to the curious manner in which
one small event or trifling circumstance had led
to another, until at last I was landed in a very
quagmire of serious result. But there I flew away
at another tangent, and began to ask myself
whether there is any event or action so trifling
or unimportant as not to have any effect on our
happiness or misery. Certainly the events of the
twenty-four hours then drawing to a close had
seemed small in themselves, and were yet pro-
ductive of results the most serious. If my horse
had not fallen dead by the wayside I should not
have stayed to think under the trees at Barnsdale, and if I had not stayed there I should not
have thought of Reuben Trippett's farmstead
and in due course gone there, and if I had not
gone there I should never have heard of Anthony
Dacre's plot, and if I had remained in ignorance
of that I should certainly not have been sitting
in my uncle's manor-house that morning waiting
for daybreak, and feeling myself already a lost
man. "Alas!" I sighs, coming at last to a definite
opinion, "'tis most true that no event is so
trifling as to be wholly unimportant. There is
naught so sure as that one thing leads to another

—the mischief is that we never know what that other is going to be."

I think I had gotten into this state of mind during my patrol of the house during the night. At first my thoughts had perforce been directed to the immediate necessities of the hour; but as things grew quiet, I could not help thinking about my own peculiar predicament. And the more I thought, the more certain was I of the result of my present proceedings. " Thou art a dead man!" says I to myself, shaking my head mournfully. " There is not a shadow of doubt about that. As dead as if old Tobias had turned his first shovel-ful——"

But at that moment—and it was a truly welcome relief, for I was, indeed, waxing melancholy —the door of my uncle's chamber opens gently, and out into the corridor steps Mistress Alison. She shut the door behind her with a pretty care, and seeing me in the grey light, came softly in my direction.

" Good morning to you, cousin," says I, rising from my chair and approaching her. " I trust my uncle is somewhat recovered by this time?"

" He sleeps, sir," says she, still very formal. " He has had but an ill night, and once I feared he was near to death. But he is now asleep, and I have left Priscilla watching by him for awhile."

By this time we stood over against the window, and I saw that her face was pale with watching, and that much anxiety was on it. She looked without, and something in the grey skies and dark fields made her shiver and draw the cloak about her shoulders closer together.

"You are weary, cousin," says I. "Will you not seat yourself in this chair?"

She looked at the chair and at me, but made no offer to take it.

"I was going downstairs," says she, meditatively, " but——"

"Why," says I, innocent enough to all outward seeming, "I have dismissed John and Humphrey for a brief rest, and it would not be amiss to have some one here besides myself, so that if there is need, we can give alarm without leaving the post. With the dawn," says I, "they will no doubt commence operations against us."

"I will remain in that case," she answers, and sat her down in the chair that I had just left. "We must all do our part to defend the house," she says, more to herself than to me.

"Aye," says I.

After that we were for some moments very

silent. For my part, I leaned against the wall watching her. After a time she looked at me gravely.

"How long will this continue, think you?" she says. "Will it be for some time, or shall we be relieved speedily?"

"Why," says I, "I see no prospect of relief, cousin. These fellows will doubtless be reinforced, and they will then make a desperate assault upon us. However," I says, seeing her grow pale at the thought, "we will hold out as long as we can, and we will do our best to contrive some way of escape for you and Sir Nicholas. Faith!" I says, "I don't see how it's to be done, seeing that we are hemmed in; but I'll talk it over with John and Humphrey—the three of us may contrive something. As for myself," I says, dolefully, my thoughts going back in their original direction, "I am a dead man already, and so naught that concerns myself matters."

"A dead man?" she says, staring at me. "What do you mean by applying such a term to yourself?"

"Why," says I, "I mean what I say. You see, cousin, I was sent north with a despatch from Cromwell to Fairfax, and——"

"Sir," she says, suddenly clothing herself with

a great dignity ; " I should prefer to know naught
of your rene——" But there she checked herself.
" I think you are loyally serving my uncle," she
says, " and myself," she adds, after a pause ; " and
I—I thank you for it, Master Coope ; but——"

" But I am still a renegade, eh, cousin ? " says
I, bitterly. " Why, so I am, I daresay, in your
eyes. But, egad ! a bit o' sympathy comes amiss
to no man ; and if one may not expect it from a
relation—but I'll not intrude my confidence upon
you," I says, and I swung round on my musket,
and looked out of the window. I think her eyes
must have followed me, for after a moment she
spoke, and when I turned she was looking at me
with some curiosity and concern.

" If you put it in that way," she says, meditatively, and she looked at me again. " I should
be sorry to appear unkind to—to anyone who
had done me a service," she says slowly.

" Oh, no thanks, cousin ! " says I. " I should
have done the same for any woman. Faith, you
did not think that I came here to save you from
insult because you happened to be my mother's
sister's daughter ? "

Now, beshrew me if I did not see her catch her
pretty lips together between her teeth as if in a
sudden vexation !

"I am aware that I am naught to Master Richard Coope," she says, cold and icy.

"I should have done it for any woman," says I. "So no thanks, if you please, mistress."

And I looked out of the window again. The dawn was come by that time, and the east was covered with a broad belt of dun-coloured light. When I looked round again I could see her face quite plainly under the hood of her cloak.

"But this danger of yours?" she says, looking at me and then away from me. "I think I— perhaps it might be well—will you tell me what it is?" she says, turning her eyes full on mine again.

"Why," says I, "'tis just this, cousin. I bear a despatch from Cromwell to Fairfax—here it is, stitched in my doublet. I should have delivered it last night, and because I have not done so, I shall certainly be hanged if Fairfax or Cromwell get hold of me. 'Tis a most grave dereliction of duty that cannot be pardoned. I shall most certainly die for it. So that you see, between being shot here and hanged before Fairfax's tent door, I have a pretty choice; and faith!" I says, "it causes me some concern, for I am not tired of life, I assure you."

"And if you had not heard of our danger, you

would have delivered your despatch last night ? "
she says.

" Why," I says, " I was horseless ; but I should
have made shift into camp somehow."

" And did you reflect ? " she says, rising from
her chair and standing before me, " upon what the
consequences would be if you came here to warn
us instead of going forward with your despatch ?
You knew that it was a question of our safety
against your own——— ? "

But what else she meant to say—and I scarce
knew what she was anxious to get at—I had no
opportunity of learning, for at that moment
there rang out a discharge of musketry from the
fold, answered by the shots from the corridor
where Peter and Benjamin were stationed.
"That's a beginning," says I, and ran off,
leaving her there without further ceremony.

IV.

I found Peter and Benjamin reloading their
pieces near the window which we had barricaded
a few hours previously, and immediately called
on them for news of what had happened. It
appeared that as daylight came they had
watched the stable door jealously, and at last

had counted six of our assailants emerge from it with their muskets. They had gazed up at the window which they had already shattered, and evidently catching sight of the lads' faces— for we had left spaces through which we might observe whatever went on without—they had discharged their pieces at it. Peter and Benjamin had discharged theirs in return as their assailants crowded back within the stable door, but they were doubtful as to whether they had hit any of them, though Peter thought he had seen one man clap his hand to his side as he hurried into shelter.

"But they were in and out again like a lot o' rabbits on a sand burrow," says Benjamin. "You saw their fronts and backs within a minute."

"Poor sort of fighting," says I, and bidding them stand to the post, I went to find John and Humphrey.

It was by that time broad daylight, and I therefore thought it well to go round the house and see how matters stood with us. I found all my men at their posts, some of them a little sleepy with their long vigil, but all keen enough to resent the enemy whenever he thought fit to attack us. I contrived that every man should be relieved in turn, and sent those thus discharged from duty to the kitchen, where Barbara saw to their needs. I satisfied myself that all our defences were in good order, and that there was little chance of the besiegers breaking in upon us at any of the weaker spots in our armour In fact it seemed to me, after going round the house for the second time, that unless some extraordinary measures were adopted against us, there was no reason why we should not hold our own against a whole troop as long as our provisions lasted.

I was engaged with John Stirk in further strengthening the defence of the window that opened into the herb-garden, when Peter came to tell me that a man was waving a flag from the stable door. "A flag of truce," says I, and hurried away to observe this new action. I then saw that the enemy had tied a clout to the shaft of a fork, and were waving it over the half-door of the stable, with an evident desire to provoke our attention. "We'll play the game fairly," says I, and hastily improvised a flag, which I bade Peter thrust out of the window while I went to find Mistress Alison. "They desire a parley," says I, "you must play spokes-woman again, if you please, cousin."

"I had rather do aught than bandy words with

Anthony Dacre," says she, following me unwil-
lingly. "Put the words into my mouth, if you
please, Master Richard."

However, there was no need for her fears on
this occasion, for instead of Anthony Dacre there
appeared one of the troopers in answer to our
signal. He came across the fold, carrying his
flag of truce in his right hand, and looking somewhat quizzically at the barricaded window. "A
queer fellow this," says I, observing him closely.
" We should have some sport with him."

Mistress Alison looked at me with a little flash
in her eyes. "Sport!" she says, and seemed
as if she would have said more. But the man
had by that time come close beneath the window,
and stood looking up at it. He was a tall,
gaunt fellow, with as long a face as ever I saw,
and a mouth that seemed to twist itself naturally
to the pronouncing of long words.

"Within there!" say he. "Ye that do suffer
investment, and are as captives in the beleaguered
city—does anybody hear me or not?"

"I hear you, sir," says Mistress Alison, putting
her face to the opening which we had contrived.
"What is your wish?"

"Why, mistress," says he, trying to catch a
glimpse of her, "as for wishes they are casual

things, and I have long eschewed them. I wish naught save to accomplish my duty——"

"I have no time to stand here chattering," says Mistress Alison. "Come, your errand!"

"I come as a messenger of peace," says the fellow. "Know, maiden, that my name it is Merciful Wiggleskirk, and that my nature is no less merciful than my name. I am a man of war, and yet my soul hankers exceedingly after peace——"

"Am I to stand listening to this babbler all day?" says my cousin to the rest of us. "Come, fellow!" she says sharply. "What is it that you want?"

"I desire your surrender, mistress," says he. "There are some of us"—he cocked his eye in the direction of the stable—"that do carnally desire the sight and smell of blood, which are matters that I cannot abide. Therefore, I come, merciful as my name, to bid you yield yourselves in the interest of peace. Let there be peace between us, I pray you," he says, rolling his eyes towards the window.

"Is that all you have to say, fellow?" asks my cousin.

"Verily, I have spoken, maiden," says he.

"Then," she says, "you can go back and say

that there will be much blood—yea, enough to turn your squeamish stomach sick, Master Merciful Wiggleskirk, unless you and your fellow rascals depart on the instant. What! you come like thieves and robbers, and then insult us with your offers of mercy—oh!" she says, "get you within shelter, lest we fire upon you."

"Peace, peace!" he says. "Peace, mistress. Woe in me that I should——"

"Get your musket in order, Peter," says she in a loud voice. Whereupon the long-faced man uttered a deep groan and hastened back to the stable, holding his flag above his head. Mistress Alison turned away without a word, and I was following her when John Stirk stopped me.

"Master Dick," says he, "there's a thought strikes me that's worth meditating upon. They're all in the stable now, and there is but one door through which they can come, and this window commands it. Why should they be allowed to come through that door, Master Dick? Why," says he, "shouldn't they have a taste of besiegement?"

"Faith!" says I, "a rare notion, John. Why did it not strike me before? However——"

"Humphrey and me," says he, "posted at this

window will stop any of them from coming through yonder door."

"And so you shall," I says, and gave the necessary orders, transferring Peter and Benjamin from the window where we stood to John and Humphrey's old post over the garden door. And since we now knew with certainty where all our enemies lay concealed, I withdrew Gregory and Jasper from the courtyard windows and bade them take the rest of which, being oldish men, they were somewhat sore in need. This done, I went back to John and Humphrey, and waited the next move of the game.

Now, after Merciful Wiggleskirk had returned to the stable there was for some time no sign of any action on the part of the enemy, both halves of the door being shut to behind him. But at the end of an hour, the upper half was swung open, and Jack Bargery's head and shoulders appeared. He was evidently in dispute with those inside, for he appeared to be talking in a loud voice, and shook his head fiercely as he fumbled at the latch of the lower half of the door. "There would be little loss to anybody if a bullet found its billet in his ugly carcase," says I. " Fire, Humphrey."

"With good will," says he, and pulled the trigger.

The fellow at the stable door staggered and clapped his hand to his shoulder. "Three inches too high," says Humphrey musingly, and began to reload his piece. "First blood to us, anyway," says John, "and 'twill read them a lesson." And so it did, for none of them showed so much as a nose-end at the stable door for the next six hours. Instead of being bottled ourselves we had bottled them fairly. And yet, as I knew quite well, we were enjoying but a temporary respite, for naught could be easier when the darkness came on, than for one of them to slip away to Pomfret and bring assistance from Fairfax's camp. I marvelled more than once that they had not done this the previous night, but I suppose Anthony Dacre had considered that matters would go better for him if he conducted his operations with a small posse instead of a large one, the command of which would doubtless have been in other hands than his.

The day wore on in quietness, John and Humphrey keeping a sharp watch on the stable door. From the time that Jack Bargery had dropped back with a bullet in his shoulder until late in the afternoon there was no sign of our assailants. But as it grew dark, the top half of the door was thrown open again and the flag once more thrust out. I was on guard at the moment, the brothers being gone to the kitchen for a bite and sup, and I immediately despatched a messenger for Alison while I waved our own flag through the window. It was Merciful Wiggleskirk who once more appeared, and he came across the ford as Alison answered my summons.

" I fear I must trouble you again, cousin," says I. " 'Tis another flag of truce. Will you make inquiry of the messenger as to its meaning?"

She frowned as she put her face to the opening. "Well, fellow?" says she. "You are come again, eh?"

" On a merciful errand, mistress," he answered. " In truth, we are at war, but should our enmity extend to the very animals? I pray you, mistress, to call a truce while we lead our horses across the ford to drink at the trough. The poor beasts do thirst exceeding sore—yea, even as the hart desireth——"

" No blasphemies, fellow," says she, and turns to me inquiringly. "What shall I say?" she asks.

" No," I says. " 'Tis but a trick that they may get out of the stable. Once under cover of the house wall they may go where they please untouched. In their present position we have them safe so long as daylight lasts."

" Yes," she says, meditatively. " Yes—but—

there's a notion struck me," she says, looking at me with a queer expression in her eyes. "Your danger, Master Richard—I think I see a way out of it. Would there be any harm if we allowed this man to water his horses, one at a time, on condition that none of his fellows leave the stable?"

"No great harm in that," I says, not quite seeing what she aimed at, but having some faith in her woman's wit; "but assure him that if any of the others leave the stable they will be shot."

She turned to the window. "Listen, fellow," says she. "You may bring out the horses yourself, one at a time, and water them at the trough, but if one of your companions shows his face we shall shoot him."

"Agreed, mistress," says he. "'Tis for the poor animals."

"And hark ye," she said, "there is a little window near the trough—place yourself near it when you come with the horses—I have something to say to you."

I saw the man's face light up with a greedy look, as if he saw some prospect of gain to himself. "I understand, mistress," says he, and hurried off to the stable, while Alison turned to me again.

"I don't comprehend your meaning, cousin," I says. "What is your notion?"

"That you should bribe this trooper to carry your despatch forward to Fairfax," says she. "It will but be a day late—and you can explain the cause of delay—and—and—it may be the saving of your own neck, Master Richard," she says.

I stood very still looking at her. "Hah!" says I, at last. "So you've been thinking of that, cousin. Why, that's kind——"

"Nay," she says, with a heightened colour, and her eyes that had wandered away coming back to me, "let us have no misunderstandings, pray! I could ill bear the thought," she says, "that any man should come to his death through rendering me a service. And so if you think it a wise plan——"

"I'll try it," says I, and made haste to summon John and Humphrey back to their posts. "If any man leaves the stable door except Wiggleskirk," I says, "shoot him on the instant," and with that I ran down to the little window that opened on the fold just against the great horse-trough. As I waited there for Wiggleskirk, I cut the stitches that secured the despatch to my doublet. Then I bethought me that it might be well to write some explanation of my conduct, so I hurried to the kitchen and found pen and ink and hastily wrote a few lines on the back of the paper. "The bearer of these," I wrote, "delayed by untoward circumstances, sends them forward by the only available opportunity." "That's all that's possible," says I, and went back to the window.

Wiggleskirk was there, keeping the horse and the pump between him and the stable. When he caught sight of my face, he started. "Hist!" says I, "come closer, but make no sound. Hark ye, lad, art willing to carry something to Fairfax at Pomfret for a handful of gold pieces?"

"To Fairfax?" he says, with some suspicion. "And what may it be, master?"

"A despatch from General Cromwell," says I, "that should have been delivered last night if I had not been surrounded in this fashion."

"From Cromwell to Fairfax?" says he, his mouth agape. "Why, that's very serious matters, master. A handful of gold, did you say? But what shall I tell——"

"There's naught to tell," says I. "Here's the despatch, and there's the money. Now, will you take it, saying naught to your companions out there, and asking no questions?"

He looked at the packet, and then at the

handful of gold that I had laid on the window-sill. "Agreed!" says he. He looked curiously into my face. "As soon as it's dark," he says. "Rely on me — though 'faith, I don't under-stand——"

"There's no need that you should," says I, and shuts the window in his face. I gave a sigh of relief as I drew the bolts to—I had, at any rate, thanks to Alison, done something to rid myself of the despatch and to secure its delivery.

Chapter V

Of my Reconciliation with Sir Nicholas, of his Last Wish, and of his Death and Our own Sore Straits.

I.

ABOUT eight o'clock on that, the second night of our investments, I sat eating my supper in the parlour, all my men being at their posts, and everything appearing of a satisfying nature. I had carefully watched the stable door during the evening, and had observed that when the darkness was fairly settled down there came out a man leading a horse which he mounted at the fold-gate. I made no doubt that this was Merciful Wiggleskirk, and that he was riding for Pomfret on a double mission. Although I recognised him for one of them that make a trade of canting hypocrisy I had reason to believe that he would deliver the despatch to Fairfax. That, then, was one errand; the other, I took to be the seeking of reinforcement for Anthony Dacre and his party. But in good sooth, it troubled me not at all that there was a prospect of our being attacked in greater force, for I had all along seen that if the enemy chose to invest us seriously we must ultimately give way to him. It had been my hope that Anthony would fail to find further help from Fairfax, or that he would think it dangerous to his own plans to seek it. Indeed, I was not without hope that the morning might find us with naught but Anthony and his own rascals to deal with, for it seemed to me more than likely that if Fairfax made enquiry in the matter of Merciful Wiggleskirk, he would withdraw him and the other trooper from Anthony's service. But whether he did or not was all one to me, for however things turned I was in a corner, and saw no way of getting out of it.

As I drained the last dregs of ale from my tankard there came to my side the lad Walter, that had run about the house on one errand or another since the siege began, and whom but a moment before I had sent up to John Stirk with a message. He seemed in haste, and there was that in his face which made me start to my feet. " 'Tis Mistress French," says he; " she wishes to see you at Sir Nicholas's chamber-door—I heard her say something to Barbara about his dying," he says, staring at me.

"Say naught to the other men," says I, and started for the stairs. I passed Peter and Benjamin at the garden window. "Keep a good watch, lads," I says. "They may attempt something under cover of the night," and I turned from them to see my cousin advancing to meet me. There was no lamp in the corridor, but she held a candle in her hand, and by its dim light I saw that her face was anxious and that she had been weeping. "You sent for me, cousin?" says I, and for the first time since I had entered the house I took her hand in mine. "I hope my uncle is no worse," I says. "May I not see him?"

"He has been asking for you," she says. "I think—nay, I am sure—that he is dying. He has been very quiet this long time, and has said but little. And his mind, somehow, seems so much clearer than it has been for some days— it frightens me to see how calm he is."

"Why," says I, wishful to comfort her, "do not lose heart, cousin, for it may be that he is somewhat better. But let me into his chamber since he has asked for me."

She opened the door and motioned me to step within. There was no more light in the room than came from the logs burning in the hearth,

K

but I saw that Barbara sat by the bedside, and that my uncle lay between the sheets very straight and still. "Here's Master Richard come to see you, Sir Nicholas," says Barbara, and got out of her chair with a sign to me to take it. "A's failing fast," she whispers, as I drew near the bed; "but a's bent on seeing thee, Master Dick."

I took the chair and leaned over towards my uncle's face. "I hope I find you somewhat recovered, dear sir," says I, feeling, as I think most men feel at such moments, very strange and ignorant of what to do or say. "Your pain, now—I trust 'tis abated since——"

"Is it Dick?" says he, opening his eyes and trying to turn his head on the pillow.

'Yes, sir," says I.

"Ah!" says he, very slow and feeble in his speech. "I hear great news of thee. We are withstanding a siege, it appears. I could wish to give thee some advice as to what should be done, nephew."

"I shall receive it gladly and with much respect, sir," says I, "if it be not too much trouble for you to speak with me on these matters."

"No trouble," says he, "no trouble, nephew—in these times we must lay aside personal——"

But here Mistress Alison steps up to the other side of the bed and lays her hand on his. "Dear sir," says she, very gentle and pitiful—faith! I could not have thought she was the same woman that had treated me to more than one sharp speech—"you will do yourself harm to talk so much. If you will but rest——"

" Pish!" says he, in his old peevish fashion. " Let me be, wench. Dick and me has matters to talk of. Hark ye, Alison, leave us to ourselves awhile—you women are for ever in the way when there is business of importance to discuss. See them out of the chamber, nephew, and come back to thy seat."

I looked questioningly at Mistress Alison across the bed. She put the tip of her finger to her lips and nodded towards the door. As I held it open for her, " I shall remain just without," she whispers. " If he seems worse, Master Richard, call me at once." " Depend upon me," says I, and shut the door on her and Barbara, and went back to the bedside. My uncle had managed to turn his head on the pillow and he stared hard at me as I approached. " Sit thee down, nephew," says he. " 'Tis poor work talking of serious matters when women are about.

And how goes the siege, Dick—shall we withstand the enemy?"

"Why, sir," says I, "I see no reason why we should not. I have taken care that all our defences are strengthened and that everything is in proper order."

"Aye," he says, "aye. Alison has told me as much—she praised thy generalship. I could like," he says, "to know how all this came about. What led to it, nephew?—these women, they have no talent for telling a straight tale."

"Why, sir," says I, "there's little to tell"—but I began and told him how I had chanced to come into possession of Anthony Dacre's plot, and of what had befallen us since then. He lay there, very quiet, listening to what I had to say, and making no more comment than an occasional curse on Anthony for his villainy. And when I had finished, "Thou hast done very well, nephew," says he. "'Twas well thought of to warn us of our danger. So thou didst join the rebels, eh?" he says with a straight look at me.

"Yes, sir," says I. "Since my duty seemed to need it—though, indeed, I was sorry to do aught that was against your wishes," I says, looking straight back at him.

"Well, well," says he. "I must not reproach thee now, Dick; and, besides, I have known some good men that have thought as thou thinkest on these matters. But I wish thou hadst been plain with me—there was something of the lawyer in thy manner of departing, nephew," he says, favouring me with another keen look.

"Why, dear sir," says I, very loth, as you may conceive, to excite or vex him, "it was for your own sake that I so behaved myself. And besides," I says, "you would have locked me up if I had dared to proclaim myself."

"Swounds!" says he, with a spark of the old fire in him, "and so I would, egad! Well, well, 'tis too late now to kick sleeping dogs, and I'm pleased with thee, Dick, for thy recent conduct. The lass Alison seems mighty taken with thee."

"I was afraid," says I, "that Mistress Alison looked on me as a renegade, and could ill abide my presence."

"Pish!" says he, "'tis a woman's way. I'll not deny," he says, "that she has had no liking for thee, because the wench is all for His Majesty, and we love not to have a renegade in the family, nephew Dick. But thy conduct of the last day or two," he says, "has changed her thoughts of thee, an I mistake not. There is a cordial by thee, lad ; give me a drink—I grow somewhat faint."

"Dear sir," says I, "I am sure that it is not good for you to talk. Let me go away, and do you compose yourself to sleep."

"Faith !" says he, making a wry face as he drank the cordial, "I shall have sleep enough enow, nephew. Let me talk while I can. What thinkest thou of thy cousin, Dick ?" he says, giving me a sharp glance.

"Why, sir," says I, "I think she is the handsomest woman I ever saw."

"Ha !" says he. "Thou thinkest so, eh ? I have left her all I have," he says, still keeping his eyes on mine. "Every acre and every penny," says he.

"I am unfeignedly glad to hear it, sir," says I, "for I am sure she deserves it."

"It would ha' been thine," he says, "if thou hadst behaved thyself."

"One must pay for misbehaviour, sir," says I.

"I am not sure," says he, plucking at the bed-clothes, "that I should not alter matters if there were a chance."

"Pray you, sir," says I, "don't think of such a

thing. I am very well provided for," I says.
And so I was, seeing that I was pretty sure to be
either shot or hanged within the next few days.

"Well, well," says he. "But things will turn
out well. I wish thee to marry Alison, nephew
Dick."

"Sir!" says I.

"Swounds!" says he. "Thou art not already
married?"

"No, dear sir," says I.

"Then there is no need for astonishment," says
he. "And, egad, she is as proper a wench——"

"Sir," says I. "She is the handsomest woman
that ever I saw, but I fear she is beyond me.
And besides," I says, "I don't think she likes
me."

"Pish!" says he. "Thou art but a lad, and
therefore knowest naught of women. There is
but one way of wooing, and that is to be masterful. Let 'em see that you're master," he says,
with a chuckle that came very feeble, "and
they're won."

"Faith!" thinks I. "If that's so I must ha'
won my fair cousin already, for I have been
masterful enough with her, in all conscience! I
will bear your advice in mind, sir," I says aloud.

"I would like to see it," he says, as if to himself. "But my days are numbered, nephew. Howbeit, if I die before this trouble comes to an end, I trust to thee to see thy cousin in safety."

"Sir," says I. "I will defend her to the best of my power. Trust me for that," I says, laying my hand on his own, which was very cold and white.

"Well," says he, "that's a comforting thought to me, Dick, for the lass has served my old age with much diligence and kindliness, though, egad," he says, "she has the devil's own temper, an you stroke her the wrong way. But there's a thing that I want to say to thee, Dick—bend down to me—ye may both be in need of money ere long, for things wear a troubled complexion. Hark ye, lad, there is gold and jewels hidden away under the hearthstone of the room where my dry herbs are kept. Use them as you think fit," he says, "there may be occasion to carry them about your person—there's more families than one homeless at this time, and nobody knows what may happen."

"Have no fear, sir," says I.

"Swounds!" says he. "What's the good o't? A dying man hath neither fears nor hopes, nephew. And faith, I think I have maybe

talked too much ; call in the women, Dick,—
Alison is the rarest nurse."

So I hastened to the door for my cousin and
Barbara, and bade them enter. Sir Nicholas
turned his head to me again. "See to thy
defences, lad," says he. "Egad, I wish I could
be with thee!" But there his face turned very
white, and the women ran to him, so I softly
closed the door and went off to see to my men.

II.

I was in some expectation during the rest of
the night that a reinforcement of the besiegers
might after all take place, and that we should be
severely assaulted under cover of the darkness.
The hours went by, however, without anything
of this sort happening, and as it wore towards
early morning I made up my mind that the night
was to be utterly peaceful. We had kept such
observation as we could upon the enemy, and it
was my firm conviction that some of them at
least had escaped from the stable during the night
and withdrawn to more comfortable quarters.
But since we had no assurance that an assault
might not be made upon us at any moment, I
kept the men to their posts, and myself patrolled

the house ceaselessly, only pausing now and then to call at my uncle's chamber-door and enquire for his health. About three o'clock in the morning as I stood at the head of the great staircase resting myself a brief moment, old Barbara came out of the kitchen and called my name softly. "What is it?" says I, going down to her in the darkness, which we preserved strictly, lest the besiegers should have any profit of our lamps and candles. "Is there aught afoot, Barbara?"

She beckoned me within the kitchen. "Master Dick," says she, pointing to the door that stood open 'twixt us and the scullery, "there is the curiousest tapping noise on the little window by the horse trough. Tap-tap-tap, tap, tap, it goes," she says. "I ha' listened to it this ten minutes. It must be a sign, Master Dick," she says fearfully. "To be sure, the blind in your poor uncle's chamber fell this afternoon, but signs may come more than one at a time, eh, Master Dick? Hark you—why, 'tis there again."

I stepped lightly towards the scullery door and heard the sound she spoke of. "Sign or no sign," says I, "I'll see what it is, Barbara," and I stepped within. But the thought occurring to me that this might signify some message from Merciful

Wiggleskirk I turned and closed the door. "Best not let in any light from the kitchen," says I, "lest the enemy see it." So I left Barbara there and went to the little window alone. After a time the tapping came again. Whereupon, keeping under cover of the wall, I put out my finger and tapped lightly in response. An answering knock coming from without, I undid the bolt and spoke. "Who's there?" says I. But lest it should be some trick of the enemy I kept closely behind the wall, for I had no mind to show my face at the window and receive a bullet in eyes or mouth.

However, as I had conjectured, it was Merciful Wiggleskirk that stood without. "'Tis I, master," says he, "and I have tapped and tapped this half-hour. I do naught by halves," he says, "and I could not ha' rested until I had told you how I sped with my mission."

"I am beholden to you," says I. "You delivered the despatch in safety?"

"It is in the hands of Fairfax himself, master," says he. "Great news or small, he knoweth every jot and tittle on't."

"That's well," says I, much relieved. "I thank you, Master Wiggleskirk."

"Why," says he, "I need naught of that sort, master, for you paid me excellent well. But I am new come from the camp, and since you are one of us——"

"What does that mean?" I says.

"I heard that you were of the true political creed," says he. " Faith, how could you be aught else, seeing that you carried a despatch from Cromwell?"

"I perceive your meaning," says I. "Go on, pray,"

"Why," he says, dropping his voice to a whisper, "as you are one of us I thought it well to tell you that ere sunrise there will be a troop here to reduce this place to submission. I was accompanied to camp," he says, " by Master Dacre, who seems to have ingratiated himself with Colonel Sands, and now you are to be closely invested and reduced. And, hark ye, Master Coope," he says, "if I were you I would——"

What more he would have said was lost to me, for at that moment Anthony Dacre's voice called across the fold. "What the murrain, Wiggleskirk! does it take an hour to water thy beast?" says he, and we heard his steps on the frosted straw as he came towards us. I shut the window and the trooper moved away. I caught sight of his figure and of Anthony Dacre's outlined against the darkness beyond, and for a moment

was tempted to see whether a bullet from my
pistol could not pick out the right man. But on
second thoughts I refrained, and went back to the
kitchen and thence to the upper storey to resume
my patrol, encourage my men, make enquiry after
Sir Nicholas, and wait for daybreak.

Now, when daybreak came there was ample
proof that Merciful Wiggleskirk's recent state-
ment had been based on truth. The house was
surrounded by troopers, who rode hither and
thither as if to take observation of their position.
There was an officer with them who plainly
assumed command—as for Anthony Dacre I saw
naught of him nor of his gang. I went round
the posts which I had already established and
exhorted my men to be brave and vigilant. The
lads Peter and Benjamin were somewhat concerned because of the array now set before them,
and so instead of leaving them together I made
Peter exchange places with Humphrey Stirk,
thinking that one tried man and a lad together
was better than two untried lads. Gregory and
Jasper I found unconcerned and ready—they had
more faith in our defences, I think, than I had.

Having assured myself that all was in order for
the struggle which I now saw we must quickly
engage in, I went to Sir Nicholas's chamber to

see how he did. He was by that time sinking
fast, having undergone a great change at cock-
crow. Alison and Barbara were in close attendance upon him, and as there was naught that
needed my immediate attention outside I prepared to stay with them for a little while. But
then came John Stirk knocking at the door and
asking if I were within. I joined him in the
corridor on the instant. "The officer," says he,
pointing to the window overlooking the garden.
"He is without there, flying a flag, and demanding to speak with you, Master Coope."

"Did he ask for me by name?" says I, mightily
surprised. "He must have meant Sir Nicholas."

"He said Master Richard Coope," says John.
"There's a fine lot of 'em without," he says, as
we went towards the garden window, and, faith,
he was right there, as I saw when I looked out.
Whether it was that he wished to make a brave
show and frighten us into resistance, I cannot
say, but he had drawn up all his men in the
garden, where their horses' feet made sad havoc
with my uncle's trim lawns. The officer himself
sat his horse a little in advance of the rest, and
when I appeared at the window was giving some
order to a man who stood at his side bearing a
white flag.

I opened the window and leaned out. "You have asked for Richard Coope, sir," says I, looking down at the officer. "What is it that you wish with me?"

"You are Master Richard Coope?" says he, looking at me with some curiosity.

"The same," says I.

"I would like to hold parley with you, Master Coope," says he. "I am Captain Holdsworth, and am charged with your arrest, and with that of Sir Nicholas Coope and his niece, Mistress Alison French. Do you purpose to submit yourselves to me?" says he, as polite as if he asked me whether I preferred white bread to brown. "Or shall we be under the necessity of using force?" he says, first cocking his eye at the brave show of thirty odd troopers behind him, and then glancing at me with an arch expression.

"Why, sir," says I, "I fear you will be under the necessity you speak of, for we have no mind to submit ourselves to you. Why should we?" I says, giving him back a smile as gracious as his own.

"This is Fairfax's own hand," says he, producing a paper, and pointing to some writing in the corner.

"I am so far away from it that I do not recognise it, sir," says I.

He put the paper within his doublet. "Can we not talk matters over, Master Coope?" says he.

"With all the pleasure in the world, sir," says I. "That is," I says, "if you love to discuss matters in so public a fashion."

He looked round him. "But I don't," he says. "Come, Master Coope, we are gentlemen and can trust each other. I will dismiss my men to a distance and you shall come down and talk with me—or I will enter the house and talk with you. I am quite indifferent," he says.

"Why, sir," says I, "'tis, I assure you, no easy matter for me to leave the house or for you to enter it. But if you will dismiss your forces, or give me your word of honour that you will not suffer them to molest or hinder me, I will come into the garden and talk with you right willingly."

"I will do both, Master Coope," says he. And therewith he turned and dismissed his men, bidding them retire into the meadow that lay beyond the garden. "You have safe conduct out and in," he says, looking at me. "I await your coming with eagerness, Master Coope."

As I passed my uncle's door Alison came out of his room and laid a hand on my arm. "Barbara tells me you are going to hold parley with the enemy," she says. "You will have no dealings with him in the way of surrender?" she says, looking at me very hard.

"Surrender?" says I, smiling. "Come, cousin, what do you take me for?"

"I have better thoughts of you than that," says she. She turned and looked at the door that separated us from Sir Nicholas. "He is near the end," she says sadly. "Let him die a free man, Richard, even if the old house is tumbling about his death-bed."

"Give me your hand on it, cousin," says I, strangely moved. She put her hand in mine and looked into my eyes. "I trust you," she says, and withdrew her hand, and went back into Sir Nicholas's chamber.

I called John Stirk to me as I ran down the stairs, and with his aid I moved sufficient of the barricade that secured the window in the herb-room to enable me to get out. "Wait there with your musket until my safe return, John," says I, and hurried round the corner of the house into the flower-garden. The officer waited me there, leaning against his horse. "So we are to talk, sir," says I, coming up to him.

"And I am glad of the chance, Master Coope," says he, frankly. "This is a strange business, and to tell you the truth, though I must and

L

shall do my duty as a soldier, I am loth to be mixed up in it."

"Sir," says I, "I am utterly at a loss to understand you."

"Are you so?" says he. "Look you, Master Coope, how would you explain such things as these? Three days ago, Fairfax issues his warrant for the attachment of Sir Nicholas, your uncle, who has been mighty active of late in vexing and annoying the Parliamentarian forces now investing Pomfret Castle. In order that the thing may be done with as little violence as possible to the old knight's feelings, he entrusts the warrant to your kinsman, Master Dacre, who on coming to the house, finds it already prepared to withstand a siege. Now within twenty-four hours of his sitting down before it——"

"Or skulking in the stable," says I, "but I interrupt you, sir," I says. "Pray proceed."

"Within twenty-four hours of its investment," he says, "you secretly hand a most important despatch to one of his troopers, bidding him——"

"Bribing him," says I.

"Why, of course," says he, laughing, "but at any rate, he was to carry it to Fairfax. And so he does, and it proves to be a despatch from Cromwell, of great moment. And so, naturally,

Fairfax wants to know how you, the bearer, came to be in the house of a Royalist when you should have been making all speed to him with the despatch—and since he wants to know, he will know, and that, Master Coope," he says, "is why I'm here."

"Sir," says I, "if I tell you the exact facts of the case, will you make Fairfax immediately acquainted with them? For I can assure you they are somewhat different to the representations made to him by that fox, Anthony Dacre," I says, looking hard at him.

"I will indeed fulful your wish," he says. "Faith, I thought there must be some other aspect of the case."

"You shall see the true one," I says, and I told him of all that had chanced since I came to the top of the road at Barnsdale. He listened attentively. "And a much more likely story than t'other!" says he, when I had finished. "I will repeat it to a trusty messenger and send him on to Fairfax at once. But, Master Coope," says he, "why not submit yourselves and go with me to Fairfax? Tell him your tale with your own lips," he says.

"Why, sir," says I, "personally, I have no objection to going before Fairfax. But within the house, my uncle lies dying, and my cousin is at his bedside, and neither will yield to you except by force. And while they're there," says I, "there I shall stay."

"Then our negotiations must fall through," says he, regretfully. "Is there no chance, Master Coope—for look you, I must do my duty—Fairfax and Sands are stern men, and I am jealously watched."

"Sir," I says, "there is no help for it — we must each do our duty in our own fashion. Your bullets," I says, with a glance at the old walls, "will find something to resist them."

"Well," says he, "'tis a pity, Master Coope, but—at least let us shake hands ere we fight," he says, and held out his own.

"With all the pleasure in the world," says I.

"We shall meet again, I think," he says—and so I left him and hastened to rejoin John Stirk and make good the window.

III.

As we were now to engage in operations to which those that we had already gone through were as child's play, I thought it well to call all my men together and give them some inkling of what was

about to take place. I had no doubt that Captain Holdsworth and his troopers would presently
attack us with much persistence, but as my sentinels were already posted to the best advantage,
and as we should mainly have to depend upon
the strength of the old house itself and of the
barricades that we had constructed, I reflected
that a few moments given over to friendly consideration of our position would not be spent
amiss. I therefore sent John Stirk to collect our
forces, who presently met me in the great hall,
each man bearing his weapon, and evidently agog
with excited interest as to the result of my parley
with the enemy.

"Now, lads," says I, facing them, "we are at
last in for some hot work. I have parleyed with
the leader of the troops outside, and found him as
reasonable a gentleman as ever bestrode a horse,
but as firm in his notions of duty as I trust you
and I are. He has to do his duty, which is to
arrest Sir Nicholas, Mistress French, and myself.
We have to do ours, and what that is," I says,
looking quickly from one face to another, "what
that is, lads, you all know. So there's naught for
it but for him to attack, and for us to defend.
But, lads, since we are all of us volunteers in this
matter, so to speak, tell me whether I have done

the right thing in refusing to submit? Have I done what my uncle would have done had he been elsewhere than on his death-bed? And have I done what's good to all of you? Speak, lads."

"'Tis what Sir Nicholas had done, and it is good to me," says Gregory, grounding his musket with a bang.

"So say I," says Jasper.

The three lads said naught, being of a shy disposition, but they nodded their heads and handled their guns, and looked from one to the other of us. John and Humphrey said "Yes—'tis good," in one breath. But so that we might all know what we were after, I spoke again.

"Now, lads," says I, "let's understand matters fairly. We may all very soon be shot or slain in some other way—is there any of you that would like to make his escape while there's a chance? If there is, let him speak." I looked at the lad Walter who was youngest of all of us. "What say you, lad?" says I. "Come, speak out—we shall not think the less of thee if thou wouldst like to be free of this business."

But the lad shook his head, and flushed as red as a peony. "I'm for biding where I am, Master Dick," says he. "And me, too," says Peter, "and me," say Benjamin.

" Why," says I, " I think we're all of a mind.
So now to our posts, lads, and let's do our best.
They will not break through our defences so
easily, and we have the advantage of safe
cover."

And there I was right, and events quickly
proved it. When we reached the upper storey,
and I could keep an eye on the operations of
the enemy, I perceived that Captain Holdsworth
was putting his men at various points around
the house, with the view of covering those of
our positions which previous incidents had
made Anthony Dacre already acquainted with.
Thus he had placed a squad in the stable, and
they were now engaged in piercing the wall
at intervals from the inside ; several men were
in the summer-house across the garden, while
others occupied the barn, and commanded the
window on the right hand side of the courtyard.
I made note of all these preparations, and
bade my men observe them with care, but
directed that no shot should be fired until the
enemy actually came to the attack. I was
somewhat curious to see in what mode they
would do this, and felt that it would repay us
to save our powder and ball until we knew
just what was going to be done.

About half-past nine o'clock I perceived that we were about to enter upon the struggle. Some twenty-five troopers were arrayed at our front, finding such cover as they' could in the summer-house, behind the wall, and in the rear of the trees. Captain Holdsworth, who had dismounted, was going hither and thither, but it was also evident that something was developing close to the house wall, which we, from our position in the upper windows were unable to see. "We must know what's going on," says I, "but how to do it I can't think." And, indeed, the thing was difficult, for all the windows on the ground floor were barricaded and strengthened, so that it was impossible to see out of any of them. "What of the garret windows?" thinks I. "I may get a peep from one of them without being seen," and on the instant I ran up the stair and into a little place immediately above the garden door. I opened the casement, and pushed out head and shoulders, and as I did so I heard the report of a musket below, and felt a sudden sharp pain as if a hot needle had been laid against the skin of my forehead. I withdrew my head instantly, and as I did so another half-dozen of bullets came rattling about the window. "Too late, my masters!" says I

and ran, laughing, down the stairs, satisfied
with my endeavour.   For in the rapid glance
that I had taken of the garden below I had seen
and comprehended what they were after.   From
the stackyard beyond the barn they had brought
one of the great pieces of timber on which the
foundations of a hayrick was laid, and a half-
score of stalwart fellows were getting it into
position, so that they might batter the door in.
As I came to John Stirk's post again we heard
the first blow, and felt the old walls shake with
its force.   "Let them batter," says I, and wiped
away the blood that ran down my nose from the
scratch on my forehead.   "They will want a stout
ram to break through our barricade," says I, and
I picked up my musket and prepared for action.

As our defences seemed to be most needed at
the front of the house, I sent the lad Walter to
fetch Humphrey Stirk from his post overlooking the fold, and Gregory from the courtyard window.   There were now five of us in
the corridor, and to each man I assigned a
window, bidding all to shoot straight, and
keep under cover as closely as was possible.
"And since we're all ready," says I, raising my voice, and presenting my piece,
"pick your man, lads, and let them have

it." And therewith, keeping behind the wall as well as I could, I knocked out a pane of glass, and took aim at Holdsworth, who was directing operations, partly covered by a tree. The others fired at the same time, and almost on the instant there came back a volley from the enemy, and the garden, from the high wall to our windows was filled with smoke that hung heavy in the damp air. And after that there was no need for us to knock out more panes of glass when we wished to point our muskets, for with the first fusilade the enemy shattered our windows to pieces, and the corridor was strewn with splinters of wood and glass, and fragments of the plaster that came tumbling from the wall behind us.

It was on this scene that Mistress Alison's eyes fell when she suddenly opened the door of my uncle's chamber, and came hurriedly towards me. "Back, cousin!" says I, rushing to meet her. "Your life——" But she came on, holding out her hands to me. "Quick!" she says. "Oh, be quick, cousin!" And then I knew what she meant, and threw aside my musket, and with a hasty cry to my men to stand to their posts I took her hand and hastened with her into Sir Nicholas's room.

Faith! in the days that came afterwards I have often thought, always with a deal of softness, of the good old knight's death-bed. He lay there, very straight and calm, with me on one side of him, and Alison on t'other, and poor old Barbara, weeping and bemoaning him, at his feet, and thanks to the stout door and the heavy curtain the chamber seemed peaceful, and yet through all its peacefulness there came the thump, thump, thump, of the battering ram and the crash and rattle of the musketry. When I first approached him I think he knew naught, but presently a fiercer discharge, that seemed like to bring the old house tumbling about our ears, called him back to life, and he opened his eyes, and looked at me.

"Ah!" says he, very feeble and low in voice. "So we are at it, Dick?" There was a sudden flash of fire in his old eyes, and a blot of colour showed itself on his cheek, that had grown thin and pale. He looked at Alison, and from her to me again. Another fierce rattle of musketry came from without, and one bullet, glancing from the casement in the corridor, struck and buried itself in the door of the chamber. My uncle made some faint show of raising himself in his bed. "To thy post, Dick!" says he, and suddenly drops back on his pillow, and died as quietly as a child goes to sleep.

"'Tis over, cousin," I whispers across the bed. Alison looked from his face to mine, and I saw that the girl had a rare faculty of keeping her feelings in control. "Leave us now, cousin," she says. But since that might be the last chance that I should ever have of seeing my uncle again, I took another look at him and laid my hand on his. Then I turned to the door, and passed from the quietness of the death-chamber into the hell that raged without.

The corridor was thick with smoke: my feet kicked against the splintered wood and glass, or stumbled over the heaps of plaster that were being rapidly piled up along the floor. Faith, the enemy were making hot work of it! But my men were unhurt, save that John Stirk had been struck in the side by a half-spent bullet, and that Peter's face was scratched by a shower of falling glass. "Stand to your posts!" I cried to them, and ran downstairs to see how the garden door had withstood its battering. I found it safe as a rock—what it might have suffered without I know not, but within, its heavy bolts and bars, supported by the mass of furniture that we had piled against it, still held the thick oaken frame sound, and I felt assured that naught less than a cannonade would break through it.

While I stood in the hall, examining our defences, there came the thump, thump of the battering-ram from the other door leading to the courtyard. I laughed when I heard it, for the enemy might as well have tried to break in through a twelve-foot wall as through the barricade which he was now attempting. The door opened into a porch, and the porch was filled with heavy flagstones that we had hastily torn up from the scullery and pantry floor, and disposed in such a fashion that the whole formed a tight wedge between the door itself and the stout wall facing it on the inside. But secure as I felt about the door, I was not so sure of our ability to direct a smart fire upon the men engaged in battering it. I hastened to the window on the right hand side of the courtyard, and found that Holdsworth's troopers, stationed in the barn, were keeping up such a fusilade upon us as rendered it impossible for my men to do more than get an occasional shot from a sharp angle of the casement. I accordingly withdrew them to the window on the other side, and from this point we did considerable execution, until Holdsworth brought up a number of men behind the low wall

of the orchard that ran between the gable end of
the house and the village street, and there directing their fire upon us, we were compelled to
retreat to safer cover. However, the door remained as impregnable as that leading into the
front garden, and presently the men drew off and
there was an interval of peace, after which the
fight was continued by the interchange of occasional shots on either side, both of us keeping
a sharp lookout, and discharging our pieces
whenever besieged or besiegers drew out of cover.
And as we were in a much better position than
they, we succeeded in effecting much damage
amongst them at no cost to ourselves.

About the middle of the afternoon Captain
Holdsworth himself was shot dead by Humphrey
Stirk as he incautiously made across the garden,
where he was evidently going to give orders to
the men posted in the summer house. I was
sorry to hear this news, for he had parleyed with
me in the frankest manner, and had shown some
solicitude for our position, but, after all, 'twas the
fortune of war, and might have been my own fate,
or Humphrey's. However, there was no doubt that
it made matters still more difficult for me, in one
respect—if we managed to escape with our lives
and fell into Fairfax's hands, he would not deal

any the more mercifully with me because one of his officers met his death in the effort to apprehend me.

We continued to exchange shots with the enemy until night fell, when a cessation of hostilities took place, save for an occasional fusilade when either side showed a light. That was a sad night, for everybody in the house knew that Sir Nicholas lay dead in our midst, and there was none that did not mourn him with much sincerity. As for me I was sore concerned as to what was to come, for I felt sure that Fairfax would eventually reduce us to submission, and the thought of what might then chance to Alison made me anxious. But here again I was somewhat helped by that curious fellow, Merciful Wiggleskirk, who came tapping in the darkness at the little window pane in the scullery, and bade Walter fetch me to him.

"You here again?" says I. "What is it, friend?"

"Master Coope," says he, "you paid me nobly, and I'll give you a hint. If you can get out o' the house," he says, "do so on the instant. Captain Blackburn is coming in the early morning with more men, and they are bringing cannon with them. Make your way out o' the house during the night, Master Coope."

He ran off across the fold, and I shut the window and stood musing in the dark scullery. If they were bringing cannon against us it was all over. "We shall have the old house heaped in ruins over us ere noon!" I says. But since I was not yet weary of life, I sought my cousin, intending to take counsel with her as to our next step.

Chapter VI

I.

ALISON was in the death chamber, where Sir Nicholas's body lay stiff and stark in its shroud. They had prepared him for his burial, Alison and old Barbara, with as much care as if he had been like to be buried with all the pomp and ceremony that is the due of a man of rank. The good old knight lay in his finest night clothes, the best linen the house afforded was spread on his bed, and they had lighted candles on either side of him, and hung the walls with black cloth. And since everything in that room was so mournful I would not talk there, but took my cousin down the stairs to the hall, where I made her sit near the fire while I addressed myself to her on the business then troubling me. She was looking pale and wearied, which was no matter of sur-

M

prise, seeing that there had been precious little
rest for anybody in that house since the investment began.

" Now, cousin," says I, " there is need for some
counsel 'twixt you and me. We are come to a
sharp pass, cousin," I says, " and unless we use
our wits we are like to be undone."

" What is it ? " she says. " Has aught of
moment happened to us ? "

" Why," says I, " 'tis difficult to say what is
and what is not of moment—one thing so leads
to another. But I fear that the worst will happen
to us in the morning."

" The worst ? " she says. " And what is that ? "

" We killed their captain this afternoon," says
I. " As pleasant a fellow as e'er I spoke to, poor
gentleman ! And now I hear from that knave
Wiggleskirk—though, indeed, he has done us
more than one good turn—that another com-
mander is coming with the dawn, and will bring
cannon with him."

She raised her head and looked at me steadily.

" So we shall have the old house tumbling
about our ears ? "

" We shall," says I.

" Well ? " says she, after regarding me again at
some length.

" Well ? " says I.

" Is that all you had to say ? " she asks.

" Nay," says I, not seeing aught of her meaning, " I wanted to speak with you of our escape."

She lifted her head somewhat, and stared at me for a full minute ere she broke into a shrill laughter.

" Escape ? " she said.   " Escape ?   Did you say escape, Master Richard ?   So you would flee the old house, eh, and leave "—she turned and pointed her hand towards the stair—" and leave his body to—come, I think you did not mean escape ? " she says, with a searching look at me.

" Faith ! " says I, not taking her at all, " but I did, cousin.   Bethink you—what can we do against cannon ?   The old walls will be shattered to pieces with half a score discharges.   'Tis our duty, I take it, to think of our own lives—and besides, there are those in the house," I says, " that we must needs consider, for we've no right to peril their lives for the sake of ours."

" Let them begone, then," says she.   " Did I ever ask them to come here ?   Escape ?   We might be rats that have crept to the very bottom o' the stack ! " she says, with a flash of the old temper.

" Egad ! " says I, laughing in spite of myself.

"And that's a marvellous neat comparison, cousin. Rats we are, and prettily caged, too, and so——"

"And so keep your comparisons to yourself, Master Richard," says she, rising with a mighty fine air of dignity and marching across the hall. "And your escape, too," she says, with a glance over her shoulder. "As for me," she says, pausing with one foot on the stair and looking me steadily in the face, "here I am, and here I stay while one stone stands on another," and she went up the staircase and vanished, leaving me there full of wonder. "What the devil am I to do?" says I, biting my nails with vexation. "Was ever such a contrary piece of woman flesh? And I thought she was beginning to show me some softness—Lord!" I says, with a sigh that seemed to come from my boots, "the vagaries of these women——"

However, there was no good to be got in standing there, so I went out into the kitchen and sent for old Gregory, whom I presently led into a quiet corner. "Gregory," says I, "set your wits to work, for, faith, there's need!" And I told him of the news that I had received from Merciful Wiggleskirk and of my cousin's attitude.

"Was ever such a coil?" says I. "You see, Gregory, I swore to my uncle that I would defend and protect her, and how can I do that if she won't listen to reason ? I must get her out of this house and across country to her father's, and there might be some manner of doing it if only she were not so averse to the notion."

"True," says he, "but I would not trouble myself over much with that, Master Richard. The best way with women," says he, "is to make 'em do a thing without argument about it."

"Humph !" says I, feeling somewhat doubtful on that score.

"What we want to find out," says he, "is whether there is some manner of escape that we can avail ourselves of. Is there any chance of leaving the house during the night ?" says he.

"Not the least," says I. "They have patrols on every side, and our doors and windows are so barricaded that we could not remove the barricades without attracting the enemy's notice."

"Then what was it that you had in your mind, Master Richard ?" says he.

"Faith !" says I, "I don't know, Gregory. We're in as pretty a trap as e'er I heard of. Now I come to think on it," I says, "I don't see how we are to escape."

He sat silent for a time, stroking his chin, which was his habit when he thought hard.

"Master Dick," says he at last, "did you ever hear of that old passage that leads from our cellar to Farmer Wood's house?"

"A passage?" says I. "Do you mean that there's an underground passage betwixt our house and Farmer Wood's? No," I says, "I never heard of it that I know of, Gregory."

"But there is one," says he, nodding his head. "When I first came here—and that's nigh on to sixty years since, Master Richard—it was open at one end, and I've been in it. Sir Nicholas's father had it closed up. 'Twas a relic of the Popish days," he says, "and there was some old woman's tale about it that I ha' forgotten."

"But if it's closed up?" says I.

"It was only a matter o' stout boarding put over the mouth," says he. "I make no doubt that it's open all the rest of the way, though I say naught as to Wood's end on't. If we could get a clear passage," he says, looking at me, "there's an easy deliverance out of our present difficulties, Master Richard."

"Marry, so there is!" says I. And indeed there was naught that could be easier. I sat thinking the matter over for a moment. "Egad, Gregory!" I says, "if only this passage is open we can circumvent the enemy and put Mistress

Alison in safety with no trouble beyond a trifling discomfort. Come," I says, starting up, "let's down into the cellars and examine things for ourselves."

Now, I am a bit slow at taking some things in, as for instance, a woman's meaning, which always seems to me to be the exact opposite of what it really is, but at contrivances and strategies I am, I think, as sharp as any, and I lost no time in making up my mind as to what I would do supposing this passage proved open to us. Our position was this—the Manor House stood at the west side of East Hardwick village, some one hundred and twenty yards away from Wood's farmstead, which was the only considerable house in the place beside our own. Between the two houses stood certain cottages, tenanted by labourers that worked in the fields. Beyond Wood's house the land dropped away to the foot of Went Hill, a long low range of hillside extending from Darrington Mill to the village of Wentbridge. If Alison and I could escape by the passage and make our way across the fields to Wentbridge, we should there come into the Great North Road which ran thence in a straight course, through Barnsdale, to Francis French's house, where I could deliver her in safety. It was possible that we might find horses or some conveyance at the "Blue Bell," on Wentbridge Hill, but if that plan failed we were neither of us unfitted to walk some twelve miles in the darkness.

But as we went down the steep steps into the cellar my thoughts turned back to Mistress Alison. If it was her pleasure to stand by the old house, how on earth was I going to persuade or oblige her to leave it? It was all very well for Gregory to say that a woman must be commanded and not argued with, but there was something in me that whispered grave doubts as to the wisdom of trying his advice on my cousin. "But I'll leave that till last," thinks I; "the passage comes first," and I hastened to join Gregory, who was fumbling at the cellar door.

II.

The cellar lay in a thick darkness on which the light of our lanthorn made but a little impression. It was a great dismal hole, hewn deep into the rock, and was damp as a garden wall in February. I could never remember that it was used for aught in my time, save that one corner of it had been set apart and prepared for a wine-cellar. It was too cold or too damp for the keeping of ale—a hogshead of October kept down there would have come out more dead than it went in. Then there was nobody but Gregory ever descended the steps, though in bygone times there must have been considerable wear of them seeing that they were hollowed out in the middle to such an extent that it was dangerous to walk down them without exceeding care.

"A dismal hole, Gregory," says I, holding up the lanthorn and gazing round me at the damp walls, up the chiselled face of which crawled a multitude of slugs and snails that left a slimy silver track behind them. "I should not care to spend much time down here."

"I ha' spent many a merry hour here," says he, glancing at the door of the wine-cellar. "'Tis a quietish spot enow, but a man gets used to that. Give me the lanthorn, Master Richard," he says, "and look to your footing as you come after me, for the floor's ill-paved and as slippery as mud can make it."

As he went before me in the gloom and I followed, keeping a strict watch over my ways,

I saw and heard things that made me turn cold and shiver with a nauseous dread. There was the scatter of rats amongst the old timber that lay strewn here and there, there were slimy creeping things that seemed to writhe and quiver in helpless silence under one's foot, and more than once a foul, cold shape that had hung or crawled on the roof detached itself and fell on my face or neck.

"This cellar of yours is like to give me the horrors, Gregory," says I. "Egad, it seems to be the home of all that's foul—I should not wonder to see ghouls and afrites in it!"

"I never heard of them," says he, "but, faith, Master Dick, there be things here that pass a christened man's understanding. Look here," says he, going a little way aside and holding his lanthorn to the floor. "What do you make of that?" says he.

I looked and saw that which turned me sick. There was a pool of black water in the floor, and on the edge of it, their staring eyes and wide mouths turned upward to the glimmer of the light, sat a row of great toads, fat and slimy, that stretched their webbed feet along the damp brink of the rock. "In with you!" says Gregory, swinging the lanthorn towards them, and they plunged in, sending the foul water in brimming beads about our feet. "They feed on the slugs," says he, with a chuckle, "faith, there's some nice picking down here! But that's naught, toads and slugs is common enough, Master Dick. Now, here's something that's of a vast difference. Look at it, Master Richard—faith, I never can make it out!"

He turned away in another direction and swung his lanthorn over a little basin in the rock, full of clear water, that came bubbling to the surface. "It looks like a spring," says I. "Aye, but look closer," says he, whereupon I bent my head and saw a hundred little fishes that darted hither and thither, turning their heads towards the light. "Why, that's curious!" says I. "But not half so curious as you shall find," says Gregory, and bends down to scoop up a palmful of water. "Look thee there, lad," says he, holding the light over his hand. "The Lord have mercy!" says I, as I stared; and faith, there was excuse for my fear. For the fish that he had taken up, smaller than the minnows that lads draw out o' the streams, was blind as a bat, having a thin white skin drawn over its eyes, and 'twas pitiful to see its head dart this way and that, and the white scale

that blinded it turn to the glint of the candle.
"For God's sake, Gregory!" says I, "No more
o' thy horrors. Let us to this passage, ere I go
crazy. Why, man, this is the very infernal pit
—to think there is a gentleman's house above
it!"

"We are a good way from the house, Master
Richard," says he; "Hark, that's the horses
stamping in the stable over us. But the passage
should be here under this heap o' timber, which
we must remove."

There was a pile of logs leaned up against the
corner of the cellar, damp, rotten, falling to
pieces, and giving harbour to more foul things
that crept about the scaling bark. "This is a
very palace of vermin!" says I, as I helped
Gregory to shift the logs. "God send the
passage have less of horrors than its porch!"

"You can soon find out about that," says he,
as we laid bare the boards that covered the
entrance. 'Twas dry enough when I was last
in it, nigh on to sixty year ago."

The boards were damp and rotten. They
came down with small effort on our part, and
we were presently gazing into the mouth of
the passage. It presented itself as a low-roofed
tunnel of some five feet in height and four in

width, hewn out of a sandstone bed which there separated itself from the rock. It was carpeted with a fine thick sand and seemed dry, though its looks were belied by a breath of foul moisture that came from it as we stood peering into its darkness. The entrance was strengthened by rude masonry that extended for some yards along the passage : it was evident that in days gone by there had been constant use of it for some purpose or other.

"There it is, master," says Gregory, swinging his lanthorn along the walls.

"Aye," says I, not half-liking the task that I knew I must needs undertake, "and the next thing is to find out, if 'tis possible, how far it is from this spot to Wood's house?" I says.

"Let's see," says he, scratching his head. "Why, come, we are under our own stable now, and that's a good twenty yards from our scullery window. We must be," says he, "a hundred yards from Wood's cellar."

"Ah, it runs into Wood's cellar, does it?" says I. "And how on earth are we to get out o' that, I wonder, even if we get through the passage? You were never through it yourself, eh, Gregory?"

"No," says he, prompt enough. "I never went along more than a dozen yards on't, and wouldn't now if t'were not for the fix we're in," he says, shaking his head.

"And why not?" says I.

"There were queer tales about it," he says, looking elsewhere than at me.

I stood and stared at him for a full minute, during which he affected not to know that my eyes were on him. "Look here, Gregory," says I, at last. "I'm going along this passage. Faith, queer tales or no, there can't be more that's horrible in it than there is in that cellar o' yours. So give me the lanthorn," I says, "and wait me there."

"I'm going with thee, lad," says he, holding the lanthorn away from me.

I reflected for a while. "Very well," I says. "But I'll lead the way—and here goes," and I took the light out of his hand and advanced along the passage. "It's a low roof for a big man," I says. "Keep your head down, Gregory."

The first twenty yards of the passage yielded naught in the way of adventure. The sand and dust was a foot thick on the floor, and there were great cobwebs stretched from side to side along which the spiders, big as a penny-piece, scattered and hurried as the light drew near. But there were no obstacles to surmount nor pitfalls to tumble into, and though the air was thick and musty it was possible to breathe with some slight discomfort. "If it's all like this," says I, "we shall do, though it's poor work walking with your body bent double." "Why," says Gregory, "we can crawl on hands and knees if need be. Master Dick—we must needs expect——" But there he stopped, for I had started back and thrown out a hand behind me to keep him off. "God in Heaven!" says I, "Look there, Gregory—there—there!"

As I swung the lanthorn to the floor he poked his head over my shoulder and we stared together at the thing that lay in the dust a yard from our feet. It was the skeleton of a man that had fallen forward on his face, and now lay with outstretched arms and bony fingers that clutched the yielding sand. There were bits of ragged linen here and there, and between his arms, but rolled a little way out of their reach, lay a coffer, or box, the lid of which had burst open and revealed a quantity of jewels that sparkled dully in the light of the lanthorn. As for the bones they shone as white as if they had been bleached, and I shuddered to think of the rats in the cellar behind us whose fore-fathers had no doubt picked them clean.

"There's naught to be afeard on, lad," says Gregory after a while. "'Tis some poor body that has striven to escape with his treasure many a generation ago and had fallen here to die. But there's matter there, Master Dick," he says, pointing to the jewels, "that's well worth the picking up, and you've a right to them, sir, for this must ha' been a Coope in bygone days. But let's on, lad, and see where this passage ends, for that's the main thing after all."

I stepped over the skeleton with a shudder, being already made squeamish by the horrible things in the cellars, and we went slowly along the passage, I half-expectant of discovering some further horror. But despite an occasional obstacle in the way of a fallen mass of stone or earth there was little to hinder us, and at last we came to where the passage narrowed and seemed to end in an approach no wider than a fox hole.

"It's useless after all, Gregory," says I, sore disappointed. "The tunnel has been blocked at this end. There's no way out here that I can see."

"Softly, lad, softly," says he. "Let me come

by you," and he pushed his way along the rapidly narrowing passage until I thought he must have stuck fast. " By the Lord Harry ! " he says, " but there is an opening here, Master Dick, and 'tis into the open air, too — I can smell it. And if so be as you'll put out the light for a moment, I'll lay aught we shall see a glimpse of the sky, for the moon was rising two hours ago."

But I had no mind to put out the light, though we had flint and steel with us, so I settled matters by taking off my doublet and wrapping it about the lanthorn. " There ! " says Gregory, " Said I not so ? " and I looked and saw a space of grey light, the size of a man's hand, high above us where the passage shot upward.

" What's to be done now ? " says I : " We can't squeeze through that."

" No," says he, " but we can make it bigger. This is naught but soft earth that's gradually fallen in to the mouth o' the passage, Master Richard. Do you scoop it away at that side," he says, " and I'll scoop at this, and it shall go hard if we don't make a good road on't."

We set to work at this without more ado and toiled hard for a good hour. " There," says Gregory at last, " if I cannot push my shoulders

N

through what's left may I never lift sack of corn again i' my life!" He gave a mighty heave and the loose soil came tumbling about him. I saw his neck twisting and turning about. "May I die!" he says, as he drew it within, leaving a good two feet square of moonlit sky to fill the hole, "if it doesn't open into Matthew Wood's orchard! I ha' been over this place many a time," says he. "From without it looks like an old drain that's been filled in long ago. And now, lad," he says, as we drew back into the passage beneath, "there's a free road for us. What's to be done next?"

"Back to the Manor," says I, and took my doublet off the lanthorn. "The road's there, to be sure," I says, "but whether we can persuade Mistress Alison to take it——"

"Why," Master Richard," says he, "if she wont——"

"Aye, what?" says I.

"We must carry her through," says he. " But I think she'll listen to reason," he says—and so we made our way back along the passage to where the skeleton lay white and ghostly. I picked up the coffer and hurried on—there was no time to remove the bones and inter them decently. It struck midnight as we came into the kitchen, and there was much to do before daybreak.

III.

We had no sooner returned to the house than I sent Walter to John and Humphrey Stirk, bidding them come to me in the hall, where I went with Gregory to meet them. They reported that all had been quiet during the evening, save that the lad Peter incautiously carrying a light past one of the upper windows had been shot at and hit in the shoulder, though not dangerously.

"He will quickly mend of that," says I. "We have something more serious than flesh wounds to think of. Now, John and Humphrey, listen to me. We are in sore need," I says, looking on them earnestly, "and must use desperate remedies. In the morning the house is to be assaulted with cannon—nay, for aught I know the cannon may be on its way now. There is naught for us but to escape before the old place comes tumbling about our ears. What say you?" says I, looking from one to the other.

John shook his head. "I fear 'tis impossible, Master Richard," says Humphrey. "We have observed that they are keeping a strict patrol

round the house, and besides, 'tis a light night—
we should be seen ere we could cross the garden."

"That's certain," says I, "but what if we tell
you of another way, lads?"—and I forthwith re-
counted to them the recent doings of Gregory
and myself, and informed them of my intentions
with regard to placing Mistress Alison in safety.
"What do you think?" I says, when I had told
them all. "Is it a good plan?"

"Naught could be better," says John.

"And now for the rest of you," says I, "I have
no mind that any of you should fall into the
hands of the enemy, and therefore I propose that
you should all make your escape in the same way.
You, John, and you, Humphrey, will have no
difficulty in reaching home, and faith, since there's
none can prove you have been here, why, there's
none can injure you for it," I says. "But what
about thee, Gregory, and the rest?"

"Why, Master Dick," says he, "I ha' thought
of all that while you have talked, and it seems
to me that the best plan is to let John and Humphrey here, and yourself and Mistress French,
make your escapes during the night, leaving the
rest of us in the house. In the early morning,
Master Dick, ere they begin to torment us with
their cannon, we will put out a flag and submit to

them—gog's wounds, they will do naught against us serving-men and women!—and 'twill save the old house," he says, "that would otherwise be blown to pieces with their artillery."

" A good plan," says John Stirk.

" But," says I, " I don't like the notion of leaving any of you in the house, Gregory."

" I am sure 'tis the best way out o' present difficulties, Master Richard," says he.

"Well," says I, " then so be it. If I only live and have power," I says, looking at all three in turn. "I will see that your devotion is richly rewarded. But now, lads, there is another matter to settle. Upstairs lies my uncle's body—we cannot leave it to be stared at by the enemy. What shall we do with it ? "

We stood looking at each other. " It should be carried to Badsworth churchyard," says Gregory, "but that's impossible, Master Richard. If we could lay him somewhere until all this trouble is at an end——? "

"And so we will," says I, a sudden thought coming to me. " We will lay him in his own house until such times as we can inter him with his fathers. Gregory, do you and Jasper take up the pavement here in the hall and prepare a grave while I see Mistress Alison, and have him made ready," and therewith I requested John and Humphrey to come with me, and went upstairs to my uncle's chamber.

Faith, it was no easy task that lay before me in making Alison acquainted with my plans, but I was resolved that she should obey me in everything—it meant ruin to all of us if she refused compliance. So I tapped at the chamber door and asked her to come forth and speak with me and to bring Barbara with her, these two having kept close watch over Sir Nicholas's body ever since they had put it into his grave-clothes. I led them into a neighbouring room, where I had already bestowed John and Humphrey, and entered upon the matter at once.

"Cousin," says I, "I wish to tell you and Barbara what I have decided upon. Events are now come to a desperate pass, and it is necessary that you and I, together with John and Humphrey, should escape the house ere daybreak. Therefore," I says, "be pleased, cousin, to hearken attentively to what I have to say, and be sure that in everything I have taken most careful thought for your own safety."

"I must decide matters for myself in spite of all that," says she.

"Let me tell you what I have decided upon

first, cousin," says I. "There will be time enough
to discuss personal likes and dislikes when we
have got over our present difficulty." And with
that I set to and told them all that we had
decided upon. John and Humphrey standing by
me and nodding their heads in approval. But
while old Barbara showed us that she also
approved our plans, my cousin's face plainly informed us that she had no liking for them. However, she heard me to the end, and faith, I spoke
as long and as persuasively as I could, for I could
see that she intended telling me her mind after
the old fashion.

"And so that is all you have to say, Master
Richard?" says she, when I had made an end.
"'Tis a pretty story to have been put in such a long-
winded fashion. Methinks I can make it shorter.
'Tis your notion," says she, looking at me keenly,
"to bury Sir Nicholas Coope like a dog, under
the floor, without rite or ceremony, and then to
skulk out of the house which he would have
defended as long as one stone had remained
upon another. Am I right?" she cries. "Am I
right, sir?"

"Pray you, mistress," says old Barbara. "Be
guided by Master Dick—a man knows more o'
these things——"

"Answer me, sir!" says she, disregarding Barbara. "Have I caught your meaning?"

"Faith!" says I, somewhat nettled at her obstinacy. "I never knew man or woman who was less apt at apprehending anything. Prithee, cousin, since you think so badly of my schemes, will you be good enough to give us some plan of your own? Something," I says, with a wave of my hand, "that will savour of more wisdom than aught my poor brains can invent. I am but a man and think after a slow fashion. You women, I am told, have a better ingenuity——"

She gave me a look that stayed me from saying aught further.

"I have naught to say," says she, very quiet and dignified, "save that I shall do what I believe to be in accordance with my uncle's wish and desires."

"Why, cousin," says I, sore inclined to lose what little temper I had left, "do you mean to say that I am not of the same mind?" My temper went as a bit of thistledown is swept away before the wind. "By God!" says I, "I am fulfilling my uncle's last command, and that was to protect you, cousin, at all cost. And now we'll talk no more," I says, cooling as quick as I had grown hot, "I'm for action rather than words.

Come, lads," I says, starting for the door, "we have no time to lose."

But ere I could lay hands on the sneck she was at my side, and her fingers held me tight by the arm. I looked into her eyes and saw them as full of entreaty as a moment before they had been bright with resentment.

"You will not bury him—where you said?" she cries. For a moment I stood irresolute, staring at her. "We waste time," whispers John Stirk at my elbow. "I must carry out my plans, cousin," I answers, roughly.

She drew away her fingers from my arm. "Cruel—cruel!" she says, and falls a-weeping on Barbara's shoulder.

"The devil!" says I, under my breath. "Cousin!" I says, approaching her, "what can we do else? Would you leave my uncle's body to be stared at by the fellows outside, and maybe suffer indignity at their hands? Lord!" I says, well nigh beyond myself, "why wont you listen to reason?"

But she put out her hand and waved me off. "Do what you please," she says. Old Barbara gives me a look. "Come," says I, and went out, followed by John and Humphrey. I wiped my forehead when I got outside—faith, it was warmer work debating with Alison than fighting a company of troopers!

Gregory and Jasper had made swift work with the grave, which they had dug under the very spot in the hall where my uncle's chair used to stand. There was a rich, soft loam under the pavement, and they had dug into it some four feet and lined the hole with boards since there was no time to make a coffin. "All's ready, Master Richard," says old Gregory, and the five of us went softly upstairs. At the door of the chamber, where I had left Alison, I paused and knocked ere I went in. She was still weeping on Barbara's shoulder, and the old woman talked to her as if she had been a child.

"Cousin," says I, "we are ready, and there is no time to lose. If you wish to see him——"

She turned her head and looked at me with a frightened enquiry in her eyes. "Give me your hand," I says, and took it in my own. "Come," says I, and led her out of the room and to the door of Sir Nicholas's chamber. The men stood aside and bent their heads. I opened the door and let her in, and then shut it and waited. It was some minutes ere she came out, and then she was calm enough and faced us all with great composure. "Stand thee with her, Dick," whispers old

Gregory, and he motioned the rest of them to follow him into the room. And so I stood at Alison's side, and neither of us spoke. But when the four men came out carrying my uncle's body, closely wrapped in his grave-clothes, she gave a little shudder and put out her hand and I took it in mine and held it there, and so we followed them down the wide staircase and into the hall, and as we came in sight of the staring hole in the floor where his chair used to stand I felt her fingers close tighter on my own.

There was no more light in the hall than came from the two lanthorns brought there by Gregory and Jasper, and the grave-clothes looked ghastly white as we laid the good old knight in the only resting-place we could give him. As we stood looking down into his grave a thought came to me, and I stepped across the hall and took down from its shelf the great prayer-book which he was wont to use. And coming back, I knelt down by the grave with Alison at my side and the others about us, and read certain passages out of the service for the burial of the dead, and when we had all said the Lord's Prayer, and Gregory had twice repeated "Amen," we got up from our knees, and I led my cousin out of the hall, signing to the men to do what they had to do with all speed.

Outside the hall I released Alison's hand.
"Now, cousin," says I, "you must prepare for
your journey. I hope to see you in safety to
your father's house ere daybreak, but there may
be obstacles that I have not reckoned for, and
we must be prepared."

"So we are to desert the house?" she says,
looking at me.

"Let's have no more of that, cousin," says I.
"We must leave the house within half-an-hour.
Cloak yourself warmly, and cause Barbara to
prepare you a flask of wine and some food in
a parcel. In twenty minutes from now," I says,
"You will meet me in the kitchen."

I watched her go slowly up the staircase ere
I hurried back into the hall, where the four men
were hastily filling up my uncle's grave. When
they had finished I sent them all to the kitchen,
bidding them refresh themselves, and then shut-
ting myself into the hall, I proceeded to take
up the hearthstone, according to Sir Nicholas's
directions, and to secure the treasure which he
had spoken of. In a strong box I found three
hundred guineas in gold, together with a casket
of jewels, to which I immediately added those
which we had discovered in the passage. When
I had replaced the hearthstone I called Gregory

to me, and put in his hands fifty guineas to be divided amongst the servants for their present necessities. But John and Humphrey Stirk, whom I approached on the same subject, would take naught, having done what they had out of pure neighbourly feeling.

And now all was ready for our flight, and I arranged the last details with Gregory and the Stirks. Alison and I were to start at once and make what speed we could towards her father's house; John and Humphrey were to follow soon afterwards and return to their farm at Thorpe ('gad, who could ha' thought that it was but three days since I ran in upon them to crave their help!), and at daybreak Gregory was to surrender the house, craving leave for the servants to go their ways unmolested. This settled there was naught for us but to say farewell to each other, and for Alison and myself to descend into the cellar with Gregory, who was in readiness to light us to the passage.

Now I had said naught to my cousin of the passage itself, but had merely told her that I had found a sure means of escape. She trembled somewhat as we crossed the slimy floor of the great cellar and came to the entrance to the passage. " We are to pass through this ? " says she, looking

at me. " 'Tis our only means, cousin," says I, and
turned to take the light from Gregory. I shook
his hand—faith, it was the last time, for I never
saw him again!—and bade her follow me. Then
we turned into the passage, and I heard Gregory's
voice, calling down God-speed on us, die away
as we advanced.

Within a few minutes the bones of the dead
man's skeleton gleamed white in the light of
the lanthorn. "Cousin," says I, "take my hand,
and shut your eyes for a while. There is in
the path what I have no mind for you to see."
And so we passed by, and ere long I put out
the light for the patch of grey sky showed at
the mouth of the tunnel. "Would it had been
a darker night!" says I, as I went first and
looked about me. But all was still and quiet,
and so I helped her out of the passage, and
together we stole across the land. As we
hurried along behind the tall hedgerows an owl
hooted from Matthew Wood's barn. "An omen!"
thinks I, but said naught to her save to encourage
her to press forward. Thus we dipped into the
meadows, wet and marshy with the November
fogs and mists, and made with what speed we
could for the foot of Went Hill, that loomed
before us through the night.

Chapter VII

Of our Adventures under
the Bridge and the Privations
we there Endured, and of my
Interview with Fairfax and
its Sad Results.

I.

THE meadows were half under water : the Carleton Dyke had overflowed its banks, and ere
we had well dipped into the low fields, our feet
were sinking at every step into the marshy ground,
or splashing loudly into some pool that stared at
us in the faint light. 'Twas bad going, i' faith,
but neither of us paid much heed to it, our minds
being set on gaining the road beyond. But when
we came to the Dyke itself, which we were bound
to cross, we found ourselves in a pretty position,
for it had widened a good six yards, and there
was no means of crossing it nearer than the ford,
which was too near Hardwick village for my
liking or our safety. " There's only one way,"
says I, " I must carry you over, cousin, otherwise
you will not get across dryshod."

" I have not been dryshod since we came into

these meadows," says she, "and methinks you'll have no easy task in carrying me across there."

"Why," says I, "I don't look for ease in adventures of this sort," and I stepped into the Dyke and took her from the bank into my arms. "Faith!" says I, "I had no idea that you were so heavy, cousin. 'Tis well that I have but a half-score of yards to carry you."

"Set me down!" says she, trying to slip out of my grasp. "I had rather be drowned——"

But what else she meant to say was lost to me, for at that moment there rang out a musket shot that had been fired somewhere in the fields over which we had already passed, and ere the sound died away, it was followed by another discharge.

"They cannot have discovered our flight!" says I, and pushed on through the water to set her down on dryer ground. "Now, cousin," I says, taking her hand, "we must run for it. There's so little shelter in these meadows that they can see us at fifty yards' distance, but if we can make the road, we can hide behind the trees under Went Hill, if they follow us. And so run, cousin," I says, "run, if you've no mind to fall into their hands."

Now there was then but one field 'twixt us and the road, and that not a very wide one, but they had been stubbing trees in it that autumn, and as ill-luck would have it, I ran in my haste upon a root that had been left half-out of the ground, and so twisted my ankle that I fell, groaning with pain. " I believe my leg's broke," says I, when I could speak. " Egad, cousin, was ever aught so unlucky ! And what shall we do now ? "

" First find out where you are hurt," says she, and kneels down by me in the wet grass. "Try to move your leg," she says. " 'Tis not broke, I think—you must have twisted your foot, cousin."

" I am stopped," says I, pulling myself up and trying to walk. " I am not good for twenty yards," and I took her arm and endeavoured to step out, with no more effect than to make me cry out with the pain. "And hark ye there, cousin ! We're followed." I heard the sound of voices beyond the Dyke. "We are undone !" says I, cursing our ill-fate to myself. " They will be upon us in a few moments."

She stood supporting me and looking about her as if she sought for some means of escape. Suddenly she clutched my arm. " If you could contrive to get forward to the top of the field," she says, "we might hide under the bridge for awhile. Nobody would think of looking for us there."

"Egad!" says I. "The very notion—naught could serve our need better." But when I tried to walk I found that I was crippled as surely as old Matthew that goes with two crutches and hobbles at that. If I did but set my foot to the ground I was like to scream with the pain of it, and though I leaned heavily on Alison's arm, the agony I suffered was so great that the sweat rolled off my forehead, and I turned sick. "Alas!" says she, "If I could but carry you."

"Why," groans I, "I wish you could, cousin, but since you can't, I must make other shift. Let's see if I can't crawl on my hands and knees," I says, getting to the ground with some difficulty. And finding that I made progress in this lowly attitude, we went on to the corner of the field, pausing now and then to listen to the voices in our rear.

Now at that point there runs a narrow stream from the coppice on Went Hill into the Dyke in the valley, and it is carried under the road from Darrington Mill to Wentbridge by a bridge of stone, so deeply sunk into the ground that you might walk over it a thousand times and see naught of it. There is a thick hedgerow at each end of this bridge, and moreover another hedgerow runs along the side of the stream, going up to

the coppice on one side and down to the Dyke on
the other, so that the entrances are shielded from
observation. You may stand there and see naught
of the bridge itself, and if you find occasion to
wonder how the stream comes under the road,
you will tell yourself that 'tis by means of a pipe
or culvert, or some such contrivance. But Alison
and I knew of this bridge, for we had hidden in it
in our boy and girl days, and there was room in it
to hide a score of folk, though the quarters were
damp enough to give a whole village the rheu-
matics.

I made shift to crawl through the bushes into
the arch of the bridge, carrying with me sundry
thorns and prickles, whose smart I regarded no
more than a pin-prick, so acute was the pain
which I suffered from my foot. The water rose
high in the channel, but I managed to clamber to
some stones that stood above the stream, and
there I sat me down, groaning as loudly as I
dared, while Alison stood at my side. And after
a time, hearing no sound from without, and
judging that our pursuers, if indeed we were pursued, had gone another way, I contrived to get
off my foot-gear in order to examine my hurt.
Then I found that my ankle was swollen to such
a thickness as reminded me of Sir Nicholas's gouty

foot, and the remembrance of that, and how he used to curse it when it tweaked him, put me into a more hopeful humour. "Come," says I, "there's naught broken, cousin—'tis but a bad sprain. Let's be thankful," I says, "that there's so much cold water at hand—'tis a good thing for a hurt of this sort." I put my foot into the stream and found much relief, though the water was icy cold. "If I can but get the stiffness out of it," says I, "we'll make good progress yet."

"It will be morning soon," she says, glancing out of the bridge. "The sky is already growing light. We shall have little chance of escape in the daytime, shall we?"

"Why," says I, "I had certainly meant us to be clear of Barnsdale ere day broke. But we must do the best we can. 'Tis the fortune of war—and yet I did not think to escape all that we've gone through these four days past, and be brought down by a tree-root. But it's these small matters," I says, with the air of a philosopher, "that lead to great results."

"I am in no humour for speculations," says she.

"Why," says I, "you must certainly be suffering much discomfort, cousin, but I don't see how we can help it. Will you not endeavour to sit down by me here?—'tis a dampish seat, this heap of stones, but I think you will prefer it to standing. And you have a flask of wine there, and some food—we shall neither of us be the worse for a drop of one and a bite of t'other," I says. She made no answer for a while, but presently she contrived to seat herself at my side, and brought out the wine and food from beneath her cloak.

"You take everything in a very philosophical spirit, Master Richard," says she, giving me the flask.

"Why, faith, cousin," says I, "why not? 'Tis my humour to take things that way. There was my uncle, now, would fume and fret himself into a fever if all went not as he wished, but it never did him any good that I could see. Take things as they come, say I."

"'Tis a poor fashion," says she, "for it shows that you have no special care for aught."

"Now methinks 'tis you that wax philosophic," I says. "And, faith, I don't follow you. As for caring for aught, why, I have cared for a deal o' things, but as I never got most of them I came to the conclusion that it was better to want naught."

"Oh," says she, "and what, pray, did you care for and want that you didn't get?"

"Why," says I, "I wanted to be a country gentleman, with no more anxiety than the rearing of cattle and the making of an occasional ballad or sonnet."

"Oh, a poet!" says she.

"Why, say a rhymester," says I. "Heigh-ho! I was all for a quiet life—and here I am in a wet ditch, with a lame leg—plague take it!—and as good a chance of being hanged or shot as any man in England. Nevertheless," says I, "there's the present enjoyment of conversing with you, cousin, which is——"

But there, like a woman, she went off at a tangent.

"Master Richard," says she, "what made you turn rebel?"

"Cousin," says I, drawing my leg out of the water where I had kept it till it was numbed through. "Why do you ask me such a question?"

"Because," says she, "you observed just now that you cared for naught, and I don't understand how a man can join a cause unless he has some care for it."

"Lord!" says I. "You are too deep for me. I must have meant—nay, faith," I says, "I don't think I know what I did mean."

She laughed merrily at that—I think it was the first time since I came to the Manor. "Why, let me help you to your wits," says she. "Would you join the rebels to-morrow, if you were able?"

"Aye, indeed!" says I.

"And why?" says she.

"Because my sympathies are with them," says I. "I am for liberty and against oppression. Being a true Englishman," I says, "I hate this Star-Chambering and extortioning of honest folk's money."

"I wonder how much you know about it," says she.

"About as much as yourself," says I.

"God save the King!" says she.

"Faith, he needs it!" says I.

After that we sat in a miserable silence for full half-an-hour. It was then growing light, and the dawn came with a sharp burst of sleet that penetrated the bushes and stung our faces as we sat huddled under the bridge. "A dreary morning, cousin," I says.

A low booming roar came echoing across the fields. I forgot my hurt and tried to start to my feet. "Cannon!" says I. "They are bombarding the old place after all. And yet surely——"

But she had rushed to the mouth of the bridge and forced her way through the bushes, and there she stood, gazing across the dank fields towards the old house. The roar of the cannon came again. She drew back within the bridge, and dropping at my side burst into a passion of bitter weeping.

"Come, cousin," says I, laying my hand on her arm, "be comforted——"

She turned her face suddenly upon me, all aflame with anger.

"Comforted?" says she, "Shame upon you, Richard Coope! Oh, cowards that we are, to have skulked from the old place like rats from a sinking ship! Doesn't it shame you," she says, "to sit here in a ditch when you ought to be there defending your own?"

"Why, cousin," says I, "considering that it's through no choice of my own that I sit in this ditch, it doesn't; and as to defending my own, why, there's naught in the old house that's mine save a book or two. It's not my property," I says, nursing and groaning over my lame leg.

"But it's mine," says she, drying her tears.

"Then go and defend it," I says, sulkily. "You were better employed in that than in preaching to me."

She turned her face and stared at me long
and hard.

"You have the rarest faculty for saying
insolent things," says she.

"Faith, it's a poor one in comparison with
yours!" says I, testily enough.

She coloured up to the eyes at that. Egad,
she had no liking for such plain talk! But she
stared at me again and then at my foot, which
was at that moment exceeding painful.

"Can I do aught to relieve you?" she says.

"I wish you could," says I. "But you can't,
and so there's an end on't."

"Oh," she says, bridling, "if you don't wish to
talk with me——" and she drew herself away.
But after a time she looked round at me again.

"Will they destroy the old house?" she says.

"I don't know, cousin," says I. "They seem
to have given over firing at it, but these two
shots will have knocked some lath and plaster
about."

She looked at my foot which I was dipping
in the water again.

"What a misfortune!" she says. "I cannot
abide this idleness. It irks me to sit here, doing
naught, as if we were rats in a cage."

But since we were helpless I made no answer

to her, and so there we sat, miserable as you please, and without the grey dawn widened into a dull morning.

II.

The morning wore away in a sore discomfort until it came near to noon. Upon several occasions we heard folks pass along the road above our heads, and now and then a cart rumbled by, or a horseman made our hiding-place echo with the ring of his beast's feet. But we heard no more of the cannon nor anything in the neighbouring meadows of our pursuers. As for my lame foot it was so damaged that I could see there was no chance of our going onward that day. The plentiful doses of cold water which I had administered to it had seemed to keep down the inflammation, but the swelling was still so great and the stiffness so stubborn that I could make no use of my leg from the knee downwards.

"Cousin," says I, "look upon me as done for. I am winged as absolutely as a partridge that can only use its feet. It will be days before I can walk," I says, groaning more with chagrin than with pain, though I had enough and to spare of that.

" Well ? " says she.

" I don't know what we're to do next," says I, sore perplexed. " There isn't a house nearer than Darrington Mill, and you musn't go there. If you go along the road to Wentbridge you'll be seen. But when night falls you might try it, cousin. Dare you travel alone ? " I says.

She looked round at me and laughed.

" Dare ! " says she. " Dare, indeed ! "

" Then will you ? " says I.

" No," says she, prompt enough.

" And why not ? " says I.

" Because I shall not leave you," says she.

" Why," says I, " that's very kind of you, cousin, but I wish I could see you in safety."

" 'Tis not my fashion to run away when things come to the worst," says she.

" 'Gad, mistress ! " says I, somewhat nettled. " I don't know which smarts the more—your tongue or this plaguey leg of mine. But you might be more civil," I says.

" Was I uncivil ? " says she, making a great show of innocence with her eyes.

" I know what you meant," I says, turning surly again.

" Well," she says, speaking very polite and gentle, " confess, cousin, that if you hadn't persuaded me to leave the house, we should not have been burrowing in this ditch, half-starved to death."

"No," says I, "that's true enough. But I would rather burrow in a ditch and have my life, than swing to the branch of a tree, or stand before a file of troopers with my kerchief tied about my eyes. And I think," says I, regarding her narrowly, "that you would prefer your liberty even in a hole like this to being handed over to Anthony Dacre."

She gave me a cool stare.

"And what harm would there be in that?" says she.

"What?" says I.

"I say what harm would there be in that?" she says.

"Oh, you did say so, did you?" says I. "Faith, I thought you did, but then I thought you didn't."

"And why shouldn't I?" says she.

"Nay," says I, "how do I know? I have given up trying to understand women."

"Anthony Dacre," says she, musingly, "is a handsome man, and a most devoted cavalier."

"I wish I had my fingers at his throat!" says I.

"No man could be more attentive to ladies than

he," she says, still musing. "His manner is of the best."

" Is it ? " says I. " I wish he would come here and show us some of it."

" He looks better in a withdrawing-room," says she, giving the merest glance at my torn and mud-stained garments.

" I daresay he will grace some corner of hell," says I, savage as a bear with a sore lug.

She turned and looked at me.

"You and I don't seem to agree," she says.

" Faith ! I don't care whether we do or not ! " I says, like to weep with the pain of my foot, and the vexation into which she threw me.

She gave me a sharp glance, and suddenly I saw her eyes melt in the curiousest fashion. She was sitting near me on the wet stones and she put out her hand to mine with a quick gesture. But what she had it in mind to say or do——

There was a rustle at the mouth [of the bridge, and we turned our heads to see a great hound glaring at us from between the bushes that his shoulders had pushed aside. " Tracked, by God ! " says I, and without a thought I snatched a pistol from my belt and fired at the brute's open jaws. He fell, a quivering heap, into the stream at our feet, and the noise of the pistol rolled and echoed along the bridge, "Oh, foolish!" she cried, "they will hear it—they cannot be far off." She looked at the dog and I saw her eyes fill with tears. "Poor dog!" said she.

But now that danger was at hand I was quick to think and to act. I drew out the bag of gold that I had carried—she already had the jewels in another bag—and handed it to her. "Here," says I, "take this, cousin—and cousin," I says, "whether we've agreed or not don't forget that I tried to serve you. A curse on this foot o' mine!" I says, struggling to get into a standing posture, "I'd give any-thing——"

There came the tramp of feet without and the sound of men pushing their way through the hedgerows. "The dog headed this way," says a voice. "Why, this is the old bridge!" says another. But by that time I had got to my feet and drawn the other pistol from my belt. "Behind me, Alison!" says I, "We'll have a life or two ere we yield."

The bushes were suddenly filled with men. I saw Anthony Dacre's face amongst the throng, and Merciful Wiggleskirk peering round the corner. I levelled the pistol full at Anthony and laughed to see him duck his head. "Coward!"

says Alison in my ear.   "Spare your powder for
better men, Dick."

She had never called me Dick before—at any
rate, since we were children.   I turned hastily to
her.   "Sweetheart!" I says, "this is the end, but
by heaven, I love you!"

After that, I think I must have swooned and
fallen.   When I came to my senses again I was
lying on the road above the bridge, with Alison
and Merciful Wiggleskirk at my side, and
Anthony Dacre talking to an officer on horseback close by.   I strove to rise, half wondering where I was, and it was only the pain in
my foot that suddenly reminded me of our
position.

III.

Having fairly recovered my senses I looked
round me and found that we were in the midst of
a score or so of troopers, apparently under command of a middle-aged officer who seemed fierce
enough to eat hot lead.   This worthy, turning
from Anthony Dacre, with whom he had been
conversing, presently approached me and enquired if I were now in a condition to travel.

"Aye," says I, "but not a-foot, sir."

"You shall have a mount, Master Coope," says he, and beckons a trooper to bring up a horse, upon which I clambered with some pain and difficulty. "We must make what haste we can," says he, "for Fairfax is somewhat impatient to meet you."

He gave me a curious, knowing look as he turned from me to Alison.

"As for you, madam," he says, "I fancy that some arrangement has been made for you by your kinsman, Master Dacre; you are free, at any rate, so far as I am concerned."

"If Mistress Alison will accept my poor protection as far as her father's house—" says Anthony, coming forward. But half-a-dozen paces away he stopped, frightened, I think, by the look she gave him.

"Liar!" she said, and looked him up and down ere she turned away. She came up to me and laid her hand on my arm, "I am going with you," she says in a low voice. "I am afraid—that man frightens me. What is it they will do to you, Richard?"

"Shoot me, I expect, cousin," says I. There was naught to be gained by keeping the truth from her.

She went over to the officer. "Sir," says she,

"you will make me your debtor if you will carry me to Pomfret with you. I have a mind to go there," she says, looking hard at him.

The man looked from her to Anthony. "Why, madam," says he, "sure you are free to do what you please, and I should feel it an honour to give you any assistance, but——"

" You are to go with me to your father's, cousin," says Anthony, with a frown on his black face. " It was on these conditions only that I secured your liberty."

But she paid no more heed to him than if he had been a stone. She still looked at the officer. " Then you will take me with you, sir?" she says.

" Faith, and so I will, mistress," says he, "if you can make shift to ride on one of my men's saddles."

" You are wrong, Captain Stott," says Anthony Dacre, " I agreed with Sands——"

" Look you, Master Dacre," says the other, " the young woman is free, and I know naught of your arrangements with Sands or anybody else. And since she asks me for a lift into Pomfret," he says, "why, she shall have it, and there's an end."

This matter being settled, much to Anthony

P

Dacre's chagrin and the further souring of his naughty temper, we presently set out for Pomfret, going thither by way of Darrington Mill and Carleton village, in passing through which the folk came out of their houses to stare at us. It gave me much pain to ride, and Captain Stott urged us forward at a brisk pace. But going up Swan Hill we came to a gentle walk and Stott brought his horse alongside mine and inquired after my condition.

" Why, sir," says I, " I suffer somewhat smartly, I promise you, and this jolting does naught to help me."

" Well," says he, " you will have a speedy quittance of your pain, young gentleman, for as I am an honest man I believe Fairfax will shoot you."

" I expect naught else," says I.

" You're mighty cool about it," says he, " and I admire you for that. Lord ! what is there that's better than war for taking the sentiment out of a man ? I am sure you'll face a file of my troopers very brave," he says, looking narrowly at me. " 'Twill be but justice, young gentleman, for your offence was exceeding grave."

" Sir," says I, " you seem to know a deal more of my offence than I know myself. To tell you the truth," says I, "I am in that state of mind which prevents me from caring whether I offend or not."

"Oh, tired of life," says he.

"On the contrary," says I. "I want very much to live, and am cursing my fate as earnestly as I can. And yet," I says, giving him a smile that was doubtless as grim as his own, "I am wise enough to know that all the cursing in the world won't alter things."

"You will certainly be shot," says he.

"Well, sir," I says, "then I will be shot. But if you would oblige a dying man—and you seem assured that I am one—say naught of it to my cousin there," says I, pointing to Alison, who rode a little in advance, and out of earshot. "She has some inkling of it already, but you have such a cold-blooded style of saying things," says I, "that she'll look upon you as a butcher."

"Why, 'tis my trade, lad," says he, and laughs. "But I'll respect your wish, seeing that it's one of the last you'll ever utter."

We were now come to Pomfret, and for some moments I forgot my own affairs in looking about me and noting the evidences of warfare which were on every side. As we drew nearer to the market-

place I saw many houses that had been shattered
by the Castle artillery and now stood in ruins.
Beyond the Moot Hill we passed the Main
Guard, which they had erected at the top of
Northgate, and out of which came several Parliamentarians to see us pass, and inquire of their
fellows as to our business. Captain Stott, however, hurried us forward along Skinner Lane,
and so we presently came to Fairfax's camp,
which was at the rear of a great horn-work that
they had thrown up for the beleaguering of the
Castle. We were now in full view of the Castle
itself, and occasionally noted the discharge of its
cannon which chiefly played, however, against
the fort on Baghill, from whence most annoyance
was caused to the besieged. Fairfax and Sands
were closeted together in a farmhouse close by
the camp, and thither Captain Stott conducted
us and bade his men help me down from my
horse. I was making shift to hobble along,
leaning on the arm of a trooper, when Sands
himself suddenly came out of the house and met
us. He looked from me to Alison and seemed
resentful of her presence.

"What do you do here, mistress?" says he,
rudely. "I cannot remember that we sent you
for any woman, Captain Stott," he says. "That

matter, I think, was arranged with Master Dacre there."

" She came of her own accord," says Stott. " She was free to go where she pleased for aught that I know to the contrary."

" What is your business here, mistress ? " says Sands. But ere she could reply he fell into a sudden fury. " Come ! " says he, " get you gone, mistress, get you gone !—what, have we not had enough of trouble with you Coopes this last day or two that you must give us more? See her out of the camp, Master Dacre," he says, turning upon Anthony. " See her to her father's house as you arranged with me." He turned from them and looked at me with a severe displeasure in his eyes. " Richard Coope, eh ? " says he. " Bring him within—we are anxious to make acquaintance with you, Master Coope."

" Sir," says I, as I hobbled into the farmhouse after him, " I claim your protection on behalf of my cousin, Mistress French, without there."

" She hath another cousin to protect her," says he, ill-temperedly. " We have given her safe-conduct to her father's house, and there's an end on't."

" But "——says I.

" I'll hear no more," says he, savage as a bear,

and he walked forward and into a room, the door
of which he closed behind him. The three
troopers that had me in charge waited in the
passage with me in their midst. I looked from
one to the other, and recognising Merciful
Wiggleskirk amongst them, I begged him to
run outside and see whether Alison had departed, and if not, to entreat her from me to
seek out some friend in the town rather than
trust herself to Anthony Dacre. This he did,
but presently returned, saying that Mistress
French had ridden away, and Master Dacre and
his two men with her, whereat I turned sick
at heart, and cared no more as to what might
happen to me.

After some little time the door of the chamber
into which Sands had withdrawn was opened
again, and an officer looked out and bade the
troopers bring me within. I hobbled into the
room and found myself standing at the foot of
a great table, at the head of which sat a man
whom I immediately took to be Sir Thomas
Fairfax himself. Sands sat by him on his right,
and two other officers were placed on his left,
while Captain Stott stood half-way along the
table. They all gazed at me with some curiosity,
and faith, I daresay I was a pretty sight to

behold, for I had had no time to smarten myself
up for four days, and the mud of the ditch was
thick on my clothes. However, I made my best
bow, and was then forced to clutch and hold by
the table lest I should fall, for the pain in my leg
was turning me sick again.

"Master Richard Coope," says Fairfax, looking
at me.

"The same, sir," says I.

"You seem to be in some distress," says he,
not unkindly.

"Sir," I says, "I have hurt my foot, and the
pain is exceeding sore at this moment."

"Give Master Coope a chair," says he.

"I thank you, sir," says I, very polite. "Faith!"
thinks I, "he is surely going to shoot me, or he
would not be so attentive." And I sat down and
tried not to groan at the agony which every
movement gave me.

"Now, Master Coope," says he, "we have had
you brought here after much trouble and annoyance to question you of your late doings."

He paused and looked at me.

"Sir," I says, regarding him steadily, "I am
prepared to answer any question you are pleased
to put to me."

"Are you so?" says he. "Be assured, Master

Coope, that we shall deal justly with you. And
since we are sitting in court-martial upon you,
you shall know what it is that you are charged
with." He took up a paper from the table.
"You are charged," he says, looking at it, "with
a grave offence, namely, that you, being duly
entrusted with the conveyance of a despatch from
General Cromwell to me, Sir Thomas Fairfax,
did desert your commission, and, attaching yourself to the enemies of the Parliament, did do, and
cause to be done, many things hurtful to the cause
which you had sworn to further. What say you
to that, Master Coope?" he says, regarding me
keenly.

"Sir," says I, "if you will listen to my defence
I shall hope to make myself clear to you."

"You shall have all the consideration that is
right," says he. "So tell us your story, Master
Coope, without fear."

"I am a poor hand at it," says I, "but this is a
plain tale and the truth," and I pulled my wits
together and put the matter plainly before them.
I told them how I had lost my horse, how I had
chanced to overhear Anthony Dacre's plot, how
I had gone to the Manor House to warn my
uncle, and had been trapped there ere I could
leave, and how I had contrived to forward the

despatch by Merciful Wiggleskirk. "And that," says I, coming to an end, "is the truth of this matter, wherein, if I have done wrong, it has been for the sake of folk that were dear to me. And, gentlemen," says I, looking from one to the other, "if there were need I would do it again— and I have no more to say."

After I had finished none of them spoke for awhile, but at last Fairfax looked at Sands. "I wish," says he, "that we knew more about this man Dacre and the plot which his kinsman Coope alleges against him." But Sands shook his head. "'Tis neither here nor there, Sir Thomas," says he. "What have we to do with plots about carrying off a young woman? Here is Richard Coope confessing, yea, and glorifying himself because of it, that he deserted his commission, and joined himself to his uncle in resisting our warrant. A clearer case," says he, "I never heard."

Then the four of them withdrew into another apartment, leaving me there with Stott and the troopers. "Thy foot will not pain thee much longer, young man!" says Stott. "Faith," says I, conceiving a great dislike to him all of a sudden, "'tis well for you, sir, that I am unable to use it!" And there might have been a pretty row between us but that Sir Thomas and the others came back and took their seats. I glanced at Sands, and knew what was coming.

Fairfax looked at me with some kindness as he began to speak. But there was naught kind about his words. I had deserted my commission, and thereby caused great annoyance to the Parliament; I had joined myself with the Royalists, and had brought about the death of a useful officer, and it was impossible that my serious offence could be overlooked. And so I was to be shot at daybreak of the following morning.

I think I got to my feet and bowed to him when he made an end. And I must have winced with the pain that every movement gave me, for he looked at me with some consideration. "I am sorry that you suffer," says he. "I will send my surgeon to see to your hurt." "I am greatly your debtor, sir," says I. And so we parted with much politeness on both sides, and the troopers helped me out, and presently installed me in a neighbouring cottage, with Merciful Wiggleskirk as a guard, and my own thoughts for amusement.

Chapter VIII

Of my Surprising Deliverance from Death, my last Meeting with Anthony Dacre, and of certain Notable Passages 'twixt Mistress Alison and Myself.

I.

THE place in which they installed me to wait for my end was a little cottage some fifty yards away from the farmhouse, where Fairfax had set up his quarters, and stood in an angle of the fields that lie 'twixt Skinner Lane and the hamlet of Tanshelf. It afforded but the most indifferent accommodation, there being naught in the way of furniture but a chair or two, a pallet bed in one corner and a deal table, but in my then condition these things were more than sufficient for my wants, and I made no complaint of them. Nay, when Merciful Wiggleskirk offered me some apology for the poor quarters he had brought me to I checked him, and pointed out that to a man who has but some sixteen hours to live a cottage is as fine as a palace.

"Why, sure," says he, "death is the greatest leveller—but is there naught that we can do for your honour? Your honour," he says, giving me a sly look, "is such a generous rewarder——"

"Friend," says I, "I verily believe that I have not even a penny-piece upon me. As for reward then——"

"I meant you to understand," says he, "that I had already received my reward, and was minded to do still more to deserve what you have already bestowed upon me. So if there is aught that you lack——"

"Faith," says I, "thou art a good fellow. Why, now I come to think on't, I should be pleased to have pen, ink, and paper, so that I may spend an hour or two in writing some necessary matters. 'Twill help me to kill the time of waiting," I says.

"You shall have what you wish, Master Coope," says he, and he went forth to his fellow at the door and despatched him for the things I needed. "I shall be on guard with you alone for the rest of the time," says he, returning to my side. "A lame man can make little shift to escape, and we need all our men in the works. There is to be a great assault made upon the Castle to-night."

"Ah!" says I, "under other circumstances I could like to ha' joined in it; but to tell the truth, good fellow, my foot gives me so much pain as to put the thoughts of everything out o' my mind. Faith!" says I, with a grim laughter filling me at the very humour of it, "I believe I'm more concerned about the pain o' this plaguey foot than that I am to be shot i' the morning."

"Why, master," says he, looking out of the window, "let's hope you'll shortly find some relief, for here's Sir Thomas's chirurgeon coming to see you," and he opened the door to admit a little, hatchet-jawed fellow, that eyed me curiously, and demanded to see my hurt. He took my leg in his lap, and prodded my swollen ankle here and there with so much abstracted curiosity that I lost my temper with him.

"Master surgeon," says I, "you torture me, and I have no mind to be tortured by anybody. For God's sake," I says, "either relieve my pain, or put my foot down!"

But he looked at me out of his leaden eyes and gave me such a nip over the ankle bone as made me roar with agony. "Yea," says he, "I thought the hurt lay there. However, in three days you shall walk as well as ever."

"Thank you for naught," says I, mightily

inclined to take him by the scruff of the neck and shake him to pieces. "Three days!—why, man, in three days I shall ha' seen things that you are never like to see—I am to be shot at daybreak i' the morning."

"Are you so?" says he, with a stare. "Pooh! I waste my valuable time," he says, and walks out of the cottage without another word. And thereat, in spite of the pain and vexation, I burst out a-laughing, and bade Merciful Wigglies-kirk shut the door on the leech's back. "Faith, I think he was in the right on't, after all!" says I. "What's the good of mending a man that's to be broken for good in a few hours?"

"Why, I don't know about that, master," says Merciful. "I conceive that a man hath a right to be eased of his pain ere his end, so that he may make a good quittance. And if you've no objection," he says, "I'll try my own healing art upon you with an ointment that I always carry about my person—a very balm of Gilead it is, and hath worked the marvellousest cures."

"With all my heart, lad," says I, "thou canst do aught thou'rt minded to, short o' cutting my leg off. I must make shift to stand straight in the morning."

He brought out the little box that contained

his ointment and began to rub my leg with it. "I have some acquaintance with the healing art," says he. "I was boy to a doctor at one time, and made experiments on my own account. Besides, my merciful nature obliges me to exercise my office upon all that are in distress."

"Thou art a queer fellow," says I. "But, come, tell me of what happened at the Manor House this morning. I am anxious to know how it fared with the serving-folk."

"Oh," says he, "at daybreak they hung out a flag and submitted themselves, and we had free entrance to the house, and were sore concerned, I promise you, to find naught there but servants. Captain Stott was for dealing sternly with them at first, but, what, they had but obeyed orders, and so he let them go their own ways, and set himself to track you and madam."

"But we heard cannon discharged," says I.

"Yea," says he, rubbing away at my foot, "your ancient house, Master Coope, is certainly not of such fair proportions as it was. Stott fired two discharges into it, and you will have some repairs to see to if you intend—but I forgot," he says, looking at me with a curious smile, "that you will not need earthly residence much longer."

"So the old house is dismantled?" says I.

"Why, say somewhat disarranged," says he.

"May the Lord reward whoever did it!" says I, and fell a prey to bitter thoughts. I had loved that old house, and it gave me sore pain to think of it, a heap of ruins over my uncle's grave. "Alack!" thinks I, sadly. "What evil days have we fallen upon. My uncle lies dead and buried under his own floor, Alison is in the hands of Anthony Dacre, and here sit I, waiting to be shot. Was ever sadder fortune?"

But there Merciful Wiggleskirk gave up his ministrations, and looked up at me from where he knelt on the floor.

"Now, master," says he, "how does your hurt feel by this time?"

"Why," says I, working my ankle about, "I believe it is a deal easier. That ointment o' thine must be rare stuff—it has certainly given me relief."

"I could have you fit to stand upright without pain by to-morrow," says he, proudly. "Ah! this is, as I said, the very balm of Gilead. I concocted the notion on't myself, and would not sell it for a deal o' money. When I grow weary of this fighting trade, master, I shall set up as an empiric——"

"It would reward you better," says I. "And were a fitter employment for a man of your powers. I'm obliged to you," I says. "The smart hath abated marvellously."

"I will minister to you again ere long," says he. "You shall walk out of this cottage straight enough in the morning. But here's your pens and paper," he says, seeing the other trooper returning. "So now you can fall to your writing, master."

It was now past noon, and ere long there was brought to us food and drink, which we consumed together with as much satisfaction as we could get out of each other's company. True, the thought of my condition did sometimes come upon me as I ate, and made my food to stick in my throat, but as there was no use in repining at my fate, I strove to be free of regret, and to behave myself like a man. And the food and drink putting some heart into me, I presently turned to the table, and began to write, in which occupation I found great comfort and relief.

Now, I verily believe that troubled as I was at my own fate (for I was troubled though I strove hard not to be) I was more concerned on account of Alison. After all that I had done to prevent it, she had in the end fallen into the hands of Anthony Dacre. I had no cause to be especially anxious for her safety when I first heard Anthony's designs against her, for she and I, on the rare occasions of our meeting, had never been able to get on together, and she had treated me with a certain haughty contempt that I secretly resented. But I had never been able to endure the thought of her being in Anthony's power, and after I had lived under the same roof with her, and seen much of her I felt that I would stay at naught to save her from him. And there was more than that, for, somehow, I had come to love her with a rare passion, even when she flouted and teased me. This made life exceeding bitter for me in what I believed to be its last hours. There I was, a prisoner in more ways than one, unable to move hand or foot to succour her whose image was constantly before me, while she, for aught I knew to the contrary, was in the hands of a man whom I knew from his own confession to be a black-hearted villain, and incapable of mercy or consideration where his own vile inclination was concerned.

There was but one thing that comforted me in this sore pass and that was the thought of Alison's own fearlessness. She was one of those

women that are accustomed — faith, there are
precious few of them that I have seen during
fifty years of life!—to think and act for themselves, and I could readily imagine her to be
more than a match for Anthony Dacre, so long
as natural wit was the only weapon employed
by both. It might be that she, finding herself
in his hands, would contrive means for her safe
progress to her father's house and even delude
him into procuring them. Thus, I was somewhat comforted, and yet it was a hateful thought
to me that the woman I loved was in the company
of a man whom I heartily despised. It was not
that I had any jealous feeling—though she had
teased me about him as we sat under the bridge,
saying that he was a handsome man, a devoted
cavalier, and so forth, which was her woman's
way of professing what she didn't believe for
very sport—but that I had so much respect and
affection for her that I would have done aught
—aye, and had done so much as to lose my own
life by it—to keep her unsmirched even by the
mere company of villainy. But caged as I was
what could I do ?—and so I hoped for the best,
and sat me down to write letters to my cousin,
having arranged with Merciful Wiggleskirk that
he would use his utmost endeavour to have the
packet delivered.

Now of what I then wrote I have at this time but the least knowledge, for the packet came into Alison's hands—though not after the fashion that I had intended—and she has since taken the strictest care of it, and values it so much that she will not permit it to pass out of her keeping even for a moment. However, what I do remember is that I spent all that afternoon and evening in writing — with some intervals wherein Merciful Wiggleskirk rubbed his balm of Gilead into my foot, much to its great benefit —and that in the end I used all the paper that the trooper had brought me, and so was obliged to lay down my pen unsatisfied.

It was then close upon midnight, and being sore fatigued, I lay down on the bed, sleepy enough, in spite of the fate that was but some seven hours distant. Merciful Wiggleskirk mounted guard over me, rarely satisfied with the result of his ministrations to my injury. "Faith!" says I, "I think I shall sleep well," and I bade him good-night.

But there was much about to happen, and since I had naught to do with that which brought it about, I shall here present to you the account of it that was written down afterwards by Alison herself.

II.

A TRUE NARRATIVE OF THE TRANSACTION BETWEEN ALISON FRENCH AND ANTHONY DACRE, NOW SET DOWN AFTER A PLAIN FASHION BY THE FORMER. —A. F.

When Colonel Sands so rudely bade me be-gone from the camp, and I saw my cousin Richard led away by the troopers to what I felt assured must end in his death, I was so sore distrest that for some moments my wits forsook me and I knew not what to say or do. It was, I think, at that moment that I first discovered my love for my cousin, and that, perhaps, had as much to do with my confession as aught else. They gave him no time to speak with me ere they led him away, but he turned himself about at the door of the house into which they were conducting him, and gave me a swift glance, and when I met his eyes I knew that I loved him with all my heart, which had never till then been stirred by the thought of any man. Then he was gone, and I felt that all was over, and that for the rest of my life I should carry with me the pain of that moment which yet mingled with the joy that comes to a woman who suddenly discovers that she is loved and that she loves in return.

It was Anthony Dacre that woke me out of my reverie. He drew near and addressed me by name. I know not what sort of countenance I turned upon him, but he stood back and looked afraid. But on the instant I grew calm. There was naught but danger of the worst sort to the man I loved and to myself (and I was now the dearer to myself because he loved me) in that moment. "This is no time," thought I, "for rashness or for ill-temper. I must keep my wits, and see if I cannot devise something to save Dick from his fate." And therewith a thought flashed across my mind. My wit against all of them — my woman's wit against Anthony Dacre's subtlety and Fairfax's decree. I had always prided myself on my strong-mindedness and my common-sense—of what avail were either if they could not help the man I loved when his need was of the greatest? Could not?—nay, but they should! I would be strong and wise: it should not be for lack of endeavour if I did not outwit them all.

I turned to Anthony Dacre with a gracious manner.

"And so you are to form my escort, cousin?"

I said, speaking to him with a civility which belied the loathing and contempt I kept for him in
my heart.

He looked at me with a great surprise,
wondering perhaps what had brought this change
over me.

" I have made some arrangements for you," he
said. " I shall conduct you to your father's house
with great pleasure. Will it please you to set out
at once ? "

" Why," said I, affecting to treat the matter
lightly, " I am ill-provided with riding-gear.
Would it not suit your convenience to stay our
progress at the Manor House so that I can fit
myself out in proper fashion ? "

" Anything that you desire, cousin," said he.

" Then we will set out at once," I said, and
gave him my hand in order that he might assist
me to the horse which stood near. " But I fear,"
I said, when I had disposed myself as well as I
could, " that we shall find the old house a heap
of ruins, and my gear may not easily be come at."

" It is certainly somewhat damaged," said he,
" and believe me, cousin, it was much against my
will. But I am but a gentleman volunteer, after
all, and things have gone beyond my power. I
wish," he said, as we rode away, followed by his

two men, "that you had thought better of me, cousin, at the beginning of this sad matter. It would have saved much bloodshed and trouble."

Now there was naught that I so much desired at that moment as to turn in my saddle and look Anthony Dacre straight in the face and tell him my true thoughts. It would have given me the greatest relief—but there was so much at stake that I must needs lie to him and to myself if I would win the game I was playing.

"Cousin," I answered, as gracious in voice as if it gave me pleasure to be in his company, "I, too, am sorry that there have been misunderstandings. But when one is misinformed——"

"Ah!" he said eagerly. "So your mind was poisoned against me, cousin? Let me now swear to you that in all this I have sought nothing but your own comfort and safety. When Fairfax determined to attack Sir Nicholas I entreated that the matter might be placed in my hands so that no insult should be offered to yourself. Alas!—I know not what it was that prejudiced you against me in this. Suffer me to believe that you are satisfied with my explanation, cousin."

"I am sorry that I did not know your true character earlier, cousin," I answered.

"I am overjoyed to think that we are re-

conciled," said he, " it has hurt me much to feel
that I lay under your displeasure."

" I have observed to others," I said, still
humouring him, " that you are a devoted cavalier,
Master Anthony," and I gave him a smile that
fetched the colour to his face, " and so I expect
you to attend me to my father's house, and
there you shall be duly rewarded —·maybe
with——"

" Ah !" said he, coming nearer to me. " With
what, cousin ? "

" Why," said I, with another smile, " with what
so devoted a knight has the right to expect," and
with that I whipped up my horse and rode
forward as if in some confusion. He laughed
and came after me, and so we pressed on to
Hardwick agreeing very well indeed.

Now when we turned into the courtyard of the
old house the sight of the ruin caused by the
cannon was like to make me weep, but I re-
strained myself and suffered Anthony Dacre to
lead me within. The kitchen and hall were least
damaged of the lower apartments, and in the
former we found old Barbara and Jasper who
were pottering about in sore lamentation, and
seemed vastly surprised to see us. I addressed
Barbara in my grandest manner giving her at

the same time a glance that she understood plainly enough.

"Barbara," I said, "Master Dacre is escorting me to my father's house, but before we go forward we will refresh ourselves if you can make shift to give us food and drink. You will not refuse to dine with me, Anthony," I said, turning to him with a smile that was meant to subdue him.

Now it is marvellous—and never so much so, I think, as to us women ourselves—that a woman's beauty and manner hath power to change a man from his purpose more rapidly than any other form of persuasion. As I looked at Anthony Dacre I knew that I could do with him as I pleased. He mumbled something in the way of a compliment that I scarcely heard, though I affected to do so, and smiled back my thanks to him for it. He was won over—but oh, the anxiety that I still felt lest my plans should miscarry!

While Barbara prepared food and drink for us, I went over the house under pretence of making myself ready for our further progress. It was a sad sight that my eyes beheld. The upper storey of the house had been well-nigh shattered to pieces, and the room in which my uncle died was a heap of stones and dust. But my own chamber was undisturbed, and thither I presently repaired and

made such alterations in my apparel as were
sorely needed. Nay, when I looked at myself in
the mirror I marvelled that I had been able to
make any impression on Anthony Dacre, for my
adventures of that day and the previous night
had made me anything but attractive. Now it
was necessary (beauty being the greatest weapon
which we women can arm ourselves and aid our
natural cunning with) that I should make myself
as attractive as possible, and so I gave some considerable attention to my toilet, and at last went
downstairs to find Anthony Dacre, and proceed
with the development of my plans.

I found him in the small parlour that adjoined
the hall, where Barbara had contrived a hasty
meal for us. He looked at me with some
astonishment as I entered, and I noticed as I
returned his glance that he, too, had taken some
pains to smarten himself up. I walked to the
head of the table, and motioned him to take a
seat at my right hand. But he came forward and
took my hand as if to lead me to my chair, and
no sooner did his fingers touch mine than he
broke out into the most extravagant profession
of love for me, swearing by all that is holy that
he adored me in the most devoted fashion, and
beseeching me to have some pity on his condition.

All this I was compelled to endure and even to
affect to receive with complaisance, though inwardly I was filled with two thoughts—the first,
that I could cheerfully have stabbed him where
he stood; the second, that he was playing into
my hands. I heard him to the end, and then I
disengaged my hand from his and drew away
from him.

"Cousin," I said, "this is not the time or place
for us to discuss these matters. It is possible,"
I said, looking at him, "that I have been mis-
taken in you, as you say, and if so, I am indeed
sorry, and will strive to make amends. But I
think it will be best if you accompany me to my
father's house, and there prosecute your suit—
if indeed, you really feel for me what you say—
after the fashion usual amongst people of our
degree. You must speak to my father first,"
says I, with a coquettish glance at him that
made him ready to obey me on the instant.

"But yourself?" said he. "What answer
will you make to me if I fulfil your wishes
in this?"

"Why," I said, looking, I daresay, very modest
and conscious, "I think that if you really obey
me, I may perhaps be found more complaisant
than you have fancied, cousin.'

"My angel!" he cried, and would have embraced me had I not anticipated some such proceeding on his part and escaped him.

"Come," I said, smiling, "let us have some food, cousin—we have a long ride before us, and for myself I have had little to eat since last night."

He took his seat near me, and I occupied myself in paying him much attention, and seeing to his comfort. As for me, it well-nigh choked me to eat a crumb of bread ; but, lest he should observe that I was anxious or pre-occupied, I forced myself to make a hearty meal. Barbara had furnished the table with a flask of my uncle's old Tokay, and more than once I filled Anthony's glass with my own hands. What a comedy it all was, and yet what a tragedy seemed to be playing itself out in my heart at the time !

When at last he would eat and drink no more, I approached the subject that lay closest to my thoughts. "Now," thought I, "Heaven send me strength and wit to carry out my project!" And I think my prayer must have been answered quickly, for I spoke with calmness, though every nerve in my body seemed to me to quiver with anxiety and apprehension.

"Cousin," I said, "what will they do with Richard Coope?"

He looked at me narrowly. I could see that the mere question raised his jealousy and distrust on the instant.

"They will shoot him," he answered, keeping his eyes on mine.

"I supposed they would," said I, affecting a rare carelessness. "Poor Dick! But 'tis I suppose, the fortune of war, eh, cousin?"

"'Tis the treatment always meted out to deserters and traitors," he said.

"Well," said I, "'tis a pity that a kinsman of ours' should die a shameful death, is it not, cousin?"

"It is not to the credit of the family," he answered. "But an offender against the cause must be punished."

"Why," I said, "I think Dick offended under some misapprehension, and 'tis rather a pity that he should die for that when you and I, cousin, have been so fortunate as to clear away our own misunderstanding. Could we do nothing to save him from so violent a death?"

"No," he said, "naught. By this time it is probably over."

It was only by the strongest effort that I was

able to preserve my composure when he said that. I affected to take no particular heed of it.

"I wish we could have saved him," I said presently. "I fear my father will visit his displeasure upon both of us for our neglect to say a word in Dick's favour. He thinks so much of family ties, cousin. But I trust he may not, for I do not wish you to meet with a frown from him when you conduct me home, under the—the circumstances that you spoke of a little time ago," said I, giving him a sly glance.

"I would do aught to please you, cousin," he exclaimed. "But in this matter of Dick Coope, what can I do, even if he be still alive, which I question ? I have no influence with Fairfax."

"You must surely have some," I replied. "One who has rendered such service."

"Why, I may have some slight claim upon him," he said. "But come, cousin, what signifies Dick Coope—let us talk of ourselves."

"Dear Anthony," said I, "we shall have so much time for that afterwards, and i' faith I am concerned about Dick — though indeed I have no cause to trouble myself about him, seeing that he and I could never abide one another's presence—for the reason that my father and our relations will be sore vexed at his death. And I am so anxious that naught should occur to vex my father at this time," I added, looking significantly at him, " that if it were in my power I would do something to save Dick, and get him out of the country. Is there aught that we could do in that way, cousin ? "

" I won't say that something might not be done," said he. " I might contrive his escape if he still lives."

" I would give something if that were done," said I. " Why, that's noble and generous in you, cousin ! Come, I think the more of you for that. But is the thing possible ? "

" There are three things that would make it so," said he, looking narrowly at me.

" And what are they, cousin ? " I enquired.

" Why," said he, " first, if he's still alive ; second, if there's money in the house to secure his release ; and third, if you will reward me for my efforts on his behalf."

" I reward you ? " said I, affecting a great surprise. " How can I reward you, cousin ? "

" By bestowing yourself upon me without delay, fair cousin !" he cried, throwing himself at my feet and seizing my hand.

" Why," said I, " affecting a pretty confusion,

" I thought that I had already given you some promise of the sort—but 'without delay' sounds so formidable—will not a year hence suit you, cousin ? " I said.

" A year hence ? 'Tis an age—a century ! " he exclaimed, possessing himself of both my hands. " It must be at once—I cannot endure my passion to remain unsatisfied, fair coz ; indeed, I love thee so much."

" I could do much for a man that gratified my whim," said I.

" And by heaven," said he, " I will gratify it if I'm in time ! Promise me, cousin, that you'll marry me to-night, and I'll save Dick Coope— that is," he said, with a sudden caution, " if he's yet alive, and if you can find me money for the enterprise."

" But to-night ? " said I, much confused. " Oh, cousin—why, was ever aught so sudden ? Let us say a month hence, or a fortnight."

" No," he said, " to-night—this very night. I will bring a clergyman with me."

" I am so taken aback," I said. " Let us say a week hence, cousin."

" No," he said. " A week ? 'Tis a lifetime— you must make me the happiest of men to-night if I do this for you. Come, yes or no, coz ? "

"Why," said I, looking away from him, "you deserve to be rewarded for your enterprise, Master Anthony, so I will say yes. But—nay," I said, as he made as if to embrace me, "let us defer all that until we have some leisure—bethink you what there is to do. We must bestir ourselves if you really mean to win me for your own ere to-morrow morning. What is our bargain, cousin? That you are to rescue Dick Coope and bring him here, and that I am then to reward you with my hand?"

"And your heart," said he, still pressing me with his attentions.

"Why, of course," said I, and laughed. "Come, cousin, let us sit down and make our arrangements," and I contrived to keep the table between us. "Now, first," I said, giving him the bag of gold which Dick had handed to me when we were caught by the troopers, "there is money for your needs in this matter. Now let us settle all other things. First, you are to set out forthwith for Pomfret and busy yourself about Dick's escape. You will, I suppose, bribe those that have him in charge?"

"Leave that to me," he answered, with a chuckle. "I know a trick or two of that sort."

"I am sure of it," said I. "Then you are to

bring him here so that he can be furnished with money for his journey out of the country."

"Must he come here?" said he. "If I manage his escape——"

"Why, to tell you the truth, cousin," said I, "I want to see him for a good reason. Sir Nicholas on his death-bed confided to Dick a secret as to the hiding of some considerable treasure, and I want to have it out of him. He cannot refuse to tell me after what we have done for him," I said.

"He shall be brought here," he answered.

"And when will you return with him?" I said.

"Why," said he, musingly, "I have a plan, and if it goes as I think it will, it will be within an hour after midnight."

"Then I will expect you, cousin," said I. I paused a moment, and then looked at him in a shy fashion. "And you will bring a clergyman with you?" I said, striving, and I hope with some success, to counterfeit a becoming modesty.

"Assuredly I will!" he cried.

"Then go, dear Anthony," I said. "But stay, there are two other matters—I do not like the notion," I said, looking about me with an air of distaste, "of spending my wedding night in this house—could not we ride to your own house at

Foxclough immediately after the ceremony?
I should find that much to be preferred,
cousin."

"Why," said he, "'tis a ten mile ride—and the
old place is but poorly furnished—but since you
wish it, cousin, I will despatch one of my men
with strict orders to have it prepared for our re-
ception during the night."

"And your other man?" said I, "will you leave
him here to protect me?—old Jasper is but a poor
guard, and there is no one but Barbara and myself in the house."

"Agreed," said he. "And now I must hasten
—egad, the time will go but slow till I return
with the parson, fair coz!"

"Hasten!" said I, "you must fulfil your bargain
if you would gain your prize. Nay," I said, seeing that he was minded to embrace me, "lose no
time, cousin—I shall be impatient for your return," and I gave him a smile as he went
out of the door that was intended to encourage
him. I watched him across the kitchen and saw
that he spoke to the two men; then he rode out
of the courtyard and I returned to the parlour,
calling Barbara to attend me there. And we had
no sooner entered and closed the door than I
swooned, the excitement of the scene I had just

gone through proving too much for me to bear
any longer.

"This will not do," I said when Barbara
had brought me round, and I sat up feeling
somewhat recovered. "There is still much that
I must undertake." I began to plot and plan
afresh, telling old Barbara sufficient of what was
going on to explain my anxiety to her. Truly I
was by that time in a sad condition, for there was
first the fear lest Dick should already be beyond
my help, and second, the thought that my plans
should miscarry ere they could be worked out as
I wished. "'Tis a desperate game," I said to
myself, "Heaven help me to play it to the end
and give me success!" And therewith I began to
consider my next movement.

Now so far as matters had turned out I had
nothing to regret, and last of all, the seeming deception which I had practised on Anthony Dacre.
It may seem to you who read this narrative that
I had played upon him in the vilest and most
heartless fashion by promising to marry him.
But there was no deception in it, save on his side,
for all the time that he spoke with me of marriage
he was in reality meditating my ruin. I knew
what he did not know that I knew—namely, that
he was already married. I had come to know it

by the most curious chance. Soon after Sir
Nicholas Coope fell ill and took to his bed, there
came to see him old Master Drumbleforth, a
neighbouring clergyman, who chanced to inform
him that he had married Anthony Dacre to one
of his parishioners some few years previously, and
that the woman still lived, though sore neglected
by her husband. And I think it was because of
knowing this that I felt it neither heartless nor
deceitful to treat Anthony as I did. My own
happiness and the life of the man I loved were at
stake—what true woman would have let squeamish notions about nice points of honour stand in
her way at such a time ?

I now proceeded to carry out my further plans,
all of which I had duly considered since my first
notion of saving Dick entered my head. Towards
the close of the afternoon I rode over to Master
Drumbleforth's vicarage and confessed to him all
that I had done and all that I had it in my mind
to do, and begged him to come to the Manor
House that night in order to help me to carry out
my last intentions. He promised to do so and
gave me his blessing and sympathy, comforted by
which I returned home. My next proceeding was
to get rid of the man whom Anthony Dacre had
left with us. I made up a parcel of my clothing,

and giving it to him, bade him follow his fellow-servant to Foxclough and bide there until Anthony and I came in the night. He went without question, and when he was fairly departed, I mounted my horse again and rode off to Thorpe, where I saw John and Humphrey Stirk. I arranged that they should come to the Manor House early that night and remain there until Anthony Dacre returned. This done, my arrangements were all complete. I had carried out everything that my woman's wit could devise, and there was naught left but to return home and wait with a fierce impatience for the outcome of my endeavours.

This is a true history of what I, Alison French, did on that distressing day. God send that no other woman be ever placed in such trying circumstances as those which I have here faithfully described. As for the end of them all, it will be much better spoken of by Richard, who has a turn for the writing of books, than by me, who have none.

THIS IS THE END OF MISTRESS ALISON'S ACCOUNT OF HER TRANSACTION WITH ANTHONY DACRE.

III.

I do not think that I had slept above half-an-hour when I was awoke by Merciful Wiggleskirk, who laid his hand on my shoulder and at the same moment bade me make no noise. There was a very dim moonlight flooding the cottage when I opened my eyes, and at first I took it for the dawn and thought that my last hour was come.

" So they are ready, eh, lad," says I, sitting up. "Faith, the night's been short, but thank God, I have slept soundly."

' Hush, master," says he. " The night's not half over. We have work to do yet. Hearken to me —are you minded to escape if I show you the way ? "

"What's all this?" I says, staring at him in the dim light. "Say plainly what's on your mind."

"Why, then," says he, "your cousin, Mistress French, has devised some plan of rescuing you, and it falls to me to carry out this part of it. Are you willing ? "

" Willing ! " I says. "Come, let us hasten."

" First," says he, "let me doctor your foot. We have still a quarter of an hour. I waked you in advance of the time so that I might be able to minister to your hurt. It may be that you'll have to use that foot whether it pain you or no."

" I'll make shift," says I, all impatient now that I knew Alison had not forgotten me. I was

anxious to proceed to our next movement, but
Wiggleskirk made me sit down while he rubbed
his balm of Gilead into my leg. He busied himself in this fashion for some minutes, and then
proceeded to bandage my ankle and foot with
linen swathes. "There," says he at last. "Now
stand up, master, and see if you cannot use your
foot a little."

Now, whether it was the healing powers of
Merciful's ointment, or my own excitement at the
thought of regaining my freedom that worked
such wonders in me, I don't know, but whatever it
was I found on putting my foot to the ground
that I could walk with some little difficulty.
There was still much stiffness and discomfort
in my foot, but the pain had abated in marvellous fashion.

"Thou art a very miracle-monger," says I.
"Come, what do we turn to next?"

"Have patience," says he. "There's much at
stake." He opened the door of the cottage and
looked forth. The moon was then dipping into
a bank of cloud. "Now," says he, "I think we
may venture," and he beckoned me to follow
him. We left the cottage, and turning the corner
crept along behind the hedgerow. For fifty yards
I contrived to amble along, but then the pain

returned, and I was forced to call a halt. "Pain or no pain," says Merciful, "we must onward," and he drew my arm within his and supported me. Soon we came to a little grove of trees. "Here are two men with four horses," he whispers in my ear. "Ask no question of them— all you have to do is to mount and ride. I shall be at your side, and we are going to your cousin."

We were now close to the horses, and one of the men, coming forward, assisted Merciful to lift me into the saddle. "All clear," says Merciful, and we set out across the fields, the three men closely surrounding me. One of the strange men led the way, and I observed that he was careful to keep clear of the town. For some time I was not sure as to the direction we were following, but after skirting the fields that lie between Tanshelf and Mill Hill we eventually came out on the Barnsdale road, and ere long I saw the top of the old manor rising up in the moonlight.

"Surely we cannot be going there!" I thought. But when we came to the corner of the village street our leader turned his horse, and in a few minutes they were assisting me to dismount in the courtyard. "Well, this," thinks I, "is the strangest adventure," but I said naught. The men tied their horses to the rings at the mount-ing-stone, and Merciful Wiggleskirk gave me his arm. And then all four of us were at the porch, and the door of the great kitchen opened, and there stood Alison, holding a lamp above her head, just as she had stood when I and the Stirks came to warn her of her danger but a few nights before. I stared at her as she looked at us and was amazed. Her eyes were bright, there was the rarest colour in her cheeks, she had never looked so handsome, I swear, but there was something in her face that I had never seen there before. It was excitement, apprehension, fear—I know not what; but when her eyes fell on me it vanished. She gave me one swift look, and then turned into the kitchen. The two strangers followed her close, with me and Wiggleskirk in attendance, and as we came into the light the foremost of them threw aside the cloak that had so effectively concealed him from me. It was Anthony Dacre!

I looked from him to her. She stood, proud and haughty by the hearth, and gave no more heed to me than if I had been a stone. Anthony Dacre spoke, setting his eyes on her boldly.

"There, madam," says he, with a bow that began at her and finished at me, "you see how well I have executed your commands. Here stands Master Richard Coope, alive and unhurt. Have I done well, fair cousin?"

"You have done excellent well, sir," says she.

"Then there is naught left, madam," says he, "but to claim my reward."

"And that," says she, "you shall have without delay. But first I must transact that business with Master Coope that I told you of. Master Richard, will it please you to step with me into the hall for a moment?"

But I looked at her and then at him.

"Hold!" says I. "What is the meaning of all this, and what is that reward you speak of, Master Dacre?"

He gave me a triumphant look.

"In return for saving your life," says he, "Mistress French confers upon me her hand and heart. Here," he says, motioning towards the man at his side, "is the clergyman who will presently marry us."

"Is this true?" says I, and looked at Alison.

"And what right has Master Richard Coope to ask such a question?" says she, in her haughtiest manner. But she had contrived to get 'twixt me and Anthony, and she gave me a look which signified so much that I saw through all this mystery in an instant. "By heaven!"

thinks I, "she has tricked him after all!" And I followed up her clue. "Nay," says I, sulkily, "it's naught to me, mistress. But what's this business that you speak of?"

"Step with me into the hall," says she. She turned to Anthony, and gave him the sweetest look. "We shall need but a few minutes, cousin," she says.

I hobbled into the hall. She followed me close, and shut the door. I turned to her, and as our eyes met she threw her arms about my neck, and held me to her. "Oh, Dick!" she cries. "My dear, my dear, if you knew what I have gone through. But you are safe," she says, starting away, "and there is so much to do. Come——"

"Alison," I said, holding her hand. "What is all this—what does it mean?"

"Dick," she says, looking me straight in the eyes, "do you love me?"

"As my life—and more!" says I.

"And will you marry me—now?" she says.

"Now?" I says. "But I will do aught that you wish," I says, sore mystified.

"Come, come!" she says, and drags me to the door of the little parlour. "There are good friends here," she says, and leads me within.

There was old Drumbleforth, the parson, there, with John and Humphrey Stirk. Alison led me up to the clergyman. "Stand by the door, John and Humphrey," says she. "Now, Master Drumbleforth, will you wed me to my cousin?"

"You are both of a mind, children?" says the old man, looking from one to the other. "But I see you are," he says, and opened his book.

So we were married, and as the parson said his last word I took my wife in my arms and kissed her for the first time.

By that time I was well nigh amazed with the succession of conflicting emotions that I had experienced during the day and night. I could not believe that things were real. I stood staring at Alison and old Parson Drumbleforth. She smiled at me, and then seemed to recollect herself.

"John," says she, "do you and Humphrey see to your arms, and give my husband those that you have prepared for him. There may be need for them, but I think not. Now——" she left the parlour, and crossed the hall. She flung open the door. "I am ready for you, Master Anthony," she cried. "Will you step this way with your friend?"

She came back and stood at my side, putting

out her hand to touch mine. And then came
Anthony Dacre, followed by the other man,
and they stopped on the threshold and stared
at us.

Faith! I am not sure that I did not pity
Anthony as he stood there. He looked at
Alison and at me, and from us to old Parson
Drumbleforth, and at sight of him his face
turned from red to black, and from black to
white. He looked back to Alison. " Tricked!"
he says. She looked steadily at him : his eyes
dropped : he turned to the door. But Merciful
Wiggleskirk had followed them in, and had now
closed the door behind them, and stood against
it with a pistol in his hand.

Anthony Dacre turned to sudden rage. "Let
me go," he says.

"When Master Drumbleforth has answered
some questions," says Alison. She turned to the
old man. " This afternoon," she says, " Anthony
Dacre asked me to marry him. Have you aught
to say to that, sir ? "

" Child," says old Drumbleforth, " He is
married already—I married him myself in my
parish church of Darrington."

" He has brought a clergyman with him to
perform the ceremony," says she, still watching

Anthony. "Step forward, friend—let us look
at you."

The man drew nearer, with evident unwilling-
ness. He removed his cloak from his face.
"He paid me to do it," growls he, motioning
towards Anthony.

"Preserve us!" says Merciful Wiggleskirk.
"'Tis Tobias Tomkins of our troop—he is no
more a parson than I am, and not half so
much so."

"I had meant to ask Master Drumbleforth if
he recognised him for a clergyman of the rural
deanery," says Alison. "But there's no need. I
have no more to say. And yet——" she paused
and looked at Anthony once again. "I have
played with fairer weapons than yours," she
says.

IV.

And now there was naught left but for Alison
and myself to make good our escape. We had
been favoured in the most marvellous fashion up to
that time, but we were not yet out of danger, and
it was necessary that we should lose no time in
removing ourselves from a neighbourhood wherein
there was so much to imperil us. So I desired
Alison, Master Drumbleforth, and Merciful

Wiggleskirk to accompany me to another apartment where we might discuss matters in privacy. Anthony Dacre and Tobias Tomkins I left in charge of John and Humphrey Stirk, bidding the latter have no mercy on them if they made any attempt to escape.

"And now," says I, when the four of us were safely bestowed in another room, "what's to be done next? 'Tis clear that we must quit this presently and put as many miles as possible between us and our enemies ere daybreak. The question," I says, looking from one to the other, "is——where shall we go?"

"If I may speak," says Merciful Wiggleskirk, "I say let us go to the Low Countries. I say us because I am going with you, master and mistress. Don't say me nay—faith, you'll find me useful enough ere we've come through our troubles," he says.

"'Tis a long journey," says I, doubtfully, looking at Alison.

"Long or short, 'tis a safe place that we shall find at the end on't," says Merciful. "And 'tis not so long either if we can but light on a ship at Hull."

"I am of Master Wiggleskirk's opinion," says Master Drumbleforth.

S

"What say you, Alison?" says I.

But for answer she put her hand in mine. "Anywhere with you, Dick," says she.

"The Low Countries be it, then," says I. I looked round me. "Shall we ever see the old house again?" I thought to myself, cursing the fate that drove me and my bride out of its shelter like beggars. But that was no time for such thoughts. "Come," I says. "Let's be stirring—what is that you propose, Merciful Wiggleskirk?"

"Why," says he, "what I propose, master, is simple enough—that we presently mount our horses and set out for Hull, there to find a ship. And since we have a fifty mile ride before us," he says——

"Let's waste no time in starting," says I. "Come, see to the horses while I arrange for the safe custody of our prisoners."

"Pity that we cannot knock them on the head for vermin," says Merciful, and bustled out of the room on my errand. Master Drumbleforth followed him to find his own beast. I turned and took Alison into my arms.

"Sweetheart," says I, "this is but a poor wedding-night for you. I fear we have many troubles and difficulties ahead out of which I would fain keep you."

"Nay," says she, laying her hand on my mouth, "no talk of that sort, Dick. We have faced more than one trouble together—I've no fear of aught that may come," says she, smiling at me. "Oh, my dear, I love you so that troubles seem naught when I share them with you."

"Why, then," says I, leading her towards the door, "all's well indeed." I paused and held her at arm's length, looking long and steadily into her eyes. "My wife!" I says, and caught her to my heart, only to release her again and look at her smiling face in sheer wonder. For to tell truth, my head was half turned with the strange doings of that day, and I could scarce comprehend that Alison was really and truly my own.

I think we might easily have forgotten our predicament, so wrapped up in each other were we, had not Merciful Wiggleskirk come bustling back again with news that the horses were in readiness. I sent Alison to her chamber for such baggage as it was necessary she should carry with her, and while she was thus employed, I went back to the room where John and Humphrey mounted guard over our prisoners. I bade them follow me without, and locked the door with my own hands.

"Now," says I, handing the key to John Stirk,

"you will keep these fellows in safe custody for
three hours, lads, at the end of which time you
may release them to go their ways as the devil,
their master, prompts. "By that time," I says,
"I trust we shall be beyond their reach. And so
farewell, honest lads both, and pray God we meet
again under this roof ere long with happier surroundings."   And I shook their hands, and went
out to join Alison, who was busied in saying farewell to Barbara.

There was a faint moonlight as the four of us
rode away across the moor towards Darrington.
It was then one o'clock in the morning, and the
air was of a biting keenness that seemed to pene-
trate to the very bones.   Master Drumbleforth,
muffled to his eyes, stooped over his horse's neck
and said naught; Merciful Wiggleskirk rode in
front, humming a psalm tune to keep his jaws
from chattering; Alison and I rode side by side
in the rear, both occupied, I think, with our own
thoughts, which were—if I may judge by my own
—of that diverse complexion which is made up
of sweet and bitter.   For first I cursed the fate
that drove me and my bride from the house
where we should have settled down in peace and
comfort, and then I blessed the day that had
given me to wife the woman whom I loved with

a deep and abiding passion. And somehow the happiness of the last thought drove out the bitterness of the first, and as we swept past the hedgerows and trees in the faint moonlight, I began to feel a sense of elation that made me bold and resolute to encounter whatever further peril lay before us.

At his parsonage house in Darrington village, Master Drumbleforth drew rein and took leave of us, bidding us God-speed, and wishing us a safe deliverance from all our dangers. We called back our thanks to him, and rode swiftly forward through the sleeping village until we came to the Great North Road. · At the corner of the inn stables, Merciful drew rein.

"I am half undecided," says he, "whether to go forward through Womersley and Snaith or to turn along the north road, and cross the river at Ferrybridge. What say you, master?"

"'Tis more likely to be safe by Snaith than by Ferrybridge," says I. "Fairfax's troopers are in force along the river-side at Ferrybridge."

A window in the inn was thrown open above us, and a man looked out as if to enquire our business. Merciful turned his horse. "Do as I do," says he, in a whisper. "By Ferrybridge, then," he says in a loud voice, and rode away up the hill. Alison and I followed. We were half a mile outside the village before Merciful spoke again.

" We are not for Ferrybridge after all," says he. " I liked not the throwing up of that window, for the man who put his head out is in a position to say which way we have gone. Therefore, I came along the north road. We will now turn down this by-lane, and rejoin the Womersley road at Stapleton. Do you see my meaning, master ? "

" Clearly," says I. " Though I don't see who can follow us."

" Best give no chance," he says. " We can't be too careful. I shall breathe more freely when we're across the Aire, and in a fair way for Hull."

We now doubled back upon our old track, and presently came into the Womersley road, about a mile from Darrington village. For half-an-hour we rode through the woods of Stapleton, which overshadowed the road on either side, and shut out what moonlight there was. Then came the long, winding street of Womersley, and the clatter of our horses' feet against the cottage walls, and then we were into a thickly wooded country again, relieved here and there by wild

patches of marsh and moor. In a shifty light
(for the moon that night was of an uncertain
behaviour) we raced across Balne Common. It
was near three o'clock when we drew near to
Snaith, and pulled up our horses under the
shelter of a wayside coppice to consider our
further plans.

"Shall we cross the river at Snaith," says
Merciful, "or shall we go on by the south
bank to the ferry over the Ouse at Hooke?
There is something to be said for both
roads."

"I know naught of either," says I, "and must
therefore leave the matter to your own decision,
lad. I incline to the straightest road, so long as
it is fairly clear of interruption."

"I think we'll make for Hooke," says he, after
he had meditated awhile. "From Howden to
Hull there is a good turnpike road, and we shall
make better progress. God send we find no
interruption at the ferry!"

So we rode forward again, through Cowick and
Rawcliffe, leaving Snaith on the left, and made
good progress until we came to Airmyn at four
o'clock in the morning. But there, just as I was
beginning to feel sure of our deliverance, we
received a sudden check that took all the conceit

out of me, and left me a prey to more doubts and
fears than I had any fancy for.

Airmyn was all alive. There were lights in
every house, and as we came along the street
we heard sounds of shouting and singing as
though the place were filled with roysterers
rather than with peaceable villagers. Coming to
the open space before the inn we found a crowd
of men and horses, and made out from a little
distance that the former were Royalist troopers.
With a common consent we drew rein, and
looked at one another by such light as the
candles and lanthorns in the cottage windows
afforded us.

"What say you, Merciful?" says I. "Shall we
venture through this mob, or is there some by-
way that we can try?"

"There is no by-way," says he, shaking his
head. "And they see us by this time, and
would think it suspicious did we turn back.
Best go forward as if we were travellers in
haste to continue our journey. Remember," he
saying, bending over to me, "that you are a
country gentleman, travelling with your lady
and servant to Hull, and that we are all staunch
Royalists."

"Can we play the parts?" says I.

"I can play a good many parts to save my neck," says he. "Come, we are observed, master —let's move forward."

So we shook our reins and went on. There was a round score of troopers grouped about their horses before the inn, with here and there a stable lad running about, flaring torch in hand, the streaming light from which gave a grotesque appearance to the men and animals. I leaned over and laid hold of Alison's bridle, and so we approached the crowd, none of whom seemed disposed to make way for us.

"By your leave, gentlemen," cries Merciful. "My master and mistress are in haste, and would fain ride forward if you will give them room."

But the men in front made no show of compliance, and one burly fellow laid hands on my bridle reins and on Alison's, staring impudently into my face.

"Body o' the Pope!" says he. "What have we here? Whither away so fast, my pretty gentleman, with mistress madam? I' faith, art come at the right time if thou wishest a score of proper fellows to drink her health."

"Good friend," says I, very anxious to keep my temper, "I wish naught but to proceed upon my way with as much speed as possible. We are on business of importance, and have no time for aught that would hinder us."

"Shalt not pass until we have drunk madam's good health!" he cried vociferously. He turned, shouting to his fellows, "Hey, lads, see what the morn brings us—a pair o' runaway lovers, as I am a true man. Come, Master Solemn Face, let's see the colour of thy money that we may drink——"

But at that moment an officer came out of the inn calling loudly for order.

"Silence, men!" he shouted. "Is this Bedlam that you all talk together like so many madmen? Sure, I command the most unruly troop in His Majesty's service! What have you there, Sergeant Strong?" he says, pushing his way through the crowd towards the man who held our bridles. A sudden turn of one of the torches threw a glare of light across Alison's face. The officer doffed his hat on the instant and came closer to us, holding it in his hand.

"Sir," says I, seizing the advantage, "I am travelling with my wife and servant for Hull, and am anxious to lose no time on the road. If you'll desire your men to give us room we'll proceed," I says, giving him a low bow.

"I crave a thousand pardons if my fellows have offered you a rudeness, sir," says he, bowing to the ground. "Sergeant Strong, give way— get the troops together and call the roll." He turned to us again as the big man moved off. "You will pardon my fellows, sir," he says, looking very admiringly at Alison. "They are somewhat cock-a-whoop because of a trifling victory gained last night. So you are for Hull?" says he, seeming loth to say farewell to us.

"And are in much haste to get there, sir," I says.

"I and my troops are for Beverley," says he. "We go the same road as far as South Cave. Let me advise you to accept our escort—the enemy is in force across the river, and madam might find it unpleasant to fall into their hands. If you will accept our protection——"

"Why, sir," says I, very impatient, "I thank you very heartily. But we are in great haste and must needs ride fast——"

"Your beasts seem spent now," says he, with a sharp look at the horses. "I think our heavy cattle will match them.

"Take his offer," whispers Merciful at my elbow.

"In that case, sir," says I, "I accept your offer

gladly. I daresay we shall be the better of your protection."

" It shall be willingly bestowed, sir," says he, still mighty polite. " But since we do not start for an hour (I wait that space in order to join a troop that is riding to meet me at the ferry) I would advise you to give your horses a feed of corn and to refresh yourselves at yonder inn. The benefit will be yours, sir."

Now, I had not bargained for any delay, being in a great anxiety to push forward, but I reflected that our beasts were weary, and that an hour's rest would help them to bear the further strain to which we must needs subject them. I there-fore dismounted, and having assisted Alison to alight, led her within the inn, leaving our horses to the care of Merciful Wiggleskirk, who lost no time in conducting them to the stables.

The officer, preceding us into the inn, called loudly for the landlord, who bowed the three of us into his best apartment and desired to know our pleasure. As for me and Alison I think we had no stomach for either eating or drinking, but I desired the man to set his best before us, and we made some show of breaking our fast. Mean-while the officer had introduced himself to us, and seemed highly desirous to make as good an

appearance as possible, protesting that as a true
servant of His Majesty it was his duty to protect
the King's loyal subjects—all of which, I take it,
was in the way of so much tribute to my wife's
beauty, and a sure proof that a woman's prettiness
can achieve more than all the common sense and
reason in the world put together.

"I' faith!" says he. "I am glad to meet you,
sir, and am unreservedly obliged to you and your
lady for your kindness in giving me your company. 'Tis poor work for a man of quality to
ride at the head of his troop with none fitting to
hold converse with him. I promise myself," he
says, with yet another bow, "a most profitable
ride 'twixt now and our parting."

"Why, sir," says I, "'tis very good of you to
say so, though I fear we shall prove but poor
company." And indeed I felt but little disposed
to hold converse with him or any other, being
sore anxious as to our future movements. But
Alison, full of her woman's wit—albeit as anxious
as I—came to my aid and talked to him, making
herself mighty agreeable—much to his pleasure—
until the hour was past and the troop departed,
the officer with Alison and myself bringing up the
rear.

As we rode along the river side into Hook

village the dawn came, grey and misty. There was a bank of white fog over the Ouse, which was there a wide and swift river, mightily swollen at that moment by the recent rains. Down at the ferry the air was cold and thin, and I saw Alison shiver as we sat our horses by the water's edge. I looked round me at the dull, flat landscape, and the wintry river at our feet, and felt a sense of coming trouble. " I have led thee into perilous doings, sweetheart," says I, laying my hand on hers. But she looked at me with the rarest smile, and I knew then that because of her love for me she was willing to face whatever might come.

Our friend the officer, while we waited at the ferry for the troop that was to join him, amused himself by drawing up his men in order of battle and putting them through various movements. I think he designed these things in order to draw our attention to his own person and importance, for he was in sooth a perfect coxcomb, and seemed to delight in showing off his airs and graces. So concerned were we with our own thoughts, however, that we perceived little of what went on immediately before us. Alison and I sat apart, conversing now and then. Merciful Wiggleskirk walked his horse up and down the road in a fashion that clearly proved his uneasiness. And presently, after an excursion to the end of the turn he came back to my side, and drawing rein as if naught had happened, leaned over and spoke to me in a low voice.

" Master," says he, " we are pursued."

" Pursued ? " says I. " What makes you think that ? "

" I have just been to the top of the road," says he, " and caught sight of a troop of horse coming along under the woods a mile off. In another minute or so you'll hear the sound of their horses' feet," he says, nodding his head towards the highway.

" Why, man," says I, " 'tis the troop of horse that this officer is now waiting for that you have seen. He expects them to join him here every moment."

" No," says he, " for these are Roundheads— I can tell the difference 'twixt Roundheads and Cavaliers at three miles. We are pursued, master, as I feared we should be, and if Anthony Dacre has a hand in it we shall have to fight. And the question is," he says, with a glance at Alison, " what is to be done with madam ? "

" Have no fear on that point," says I. " Fetch the officer to us, Merciful, and let us tell him our fears. If we are pursued we may as well ask our new friends to defend us."

While he rode off I turned to Alison and told her our fears. "I doubt," says I, "that Anthony has escaped the Stirks and raised a hue-and-cry after us."

"We will not be separated, Dick," says she. "If it comes to the worst give me a pistol and they shall see that I can use it. Only promise to let us keep together," she says, imploringly.

But ere I could answer, the officer comes riding up with Merciful at his heels. I lost no time in telling him our fears. "Sir," says I, "you have been so kind to us that I scarce like to trouble you with more of our misfortunes, but we are like to be in a sore plight. The fact is that I and my wife—and 'twas but yesterday that we were married—are closely pursued by a troop of Roundheads from Fairfax's camp at Pomfret, and my man has just sighted them along the road there. You can even now hear their horses' feet."

"Faith," says he, "I do hear something of that sort, but I think 'tis the troop that I am to meet here."

"No, master," says Merciful, "they are Roundheads—I observed their headgear narrowly."

"Then we are in for another fight!" cries the

officer, rubbing his hands. " Have no fear, sir—
do you and your lady sit apart, and you shall
see as pretty a bit of war-play as you could wish
for. Hold—I have it ! Do you conduct madam,
sir, into yonder house, and let your man stable
your beasts at the rear. I promise you we will
soon settle these crop-eared rogues, and be ready
to escort you onwards within the half-hour. Hah !
—now I hear them plainly—suffer me to get my
men in order."

Now, I should dearly have liked to draw my
sword, and had a share in the coming fight, but
the officer's advice seemed good, and in a trice
all three of us had ridden round to the rear of
the house overlooking the ferry, and were off our
horses. While Merciful hurried them into the
barn, Alison and I made for the house. There
was no person to be seen within but an old
woman, who scuttled away at the mere sight of
us. And that being no time for ceremony we
made our way to an upper chamber, whose
windows looked out upon the street, and from
behind the curtains gazed at the progress of
events below. From our point of vantage we
could see along the highway by which we had
ridden from Snaith. Almost immediately before
us it made a sudden turn, where it dipped

T

towards the ferry, and it was in this turn, hidden by a tall farmstead that the Royalist captain had drawn up his men along the roadside. I saw his plan on the instant : it was to let the advancing troop sweep by, and then to hem them in between the high ground and the river bank.

The Roundheads came on at a gallop, evidently unconscious of the fact that the ferry lay close before them. They rode in a close-packed body, some thirty in number, and at their head as they swung round the bend, I saw the evil face of Anthony Dacre, whose eyes were like those of a hound that scents its prey.

With a swing and clatter that woke all the echoes of the neighbouring houses, the troop dashed round the corner of the farmstead and into the presence of the Royalists. Every man of the latter had his sword drawn, and as the Roundheads swung by, pulling on their horses' reins lest they should go over the river bank, they charged with a crash that made the blood tingle in my veins, and Alison cover her face with her hands. And in good sooth 'twas no pleasant sight that we gazed upon. Three men had gone over the bank and were perishing miserably in the grey stream, calling on their friends for help that could not be given. Here and there, trampled underfoot by the horses, and presently battered into unrecognisable masses of flesh and blood, lay men that had been cut down ere ever they could draw weapon. High above the curses and cries, the shouting of the men and the neighing of the plunging horses, rose the clatter of the swords as Roundhead and Royalist hewed away at each other, and the battle cry of the latter, roared from the leathern lungs of Sergeant Strong, who was here and there like a mad bull, slaying at every stroke.

I suppose it was all over in a few moments, for the Roundheads, riding full tilt into an ambuscade, had never a chance, and were overwhelmed in point of numbers into the bargain. But as the fight ebbed away I seized Alison's arm. " Look, look ! " I cried, and pointed to the road beneath.

There was a sort of small courtyard immediately before us, and within it, swept aside by the struggling mass of men and horses about them, Anthony Dacre and the Royalist officer fought, foot to foot. Both were covered with blood, and both fought fiercely as if for life. But the Royalist was pressing Anthony hard ; he retreated yard by yard until the wall lay close behind him ; I saw in his face the look that comes to a man's eyes when he knows that death is at last before him, not to be denied. And at that I threw open the casement to lean out and see the end. At the sound, Anthony Dacre looked up. He saw me, and Alison at my shoulder, and I saw his lips form a curse. And at the same instant the Royalist's sword passed through his heart, and I caught Alison away lest she should see him fall and die. But at the sound of a bugle I went back to the window, and saw the troop that we had waited for riding up to the ferry to find their comrades hot with the heat of victory over the Roundheads who lay dead or dying in the middle of the highway.

And so it was all over, and we were free of our enemies. Late that night Alison and I, with Merciful Wiggleskirk in attendance, were in the Market Place at Hull, weary and sore bespent, but devoutly thankful. Ere daybreak next morning we were sailing down the Humber, and so at last I had some leisure to look at my wife and assure myself that all the events of the past week were realities rather than dreams. But that they were realities her sweetness did most abundantly prove to me, and in spite of the fact that we were exiles, she and I spent our first years of married life in Holland, in as sweet a contentment as lovers could wish for.

But after many years we came back to England and to the old house. And since it was half-ruined, I set to work to rebuild it, and somewhat altered it in appearance and design. We transferred Sir Nicholas's body from its first quarters to its proper resting-place. On the spot where we first buried him I now spend many hours, sitting in his chair, and telling my eldest son, Nicholas, of the brave doings that I have had in our old house. And for the sake of him and of his brothers and sisters — for I warrant you we have been blessed with a numerous progeny!—I have written down this chronicle at such times as I have had naught better to do.

When I showed the first pages of this book to my wife, she took some objection.

"Sure," says she, "I never called you Master Poltroon."

"Sweetheart," says I, "you did."

"But you called me Mistress Spitfire," says she.

"And that's what you were," says I.

"Was I ?" says she. "Well, maybe I was—but you were never Master Poltroon."

Faith ! 'tis mighty comforting that she has so good an opinion of me.

THE END.

BY THE SAME AUTHOR

ALDINE HOUSE,
69 GREAT EASTERN STREET, E.C.,
AND
67 S. JAMES'S STREET, S.W.
OCTOBER 1896.

Messrs. J. M. Dent & Co.'s New Novels and Stories

IN ACTIVE PREPARATION.

L. Cope Cornford.—THE MASTER BEGGARS: A Historical Romance of the Low Countries in the times of the "Beggars." By the author of "Captain Jacobus." Cr. 8vo. 4s. 6d. net.

Gilbert Parker.—THE TRESPASSER. Revised and Rewritten Edition. Cr. 8vo. 4s. 6d. net.

Mary Beaumont.—JOAN SEATON: A Story of Parsifal. By the author of "A Ringby Lass." A Yorkshire Story. Cr. 8vo. 4s. 6d. net.

J. S. Fletcher. — MISTRESS SPITFIRE: A Romance of the Civil War. By the author of "When Charles the First was King," &c. Cr. 8vo. 4s. 6d. net. [Oct.

Hannah Lynch.—JINNY BLAKE. By the author of "Dr. Vermont's Fantasy," &c. Cr. 8vo. 4s. 6d. net.

J. F. Sullivan.—THE FLAME FLOWER, and other Stories. Written and Illustrated with about 100 Drawings by J. F. SULLIVAN. Imp. 16mo. 5s. net. [Oct.

I

J. F. Sullivan.—BELIAL'S BURDENS; or, Down with the McWhings. Written and Illustrated by J. F. SULLIVAN. Cr. 8vo. 1s. 6d. net. [*Oct.*

H. Sienkiewicz.—QUO VADIS: A Narrative of Rome in the Time of Nero. Translated from the Polish by JEREMIAH CURTIN. Cr. 8vo. 4s. 6d. net. [*Oct.*

Gordon Seymour.—ETHICS OF THE SURFACE. No. 1—THE RUDENESS OF THE HON. MR. LEATHERHEAD. Imp. 32mo. 2s. net. [*Nov.*

Jas. Lane Allen.—SUMMER IN ARCADY. By the author of "Flute and Violin," &c. Fcap. 8vo. 3s. net. [*Oct.*

Argyris Ephtaliotis.—ISLAND STORIES; or, Sketches of Greek Peasant Life. Translated from modern Greek by W. H. D. ROUSE, M.A. 2s. 6d. net.

S. J. Adair Fitz-Gerald.—THE ZANKIWANK AND THE BLETHERWITCH: An Original Fantastic Fairy Extravaganza. Illustrated with about 40 Drawings by ARTHUR RACKHAM. Imp. 16mo. 3s. 6d. net. [*Oct.*

Prosper Mérimée.—CARMEN. Translated from the French by EDMUND H. GARRETT. With a Memoir of the Author by L. I. GUINEY. Illustrated with 5 Etched Plates and 7 Etched Vignettes from Drawings by E. H. GARRETT, and a Photogravure Frontispiece of Calvé as Carmen. Cr. 8vo. 5s. net. [*Oct.*

Maud Wilder Goodwin.—WHITE APRONS: A Romance of Bacon's Rebellion, Virginia, 1676. Cr. 8vo. 3s. 6d. net. [*Now ready.*

Maud Wilder Goodwin.—THE HEAD OF A HUNDRED: Being an Account of Certain Passages in the Life of HUMPHREY HUNTOON, Esq., some time an Officer in the Colony of Virginia. Cr. 8vo. 3s. 6d. net. [*Now ready.*

By the Author of "The Wheels of Chance."

Crown 8vo, cloth, gilt top. Third Edition. 5s. net.

THE WONDERFUL VISIT.

By H. G. WELLS,
AUTHOR OF "THE TIME MACHINE," ETC.

W. L. COURTNEY, in the Daily Telegraph.

"It would be indeed difficult to overpraise the grace, the delicacy, and the humour with which the author has accomplished his task. It is all so piquantly fresh, so charmingly unconventional, that it carries one away with it from start to finish in a glow of pleasurable sentiment. Rarely, amidst all the floods of conventional fiction-spinning and latter-day psychological analysis, does one come across such a pure jet of romantic fancy as that with which Mr. Wells refreshes our spirits."

Pall Mall Gazette.

"Enthusiastic we own that we are; no book could be more prodigal of honest delight, and its promise leaves hardly any literary accomplishment beyond the aspiration of its author."

Saturday Review.

"A striking fantasia, wrought with infinite tact, charm, and wit. . . . The conversations are full of light and delicate (rather than full-bodied) wit, and it becomes sufficiently pungent at times; but underlying the sweet or acid wit, or even the pure fun (for fun abounds), there is a vein of seriousness and sadness which, with the beautiful descriptive miniatures scattered here and there, justify us in calling the story a piece of literature."

Referee.

"So fresh and imaginative a piece of work, that Mr. Wells, we begin to think, is the new man in fiction. Not only the ingenuity of the story, but the logic of it is such that we know no writer since the author of 'Gulliver's Travels' who could show such amazing power in sustaining the illusion of truth under like conditions."

Scotsman.

"The whole story is so delightfully coherent that, whether in the amusing or in the touching passages, it pleases always. So much that is clever, comical, tender, whimsical, and of healthy fancy."

3

Crown 8vo, 4s. 6d. net.

IN THE VALLEY OF TOPHET.

By H. W. NEVINSON,

AUTHOR OF "NEIGHBOURS OF OURS."

Daily Chronicle.

"Mr. Nevinson's keenness and clearness of observation of his characters comes of his deep sympathy with them. Through the mirk and mire, the folly, the ignorance, and the superstition, he sees the good human stuff. Hence his humour has always in it something of pathos, and his pathos is just lightened by a touch of humour. He plumbs profound depths. He not infrequently brings a lump to the throat."

Athenæum.

"In a series of a dozen epistles, more or less connected, he has set forth, with a vividness which one would suppose can only be the result of careful personal study, the grim humour and the grimmer pathos of the lives that are lived about Cradley, Dudley, and Walsall. It is to the author's credit that in depicting these lives he has been able, while in no way ignoring the lawless animal traits natural to a swarming and neglected population, to steer almost wholly clear of the Zolaesque crudities in which some writers whom one could name would probably have revelled. Take it all in all, this is the strongest book of short stories which we have come across for some time. . . . One feels that it would have taken a good many critics to write one of these stories."

Scotsman.

"The atmosphere of the book is as hard and grimy as a coal-mine itself; but the charm lies in this, and it is true to the nature of its subject. Its pathos—and there is plenty of it—is never forced or mawkish; and the stories never fail to be impressive. The book will enhance the reputation its author gained by his 'Neighbours of Ours,' and will no doubt be widely read."

Glasgow Herald.

"Mr. Nevinson has succeeded in exacting the marrow from his subject in a fashion that should place him at once high amongst our contemporary writers of fiction. His vein of romance, his slow but delicate humour, and his strong humanity of touch remind us more of Miss Mary Wilkins than of any other living writer that we can call to mind. His book is one to read and re-read, and then to lay aside for future enjoyment."

Crown 8vo, cloth, 4s. 6d. net.

THE TOUCH OF SORROW.

By EDITH HAMLET.
(EDITH LYTTELTON).

Times.
"The style is good and the observations are keen enough."

Daily Chronicle.
"'The Touch of Sorrow' appears to be the author's first novel, and as such she may safely congratulate herself both upon its promise and its performance."

Daily Telegraph.
"Miss Hamlet's powerful story."

Dundee Advertiser.
"The course of the story is simple and free from complication, yet it is written with freshness and engrossing charm. At some points, indeed, the interest of the reader is strained almost to intensity. Miss Hamlet has studied human nature, and particularly her own sex, to advantage, and more of her wholesome and pleasing studies will be welcomed."

Daily Mail.
"'Edith Hamlet'—under which designation is veiled the identity of the Hon. Mrs. Alfred Lyttelton—has set forth this main theme with much tenderness, insight, and emotional power. The character of Stella is perfectly natural, and is consistent throughout. The book is intensely womanly, in the best sense of the word, and many of the writer's 'thoughts by the way' are fresh and striking."

Westminster Gazette.
"It is extraordinarily refreshing, by turns jaded and perplexed as we are with sex problems and complications arising out of the married state, to watch, absolutely without their aid, the birth and development in this joyous, radiant being of the Sorrow Soul."

Glasgow Herald.
"This thoughtful and able story."

Liverpool Post.
"A charming literary effort and clever study."

The Guardian.
"Stella Morecombe is one of those rare heroines whose charm is felt by the reader as well as described by the writer."

Crown 8vo, 4s. 6d. net.

IN THE WAKE OF KING JAMES.

By STANDISH O'GRADY,
AUTHOR OF "ULRICK THE READY."

Athenæum.

" No one now living writes a better story of adventure than Mr. Standish O'Grady. . . . It has every quality that is of value in such a story. . . . It ought to be devoured for pure delight by all the young people in the kingdom."

The Speaker.

" A robust and excellent piece of work. . . . Mr. Standish O'Grady must be warmly congratulated upon so unequivocal a success as he has achieved in this thrilling romance."

Manchester Guardian.

" A striking and powerful romance of love and adventurous peril. . . . Mr. O'Grady is to be congratulated and thanked for a spirited piece of imagination, full of swing and vigour. This story, at any rate, does not ' buckle and bow the mind to the nature of things,' but quickens the pulse and stirs the blood in the name of chivalry."

Scotsman.

" The tale is vivid and vigorous above most, and there is about it a fine briny flavour of the Atlantic. . . . Old Thomas is certainly a villain of the first water, and what is more to the purpose, a villain of a new type."

Freeman's Journal.

" Without any disparagement to the power and brilliancy of any of Mr. O'Grady's work, we think that we have here perhaps the most interesting and finished of his novels. . . . The hero's adventures, mishaps, and captivity in the grim old hold of his malevolent cousin, and his final rescue by the quick-witted and courageous Lady Sheela, will be read in the volume before us, and we will not spoil the reader's enjoyment of the full flavour of those startling adventures by any attempted foretaste. ' In the Wake of King James' will undoubtedly do much to increase the already high reputation of its author."

Weekly Irish Times.

" Do you want to read a thoroughly fresh and stirring romance? If you do, get Mr. Standish O'Grady's last novel, ' In the Wake of King James.' . . . The wild work that goes on in the old castle, and the hair-breadth escapes . . . should be enough to quicken the pulses of the most sluggish-blooded reader."

6

Crown 8vo, 3s. 6d. net.

DR. VERMONT'S FANTASY,

AND OTHER STORIES.

By HANNAH LYNCH.

Athenæum.

"Original observation and a rare reticence of detail."

Daily Chronicle.

"Miss Lynch has proved in previous work that she has at command the most precious of gifts, the gift of charm. These stories are all, more or less, interpenetrated by it. Nor is the working of it in us merely while we read. It recurs unbidden in the 'sessions of sweet, silent thought.'"

Vanity Fair.

"Miss Hannah Lynch's new volume, 'Dr. Vermont's Fantasy,' is the finest piece of feminine literary work, take it all in all, that has been accomplished in Great Britain during the present generation. Miss Lynch belongs to no school; she has chosen the best models here, there, and everywhere, and formed her own style. I cannot say what model has been dearest to her; but the general effect is Greek—the massive dignity, the repose—with the exception of the story 'Brases,' which is supposed to be written by an excitable Frenchman—the cold simplicity keeping in check but never conquering the rich warm temperament of the Irish author. . . . Her matter in the average cheap and skilful hands would win immediate recognition, so abundant and full of interest is it."

Dundee Advertiser.

"The climax, great because of its very simplicity, shows that the authoress has a very rare gift as a writer of fiction. In its entirety the collection offers not only something new, but something that will remain attractive. It might be the work of any one of the best French writers. Not that the style is copied. It is the work of one who has not only studied French fiction as a scholar, but who has herself marked and pondered over the life from which she has drawn her men and women."

Scotsman.

"This writer's work is distinguished among the host of similar productions that clamour for public attention to-day by being much stronger than the ruck. The pictures of life of to-day are recognisable . . . they have no mawkishness in tone, and, while laying the shadows heavily in, do not forget that the prime office of the literary, as of the other arts, is to please. The skill they show in giving literary shape to the less obvious moods and phases of feeling that a present-day reader must recognise as peculiar to his own generation is remarkable; and there is not one of the stories that has not its own peculiar variation of this consistently maintained interest."

Crown 8vo, 4s. 6d. net.

IN THE HEART OF THE HILLS:
A NEW ENGLAND STORY.

By SHERWIN CODY.

Scotsman.

"The tale is told in a simple, straightforward way, and the peace that is in the everlasting hills pervades and inspires it."

Glasgow Herald.

"An extremely pretty and natural story quaintly and simply told, and has a rural atmosphere that is very alluring to the jaded palate."

Illustrated London News.

"A delightful story. . . . It is some time since we have read a sweeter love-scene than that with which the book happily closes; and, indeed, throughout you feel yourself in Arden."

Crown 8vo, 3s. 6d. net.

VENUS AND CUPID;
Or, A TRIP FROM MOUNT OLYMPUS TO LONDON.

BY THE AUTHOR OF
"THE FIGHT AT DAME EUROPA'S SCHOOL."

Nottingham Express.

"This fantastic romance is calculated to offer delightful amusement to a multitude of readers, and ought to have a great run of popularity. It is a long time since we have read anything so provocative of laughter. The idea of the book is most happy and humorous; and its development leaves nothing to be desired. Every chapter is full of fun and frolic, and it is impossible to find a dull page from the beginning to the end of the story. It would be unfair to disclose the particulars of this unique 'personally conducted tour'; but we warmly recommend holiday-makers and all others who are on the look-out for a lively and entertaining book to secure a copy of 'Venus and Cupid,' and if they do not find in it magic to brighten a wet day at the seaside, they are quite free to anathematise the reviewer. Our verdict is that a more mirth-provoking romance has seldom if ever been published."

Birmingham Post.

"The story is thoroughly consistent, that having accepted the position —the visit of these august personages to earth—all the details are worked out in harmony with this conception, with abundant fun and humour and fancy. Cupid—or Q, as he is called—is the most delectable little rogue, and we were quite sorry to say good-bye to him."

8

Crown 8vo, cloth, 3s. 6d. net each volume.

EMANUEL.

By HENRIK PONTOPPIDAN.

Translated from the Danish by Mrs. EDGAR LUCAS.

ILLUSTRATED BY MISS NELLY ERICHSEN.

Daily Chronicle.

"Extremely interesting story . . . most delicately delineated, and charms us by its idyllic grace and purity."

Manchester Guardian.

"As a novel pure and simple the book is altogether out of the common, and the firmness of its character-drawing, the sympathetic rendering of nature's background, and the prominence given to the life of the clergy, it reminds one not a little of the work of Ferdinand Fabre, the novelist *par excellence* of French clerical life."

Glasgow Herald.

"Among the many Scandinavian works that have of late appeared in an English dress, few have worn it with a more charming air than this tale of Henrik Pontoppidan's, for a really excellent version of which we have to thank Mrs. Lucas. . . . The tale is told in a fashion that recalls, among our own writers, the intimate knowledge and loving descriptions of Miss Mitford or Mrs. Gaskell. It is not very far from being a work of real genius."

UNIFORM WITH THE ABOVE.

THE PROMISED LAND.

Pall Mall Gazette.

"A story simple and strong, with much quiet pathos, keen analytic power, and graphic picturing of character and place. It is a book to read, enjoy, and muse over, both for its domestic and political interest."

Scotsman.

"It is told with so equable an art and with so much fidelity, both to the general life which a reader of any nationality can understand, and to the local conditions to Denmark, that it is always full of a quiet intense interest. The English version is throughout well done, and it has the advantage of a series of pleasant illustrations from the pen of Miss Nelly Erichsen."

Manchester Guardian.

"It is impossible to read it without feeling that Henrik Pontoppidan is an artist of the first rank."

9

Crown 8vo, cloth, 2s. 6d. net. each.

THE ILLUSTRATED NOVELS OF
ALPHONSE DAUDET.

TARTARIN OF TARASCON.	RECOLLECTIONS OF A LITERARY MAN.
TARTARIN ON THE ALPS.	THIRTY YEARS OF PARIS.
KINGS IN EXILE.	JACK. 2 vols.
ARTISTS' WIVES.	ROBERT HELMONT.

Globe.

" A very pretty edition, excellently printed on good paper,—the attractively bound volumes should be much in request."

Glasgow Herald.

" A very readable and enjoyable version. The little volume is neatly and tastefully bound ; and if Daudet's other works are to follow in the same style, the whole collection will be a charming one."

Scotsman.

" The book, which is a history of literary Paris of the time, as well as a record of the author's own life and work, ranks as one of the classics among French books of its kind. It will be a boon to many to be enabled to read in English a book which is a model of easy style, and delightful in its frank estimates of men and books."

Weekly Sun.

" Mr. Dent has been at pains evidently to give to the exterior of these volumes a daintiness and an elegance suitable to their tone ; and certainly the volumes are in an exquisite dress. The translations, too, are so good, that one often forgets that one is not reading an original work—which is the highest praise one can bestow on a translation."

Dundee Advertiser.

" The publishers have spared no pains to render the volume attractive. It is daintily illustrated and prettily bound, and exterior and interior are alike attractive."

Illustrated London News.

" It is hardly too high a compliment to the illustrations of this new edition to say that they are as exquisitely humorous as the text of which they double your enjoyment."

THE IRIS LIBRARY.

Glasgow Herald.

"The Iris Library volumes are so dainty and beautiful, that one always takes up with pleasure a new one. All that good type, good paper, and pretty binding can give in the way of attraction these books have."

TRYPHENA IN LOVE.

By WALTER RAYMOND.

Times.

"'Tryphena' is far the best work that Mr. Raymond has yet given us. . . . It is a work of art; nowhere redundant, nowhere deficient, steeped in sterling human nature, and instinct with quaint humour."

MAUREEN'S FAIRING.

By Miss JANE BARLOW.

Freeman's Journal.

"Some of the best writing Miss Barlow has yet done . . . filled with a fidelity to Irish nature, marvellous in its closeness. Since Rudyard Kipling gave us his Wee Willie Winkie, new fiction has contained no character to match with Mac."

MRS. MARTIN'S COMPANY,

AND OTHER STORIES.

By JANE BARLOW.

Spectator.

"The first in this little volume is a perfect gem of bright delineation of the mixed simplicity and faith of the Irish people. Nothing could possibly be told with happier touches of both human and devout fancy than this beautiful story."

A RINGBY LASS,

AND OTHER STORIES.

By MARY BEAUMONT.

Leeds Mercury.

"Half a dozen stories, every one of which is a gem, and every gem of which is set in brilliants."

A MODERN MAN.

By Miss ELLA MACMAHON.

Pall Mall Gazette.

"This extremely clever sketch, with its subtle analysis and almost pitiless dissection of character and 'motives,' is as intensely modern 'as they make them.'"

CHRISTIAN AND LEAH.

Translated from the German of Leopold Kompert, by ALFRED S. ARNOLD.

Birmingham Post.

"The tales are tenderly told, and the life of the Ghetto is made very real to us as we read, and beautiful as well as real. There is amid the sordid surroundings . . . an ever-present dignity and sublimity of conception about the great mysteries of life, and a moral purity, which win respect and admiration."

THE WITCH OF WITHYFORD:
A ROMANCE OF EXMOOR.

By GRATIANA CHANTER.

Pall Mall Gazette.

"Charmingly told with a simplicity and delicacy that marks an ability above the common."

WHERE HIGHWAYS CROSS.

By J. S. FLETCHER.

Guardian.

"A charming idyll. Thoroughly original and cleverly worked out."

A LOST ENDEAVOUR.

By GUY BOOTHBY.

Saturday Review.

"An exceedingly effective story; he grips the reader from the outset, and holds him to the end."

LIVES THAT CAME TO NOTHING.

By GARRETT LEIGH.

Pott 8vo, cloth, gilt top, 1s. 6d. net each volume.

Odd Volumes Series.

ASTECK'S MADONNA,

AND OTHER STORIES.

By CHARLES KENNETT BURROW.

Manchester Guardian.

"It is turned out with all the daintiness we have learned to expect from its publishers. If its contents are an earnest of the standard of workmanship to be maintained in the remaining volumes, we can look forward to them with pleasure. Each one of the nine stories is technically a work of art."

To-Day.

"The daintiest, lightest, and best printed book I have ever seen at the price. The first two pages are enough to show that the author has great gifts, a sense of the fitness of words, an ear for the rhythm of fine prose—a style, in fact. But he has more than these. He has observed keenly and felt deeply the moods of nature and of human nature. He writes with knowledge, and from the heart. Two main ideas I find informing the book—a love of the great peace that lies near the heart of nature, and of the courageous spirit (born of that peace) which enables a man to look life in the face, fight its battles, and enjoy its fruits."

KIRIAK;

Or, THE HUT ON HEN'S LEGS.

Translated from the Russian of COUNT SAILHAS
by Mrs. SUTHERLAND EDWARDS.

Scotsman.

"The simplicity of the story, and the truth and delicacy of touch with which its pathetic central figures are drawn, give the book a rare charm."

World.

"Told with a rugged force, and unstrained pathos, and a mastery of simple yet beautiful imagery that reflect the unmistakable literary genius of Count Sailhas, its author."

IN RUSTIC LIVERY.

By GEORGE MORLEY.

The Literary World.

" His name will have to be written down whenever a list of worthy suppliers of short stories is being made. . . . Mr. Morley has given us a little book of distinct charm and individual flavour, and we record our thanks with a marked sense of pleasure."

THE CLOSING DOOR.

Authorised Translation from the German of OSSIP SCHUBIN
by MARIE DOROTHEA GURNEY.

Glasgow Herald.

" Its chief attractions lie in the skill with which it blends pathos and humour, the vividness of its sketches of Austrian society, and the high moral tone which pervades it. As a further attraction, in as far as the British reading public is concerned, it has been excellently translated."

Scotsman.

" Both characters and action are depicted with a humanity that makes the pleasing effect of the story independent of local colouring. It is a healthy and a delightful story, and will stimulate its author's growing popularity in this country."

MAN.

By LILIAN QUILLER-COUCH.

Scotsman.

" Every sketch is cleverly built round a dramatic situation, and none of them ever wholly loses sight of the poetical aspects of its subject."

NOW READY.

AMOS JUDD.

By J. A. MITCHELL.

15

THE NOVELS OF H. DE BALZAC.

An entirely new translation of the COMÉDIE HUMAINE. Edited by GEORGE SAINTSBURY. Translated by Miss ELLEN MARRIAGE and Mrs. CLARA BELL. With 3 Etchings in each volume by W. BOUCHER and D. MURRAY-SMITH. Crown 8vo, cloth, 3s. 6d. net.

For Large Paper Edition apply to the Booksellers.

The following volumes are already published :—

The Wild Ass's Skin.	The Country Doctor.
The Chouans.	The Cat and Racket.
Eugénie Grandet.	Ursule Mirouet.
The Quest of the Absolute.	Old Goriot.
The Unknown Master-piece.	The Atheist's Mass.
	La Grande Bretêche.
A Bachelor's Establish-ment.	César Birotteau.
	Modeste Mignon.
Pierrette and The Abbé Birotteau.	The Village Parson.
	Béatrix.

The following volumes are in active preparation :—

The Peasantry.	Lost Illusions. 2 vols.
A Harlot's Progress. 2 vols.	Seraphita.
About Catherine de Medici.	The Seamy Side of History.
A Woman of Thirty.	Cousin Betty.
A Lily of the Valley.	Cousin Pons, &c. &c.

Athenæum.

"The volume is got up with the taste the publishers have taught the public to expect of them."

Times.

"Certainly few English critics are better qualified than Mr. Saintsbury to write either a general introduction such as he here gives, dealing with Balzac's life and the general characteristics of his work and genius, or a series of prefaces such as he promises for each succeeding volume."

Glasgow Herald.

"The translation ('Old Goriot') has been done by Miss Ellen Marriage, and is characterised by that accuracy and fluency of style which, in the five or six volumes already contributed by her to the series, have shown her thorough competency for as difficult a task as a translator could undertake. It has the singular merit of being so idiomatic and natural that those who do not know the original might easily take it to be an English story of Parisian life, and yet so true to Balzac's manner that those who are familiar with him will recognise many of his peculiarities even in the version, and almost find themselves doubting whether they are reading him in French or English."

Glasgow Herald.

"Mrs. Clara Bell, who is responsible for these stories ('La Grande Bretêche') has again done her work with remarkable skill and fidelity. We have read through the version of 'La Grande Bretêche' with the original before us, and we have not found a single passage with which the most exacting critic could fairly find fault."

www.ingramcontent.com/pod-product-compliance
Lightning Source LLC
Chambersburg PA
CBHW020809060726
47498CB00017B/1161